A NUN
AND AN
OFFICER

July 12, 1997
Ruth Ann
Hope we can keep
our friendship and
family lings forever
we will

love
Radmila Johnson

RADMILA JOHNSON

ISBN Number 1-57087-042-X

Production Design by Robin Ober

Golden Bobby Publishing
P.O. Box 11082
Charlotte, North Carolina 28220

Printed by Professional Press
Chapel Hill, North Carolina 27515-4371

Manufactured in the United States of America
96 95 94 93 92   10 9 8 7 6 5 4 3 2 1

About the Author

Radmila Johnson was born in the Republic of Bosnia-Hercegovina of former Yugoslavia. As a child she witnessed the wrath of the previous Yugoslavia civil war. In post war years as a young girl she moved to Belgrade and studied foreign languages, theater, and film making at Avala Film Academy. Fortunate to escape the worst of life and agony which her mother went through, she found her way to the United States.

In America Radmila's career centered on fashion, modeling, and business. As Owner/Director of Radmila's School and Agency of Beauty-Fashion-Modeling, she responded to the needs of young people and succeeded where their parents could not. As a genuine dynamic role model for young girls, she passed on many of the same values she learned from her mother while surviving hard times during WW II Yugoslavia. Personal values of love and respect for their parents; and a positive attitude towards themselves are the corner stones of her philosophy.

Radmila's models have received contracts with top New York model agencies, Elite and Ford, where they have been featured in leading fashion magazines, TV, and film productions.

Radmila is the subject of frequent interviews by the media, The Charlotte Observer, The Charlotte Leader, Creative Loafing, and ABC, CBS and NBC affiliate TV stations regionally. They have featured her work with young girls, experiences growing up in Yugoslavia, and the book project "A Nun and an Officer." In 1991 she was featured in Yugoslavia's leading life styles magazine "Svijet." She received a joint proposal from a noted Yugoslav film director Vesna Ljubic and Nikola Gurovic of TV/ Radio Sarajevo to make a movie from her manuscript.

Her interest in free-lance journalism has led her to such celebrities and film stars as Elvis Presley, Elizabeth Taylor, Anna-Maria Alberghetti, Luciano Pavarotti, and Arnold Palmer.

Writing "A Nun and an Officer" is just a continuation of her work helping others benefit from the lessons passed on by her mother and what she's learned about surviving very difficult times. Her goal is to make a movie of "A Nun and an Officer."

Currently, she is working on several other books: *Modeling and Etiquette for Personal Success, Timeless People, Secret Key for He or She, My Talking Pets,* and *South Slav's Cookbook.*

CONTENTS

ACKNOWLEDGEMENTS.. iii

FORWARD v

PROLOGUE 1

1   DJURIN AND ANDJELKA.. 4

2   MYSTERIOUS BEHAVIOR ON THE TRAIN 10

3   SMUGGLING TOBACCO 18

4   SECRET OF THE CONVENT... 28

5   EXCOMMUNICATION FROM THE CONVENT 38

6   STANISLAVA AT THE BUS TERMINAL 45

7   ARRIVAL IN NIS... 56

8   WEDDING IN NIS 62

9   FOREIGN TRAVEL... 69

10 BOMBARDIERS IN THE SKY OF NIS 76

11 THE HODJA'S MIRACLE 83

12 MIRKO'S DEATH 92

13 THE GYPSY WOMAN 98

14 ON THE ADRIATIC COAST 105

15 THE MAN IN THE CHIMNEY 112

16 CAPTURED BY PARTISANS....................................... 120

17 SAD SATURDAY.. 129

18 RADOJKA IN ORPHANAGE 139

19 DRAGINJA AND MILOJE 149

20   KRAGUJEVAC 157

21   BACK TO BELGRADE 166

22   MYSTERY MAN 176

23   MIDNIGHT RESCUE 189

24   FIRST MEETING WITH JANKO 195

25   HEJ BABA RIBA, HEJ BABA RIBA 202

26   DECEMBER PARTY 211

27   NINE MONTHS AGONY 218

28   MOTHER AND INFANT 225

29   STRUGGLING TO SURVIVE 233

30   ESCAPE ACROSS THE AUSTRIAN BORDER 244

31   MARIBOR PRISON 252

32   THE CORPS DIPLOMATIC PARTY 258

33   MAN FROM THE EMBASSY 265

34   LAST LETTERS FROM STANISLAVA 275

EPILOGUE 285

PHOTOGRAPHS, INCLUDING A MAP OF FORMER
     YUGOSLAVIA .... INSERT AFTER PAGE 116

TERMS 287

ACKNOWLEDGMENTS

hank you to all those who helped and encouraged me to complete this book. Without your support, it would still only be a thought in my mind.

A special tribute to my loving and unforgettable mother Stanislava-Draginja for instilling in me love, trust, and a strong belief of God. What she has done for me will now never be forgotten.

To my husband Kent who literally pushed me to the writing of this book and who truly believed in my abilities and accomplishments.

To my son Slobodan who diligently made a point to remind me daily to write and finish *A Nun and an Officer.*

I express special gratitude to Boyd Davis, English professor at University of North Carolina at Charlotte, who gave me great encouragement ten years ago. After viewing parts of my manuscript Dr. Boyd Davis sent me a letter full of advice and concluded by saying, "Radmila you are sitting on a gold mine, do not stop writing."

Many thanks to Michael Simpson who worked many late hours along side me as we prepared this manuscript for publication. To Jane Grau who helped proofread and edit *A Nun and an Officer.*

To three critics who read my manuscript and helped correct deficiencies: Lawrence Toppman writer and film critic with The Charlotte Observer; Dr. Barbara Thiede, English Professor at Chapel Hill; and Pamela Hilderbran, also a writer, who came highly recommended by the English department where she taught at the Queens College.

Forever thankful to Nikola Gurovic, while Chief Editor of TV/Radio-Sarajevo connected me with Vesna Lljubic, a well known European film director and producer, who has become my dear friend and partner. She has proposed to develop my book into a 4 hour TV feature.

Love and thanks to my brother Dr. Srbislav Bulic and, his family for providing our family photographs.

My constant thoughts and prayers are with my Serbo-Croatian families and friends, also to my dearest friends in Sarajevo and Mostar who have lost their loved ones in the present civil war of the former Yugoslavia.

Sincere thanks and appreciation are extended to my friends who have given me moral support and shared in my grief for my native country.

COVER: Boris Tomic noted Yugoslav artist was commissioned to provide the art for the cover of this book. It symbolizes a nun with a child and an officer in a setting of a cultural bridge (like the "Stari Most," old bridge in Mostar) linking the three cultures of the former Yugoslavia symbolized by the churches of the Croats (Catholic), Muslims, and Serbs (Eastern Orthodox).

* * *

"Love for God and for each other, is the "GOLDEN KEY" which opens every door."

FORWARD

by

Lt Col Kent Johnson, USAFR (RET)

The real people in "A Nun and an Officer" I have come to know from photos and the legacy of stories related to me by my wife. On the other hand, the "Nun" and the "Officer" are symbolic of the many contrasting and conflicting issues which have for centuries affected Yugoslavia (South Slavs). Stanislava the Nun is ethnically Croat serving God as a Catholic for love and peace, while Borislav the officer is ethnically Serb serving the Kingdom as a soldier; both are Slavic. They also represent the periods of war and peace which have swept over the Balkan region for centuries, and the ever-expanding ethnic lifestyles (over half the population is of mixed marriages), including the Muslims also Slavic whose ancestors were converted to Islam by the occupying Turks of the Ottoman Empire.

This book started as a project before the first shots were fired in the 1991 break-up of Yugoslavia. Writing has been made more difficult as a witness to the destruction of a nation one has become to know so well, especially to my wife who is seeing it happen all over again. And for me to see some of Europe's most historical cities crumble to rubble before our eyes, and to see friends and relatives who were not able to escape wither away betrayed and forgotten by a new wave of revolutionaries.

During half a dozen visits to Yugoslavia over the past 20 years, I have been fortunate to experienced many of the pleasant sights, sounds, and smells as the real people in this book. Also my life has been immeasurably expanded by the Yugoslav people I've met and who have become close friends. On the other hand I am unfortunate and share their anguish. Up until our last visit in 1990, everything seemed normal throughout the Republics, with much to take pride in. All the people I've met, from simple country people to business executives, exhibited great pride and sense of purpose in their work and life.

For example, a most memorable occasion was when I met for the first time my wife's cousin, Pero Simic, a Lieutenant Colonel in the Yugoslav Army. I was shocked to face a military officer wearing the a red star which was symbolic of the enemy, Soviet Union, I was trained to fight. Drawing attention to the Yugoslav Red Star on his cap I asked where was the infamous "hammer and sickle" as some of the others had embossed on theirs. With pride he replied that it was not necessary to be a member of the Communist party to do well Yugoslavia.

As for ethnic tolerance, it appeared to be no more of a problem than here in the States. The mix of cultures in music, love of life, generosity, foods, and Slavas (celebrations) gave life extra meaning. I am perplexed as to the origins of the villains, communists, nationalists or whatever they call themselves who were responsible for betraying such a beautiful country. What went wrong?

Maybe the experience of Medjugorje is the clue to this question. Medjugorje is a small rural village in the heart of Bosnia-Hercegovina not far from Mostar. It is the site where the Virgin Mary appeared regularly before a group of young shepherds. In 10 revelations over a period of years during the late

1980 and early 90, she warned of pending disaster and that the world should turn to God to save themselves. Perhaps....

But the history lesson of the Balkan is that man has not prospered over the last 2000 years except for brief periods of great success followed by terrible destruction. The people are cursed to repeat history, a common theme in the art and literature of this region. In historical perspective the period following World War II was a period of great success. Today the breakup of Yugoslavia and resulting civil war is just a "minor eruption" in the range of conflicts that has revisited this region. Compare this to the period of our story "A Nun and an Officer". Between 1910 through the 40's, in the order of 3 to 4 million people lost their lives to war (1-2 million during World War II alone) out of a population of 22 million in a geographic region approximately the size of the states of New York and Pennsylvania combined. This has been going on for centuries! What kind of people survive this pummeling of historical tragedy?

Not until you recognize that it is the intensity and extremes of emotion towards life which is the core to this culture will you truly understand or appreciate the Slavs. It is a curse in time of war, but a blessing in times of peace. To stoic Anglo Saxons the contrasts are sometimes so extreme they appear contradictory. As a Yugoslav friend with great insight recently said: "Yugoslavs are not happy unless they are sad. They sing and cry and have a 1000 songs to express their emotions." Slavs reveal their character when they express their hearts.

This Slavic characteristic called "dusa" (pronounced "du-zhay") is a strong emotional outpouring from the heart or soul; Slavs characteristicly express themselves with emotion. This may explain why my wife has put more tears into this book than sweat; the toil of writing has been trivial compared to the feelings she shares with the characters in the saga of Stanislava and Radojka.

Century after century has passed in Yugoslavia and not a single generation has escaped war. Only people who have suffered so much in war can love so much in peace. They give so much to the moment because life has taught them that there may not be another Spring.

This book concentrates on Stanislava's and little Radojka's love of life and their struggle to survive during World War ll in circumstances that are not unlike what the world is witnessing today in 1993. By reading "A Nun and an Officer" the reader can began to feel this "dusa," the true strength of character, this "dusa" of the Yugoslav people and their ability to survive.

Stanislava,

You would be proud of your little Radojka today.

She has given me a reason to love you and cry for you even though we've never met.

Your loving Son-in-Law, Kent

PROLOGUE

his book began years ago with lots of "cabbage leaves," the notes which I kept daily whenever I remembered incidents in my childhood and stories my mother had told me of her parents and her life.

In 1977 when my husband and I visited my native country of Yugoslavia, we stayed with my mother's brother Grgo and his family. They lived a few kilometers from the small city of Slavonska Pozega, between the Serbian capital Beograd and the Croatian capital Zagreb. The restful visit to the countryside, watching my aunt milking goats, chickens about to lay eggs and the roaster's "kookurikuu" reminded me of my childhood with my grandparents.

One afternoon, Uncle Grgo took us to visit the cemetery and to lay flowers on my grandparents' grave. I sat on the flowery grave and prayed. It was a very sad moment. While I prayed, I looked at the photographs of my grandparents inserted in the headstone. I choked with tears and said aloud, "God bless their souls! I wish I had the chance to visit them more often when they were alive."

When I finished praying, I turned to my husband and told him about my grandparents, my mother, and their lives. He firmly believed that I had lots of valuable and interesting stories and encouraged me to write a book.

Upon returning to America, I decided to take writing classes at the local college. I wrote all the promotional brochures and the curriculum for my school on Etiquette and Manners.

* * *

Centuries ago, cruel north-western winds created the Adriatic Sea and the Dinaric Alps. The restless waves splashed and molded sharp rocks, but also formed soft coves along the thousand-mile coast. The sound of the cruel sea winds quickly spread throughout Europe. Seed to seeds. From the time of caves and cabins to the time of high rising romantic villas filled with Edison's magical electric lights and Tesla's inventions. This is the beautiful Adriatic Sea of the South Slavs.

Even though there is currently civil war among the South Slavs, six major nationalities—Serbs, Croats, Slovenes, Muslim Slavs, Montonegrian, and Macedonian—have lived together for centuries and speak three main languages: Serbo-Croatian, Macedonian, and Slovenian.

Like in a good marriage, they quarrel and fight among themselves but would give their lives for their brothers. Inter-marriage between the nationalities will eventually bring the Slavs back together.

Their churches are built close together, almost in the same block. No matter what religion people are, they equally enjoy the sounds of the Catholic church bells, the Muslim Hodja calling his people from the top of the Mosque, and the smell of the aromatic incense of bosiljk in the candilo from the nearby Orthodox church.

The fortresses, the beat of Eastern music, the aromatic herbs and spices of the Balkan food such as hazelnuts, olives, and the oleander trees and vineyards—all are gently framed by the blue Adriatic sea.

The taste of Yugoslavia is still on the palette of the surrounding foreign countries. For centuries, selfish and greedy foreigners tried to split the South Slavs. And now, promising them "democracy," politicians from all sides have driven innocent people into a civil war.

It is hard to forget the South Slavs, the colorful people of what was once Yugoslavia, a beautiful garden mixed with the colors of violets and roses. The drastic changes of the present civil war and the loss of the historical Mostar bridge are painfully accepted in the hearts of all the South Slavs and the world.

This prayer is dedicated to the South Slavs.

TO THE SOUTH SLAVS

Oh, come, Heavenly Father,
help them; they are destroying
themselves.
Our mother Earth is tired and weak.
They are playing with a flammable lighter,
Small and big flames are on and off.
Oh, come, Heavenly Father,
show them and teach them how to live
in harmony and love each other.

Written on beginning of the war in 1992
Radmila

CHAPTER 1

DJURIN AND ANDJELKA

In my soul and in my heart there will always remain the memories of my grandparents and their self-made bacije or summer home. The bacije's walls were made of white rocks held together with mud, and the roof was made of sticks and straw.

I remember so well the summers I spent with my grandparents near Mostar in the Oshtric Mountains, about 5000 feet above sea level. In the spring, just before the sheep had their lambs, my grandmother Andjelka, together with her four sheep dogs, took the sheep and goats to the mountain bacije. In the mountains, she sheared, groomed, and milked the sheep. Grandmother made butter, cheese, and kajmak, a form of light butter. Then, in late summer, Grandmother returned with the sheep, goats, and lots of baby lambs.

My sweetest memory was of sleeping on the rocky floor just barely covered with hay and Grandmother's homemade wool blanket. Especially vivid are the evenings by the oil lamp and old stone fireplace where Grandmother cooked the corn meal and told her life stories. Falling asleep in her arms was warm and cozy. Then, later, we were awakened by the howling and whining of the hungry wolves under the full moon who were aroused by the smell of the newborn lambs in the air.

There was not a bathroom, not even an outhouse, in either of the two homes of my grandparents. Their beliefs were that anything the human body purges should be far away from the house. In a way, it was refreshing behind the bushes.

One night, when the moon was young, the stars were so bright and some were so low in the sky, I spread my hands to heaven and felt that I could almost touch them. I remember listening to the shimmering sound of the poplar trees and feeling the evening breeze. The whispering winds that squeezed through the thick shrubs of hazelnuts spread their sweet God-given scent into the far distant hills.

My grandparents lived in the small mountain village of Raketno, about 50 kilometers above the city of Mostar and the Naretva River valley. They were neither poor nor wealthy; they were survivors.

Mostar is nestled among the huge mountains between Sarajevo and the Adriatic coast. The city was named Stari Most, "old bridge," after the arched-stone bridge a Turkish architect built over the steep rocky gorge of the Naretva River in 1566. The river is crystal clear, with a green tint from the copper mines and minerals. Mostar, famous for its many Turkish mosques and baths, is a medieval city which seems suspended in that fairy-tale time. I could never forget my childhood spent in Mostar, the little coffee and baklava shops next to the bridge, the aroma of Turkish coffee and tobacco, the smell of the fig trees.

My grandfather, Djurin, was well-known around the many villages that surrounded Mostar and all the way to the Adriatic coast. He was almost seven feet tall and had a long thick mustache. With both hands, he swirled his moustache, brought it behind his head, and tied it in a knot. People knew him as a tobacco trader, but everyone would say, "He is the man whose son Jozo was christened by King Petar II." At that time, a christening was a personal gift from the King of Yugoslavia for whoever had nine sons.

Djurin was hard-working and ambitious, a stubborn but religious man. As a young man, Djurin spent a short time in America working in shipyards with several relatives and people from his village. Upon returning to his native country, Djurin got married and had fourteen children. He was also rumored to be a lover who had a couple of mistresses near Rakitno. Of his fourteen children, only ten survived World War II.

In Raketno, Djurin built his own two-story stone house, with a large attic and a wine cellar. There were several beehives in one corner of the attic by the window; on the other side, he had lines for drying tobacco leaves. Behind the house was a smokehouse where he kept meats for the winter. The bottom of the house was a basement where Djurin had barrels of wine which he had made. Wooden mugs hung on the barrels' spouts.

I remember my mother told me how, when she was a child, her brothers would sneak down to the cellar and secretly "test" the wine. They would leave the barrel spouts open and dripping because they couldn't close them with their little hands.

Djurin played an instrument, called a gusle, which he had carved from hazelnut wood. A gusle looks like a smaller version of a sitar. The bow and strings are made from the hair of a horse's tail, and it produces a sad, whining sound.

In the evenings, the men would meet in Djurin's house and sing ganga. The sounds of the whining ganga could be heard far in the distance. They all sat on three-legged stools at a low, round table that Djurin had made. On top of the table was an old copper pot full of tobacco with pipes extending for the men to smoke. Djurin played his gusle while they all smoked. He sang ballads of how the Slavs won battles against the Turks and how they later fought the Austro-Hungarians during World War I.

My grandmother sat with the women away from the men. While the men sang and smoked, the women spun wool into thread by hand on their kudeljas, a long piece of wood which looks like a spatula but is wider on top where the raw wool is held. The lower part is tucked into the waist of the skirt.

My grandmother was a petite, quiet woman. She would get up hours before sunrise every morning to milk their only cow, as well as their goats and sheep. I remember one occasion when my grandmother milked a goat sideways and squirted me in the face. "This is very healthy for you, Radojka," she said with a smile. "It makes you prettier."

When his sons grew a little older, Djurin sent each of them to relatives who lived near the cities on the Adriatic coast to get some schooling and learn some kind of trade. Some sons went their own way, and some came back in the summer and helped Djurin with his sheep farm. The girls were sent to a convent for schooling and discipline.

My mother, whose name was Stanislava, stayed at a convent, which was near Mostar, for several years and studied to become a nun. At the convent, she learned to read and write, embroider tablecloths, and care for the sick.

My mother was one of the most beautiful young girls from Mostar to the Adriatic. Both mentally and physically, she was a strong and stable young woman. For her, love for God was first. But my mother also loved life and people; she was always ready to help the needy, young and old.

I remember when my mother braided my hair, talked about her family, and counted the names of her brothers and sisters. Sometimes she made me repeat after her, but it was difficult for me to remember them all. When she counted the names, she closed her eyes, then started: Pero, Jure, Mate, Stipe, Ivo, Grgo, Dana, Dragica, Anka, Stanislava — oops, that's me — Lucia, Vinko, little Jozo. Then my mother would pause, say the name Mirko, and suddenly burst into tears. "Mirko was killed. It is so hard for me to think of him."

Lucia and Jozo, the youngest ones my mother helped raise, stayed on the farm until their late teens. She proudly talked about her younger brother Grgo because he was the one who helped his father on the farm more than anyone. Grgo and Jozo were the most handsome. "And Lucia," my mother sighed, "was the prettiest of all the girls."

Some of my uncles and aunts I remember well and have many memories of my life with them. On my tenth birthday, my mother took me to Zagreb to visit her older brother Stipe. It was my first time to meet him and his family. Uncle Stipe was very tall and he looked like my grandfather. My mother pulled my hand and tried to introduce me to him. I shied away, but really, I was a little bit scared when I saw him because one eye was slightly unfocused. "This is your uncle," my mother said as she poked me in the back, "He loves you. Go ahead. Give him a hug."

Uncle Stipe was so soft-spoken and easy-going that in time I got used to him. Some evenings he played the gusle for us. He only had one daughter, Mira, who was younger than me. I remember when Mira's mother sent us to the bakery to buy long loaves of bread. On the way home, both of us ate the soft part from inside and left the whole crust untouched from the outside.

Since I was good at hopscotch, Mira always enjoyed playing with me. For those few days we played so well together that I felt like I never wanted to go anywhere but always stay with her.

Later, on the way back home, my mother told me: "Whenever Grandfather Djurin got mad, he would release his anger and hit his children over the head. That could be why Uncle Stipe is slightly deaf and has a problem with his eye."

One of the more memorable of my uncles was Uncle Ivo, who my mother admired most. Uncle Ivo was also one of the first brothers who ran away from home and traveled the world. Anytime he visited her in the convent, my mother said that he looked like a millionaire. He was always well-groomed and well dressed, whenever he visited his friends and relatives, he never came empty-handed. He would bring a white shirt for my grandfather and soft soft fabric for my grandmother. Each time he came to visit us, he gave me a gold coin.

I remember when I was a little girl, my grandmother took me by the hand to one of the rooms where she kept her cedar chest full of her embroidered tablecloths. She pulled out a white gown trimmed with white lace. My grandmother had made the gown herself from fabric that Uncle Ivo brought from Italy.

"Radojka," she said, "when it is time for me to go away from this world, I like to be buried in this gown."

"Why do you think of that now?" I asked. "You are so young."

"Our tradition," she answered, "is to be always prepared when the time comes to go to the other world. Your soul and body should be clean, and you should dress in something nice."

CHAPTER 2

MYSTERIOUS BEHAVIOR ON THE TRAIN

Djurin sent all his daughters to a convent between Mostar and Sarejevo, but my mother Stanislava was the only one who stayed. When she entered the convent she was only fifteen years old and was escorted by her parents.

In the winter of 1937, after several years in the convent, Stanislava was given permission to visit her home. A messenger had brought bad news: Andjelka was very ill and desperately wanted to see her. The Mother Superior made all the arrangements for Stanislava's trip. Even though she was instructed how to travel by train to reach her destination, she was scared to travel alone.

Her train was on time. The train conductor greeted her and helped her on board. He was an older man with many lines on his face that made him look rough, but he was reassuring and soft-spoken. Since the train was only half full, there were lots of places to sit. While the conductor checked her ticket, he graciously offered to let her sit in any place she desired. Nuns were highly respected as holy people and were always given priority.

Since Stanislava had permission from the conductor, she chose an empty compartment in the first-class section. Alone for

a while, she enjoyed reading her Bible in tranquility. Her medi-
tation was interrupted as the train slowed down for the descent
through the steep mountains. The brakes were squeaking on
the icy tracks.

She was relieved when the conductor came by to chat.
Confiding in her, he said, "How I wished to have a daughter like
you, a Chasna Sestro–Holy Sister... but then I am happy — I
have seven sons!"

The train finally broke free of the mountain and came to
a stop in a pocket of snow-free meadows, streams, and a station.
A few people boarded the train. Stanislava, glancing out the
train window, noticed the reflection of a handsome man in
uniform outside her compartment. Suddenly, the doors
opened, but she still looked through the window like nothing
had happened.

"Please excuse me, Chasna Sestro, your holiness," the
man in the uniform said. "Would I disturb you if I came in and
sat down?"

Stanislava was breathless when she saw him closer. She
noticed his black hair, his thick bushy eyebrows, and his hat
tilted toward his left ear. She stared at him as if she had seen
God. At the convent, the men she had seen, a horse buggy
driver and visiting priests, were all old and unattractive. She was
very shy and did not answer the man immediately.

"Would it disturb you?" he asked again.

"No. Oh, of course not; there are plenty of seats," she
replied in a stuttering voice. As she looked at him again, she
shivered, turning her eyes away toward the window, but still
watching his reflection.

The olive-skinned young man again broke the silence
to introduce himself. "Since we are going to travel together for

a while, I am Captain Borislav Bulic and I am in the military academy of the King's army." He took his hat off and offered his hand, but she bowed her head and said, "I am Sister Stanislava."

For a few moments no one said anything. She curiously observed his epaulets with little stars on them, tilted her head, gently smiled and said, "Forgive me for looking at you, but this is my first time to see an officer of the King's Army."

"I hope my uniform doesn't make you uncomfortable," Borislav asked.

"Oh no, I am also in a uniform, except I serve God and people," she replied.

"I am Serbian," he said. Borislav wanted to converse and thought that their religion would be a proper topic. He asked, "Have they taught you about different religions in the convent?"

"Yes, I learned a little bit about the Eastern Orthodox religion. They told us—"

"In our Serbian church," Borislav interrupted, "we stand all the way through the church ceremony, even if it is sometimes three hours long. Don't you Catholics fall asleep while sitting during your mass?"

Stanislava, holding her breath, was about to answer, but Borislav smiled and said, "I apologize, Sister Stanislava. I was just joking."

She looked him straight in the eyes and said, "No, Captain Borislav; it looks like we are sleeping in our pews, but we are seriously praying for Serbian sinners."

Borislav smiled slightly, took the newspaper *Politika* from his traveling bag, and with a deep sigh said, "I better catch up with news back home in Serbia."

Stanislava felt guilty about saying her thoughts out loud.

Her heart was beating abnormally fast. To hide her feelings, she opened her Bible and started to read again. Then she prayed to the Holy Mother of God and asked for forgiveness. In spite of her strong belief in God, her human curiosity was so strong that she couldn't wait to speak with him again. Borislav turned the pages faster, rustling the paper, then caught her looking over the Bible at him. They both laughed. Borislav got up, lit a cigarette, excused himself, and left the compartment.

Stanislava was tired. She rested her head against the window and tried to close her eyes to rest, but unconsciously, her eyes were on the hallway watching Borislav bouncing back and forth as the train picked up speed. When he returned to the compartment, knowing that he was observed, he took the liberty to say, "Sister Stanislava, you know, we have a lot in common. I come from a very religious family. My father was an Eastern Orthodox preacher. He is no longer with us; he was killed by Bulgarians while preaching his faith." Borislav sat back down and was about to continue when Stanislava spoke.

"Are you going to be a preacher, like your father?" she asked.

"Oh, no. I have other interests like politics and law. This year I will be finishing military academy, then I will apply for a position in a city."

Stanislava listened, clutching her Bible to her chest, as Borislav went on to talk about his parents and his career.

"My life is much simpler," she said, "I come from a very large family of fourteen children."

"Fourteen children? I can't imagine your life being simple with so many brothers and sisters. There were only four children in my family."

"You're lucky, Captain Borislav. My life is not easy. You

did not have to fight with your brothers and sisters for clothing or food. But even fourteen children can be fed with milk and cheese, and clothed with wool from my father's sheep farm. In the convent, I found spiritual happiness, but I have missed my mother and father and cannot wait to see them." She opened the Bible and started to read again, keeping her eyes hidden from Borislav. A few moments passed before Stanislava put the Bible at her side and looked at Borislav. "Captain Borislav, do you favor your mother or your father?"

"Indeed, I am very much like my deceased mother."

"Your mother is no longer living?"

"My mother died shortly after my father was killed."

"It's sad to have both parents leave you so soon. But they are with God."

In spite of their differences in background and religion, they found each other captivating. It was like they had been friends for a long time.

In spite of being a cold day, the sun tried to peek through the gray sky. The train snaked along the aqua-green river canyon of the Neretva. Even for those who had traveled often along this route, the scenery between the majestic snow-capped mountains was always breathtaking.

Late that afternoon, somewhere in the mountains close to Mostar, the train stopped. It was rumored that radical nationalists had sabotaged the train. The conductors ran through the train, reassuring people that everything was all right.

Gendarmes and the regional police asked everyone to get out of the train. Stanislava tried to hide her fear, but Borislav sensed it and calmed her by taking her hand in his. "Please do not worry," he assured her. "I will be watching over you."

As Stanislava jumped down from the steps to his arms, she said through her tears, "We were taught not to waste our energy on emotions..." In a few moments, they joined the others.

It was an extremely cold January. The breath from people's mouths puffed out like steam from the engine. The beautiful mountains were covered with a blanket of snow. In the distance, the little smokehouse behind the country homes had meats drying inside them. Wisps of grayish-blue smoke from home fireplaces drifted in many directions as the winds commanded. It was rare and divine scenery, likely captured by many, if not with cameras, definitely in their hearts and memory.

As the sky began to darken into night, Borislav and Stanislava stood there forgetting that they were shivering in the cold. When one of the regional policemen passed by, Borislav asked if everything was all right.

"Yes," the policeman said, "but everyone will have to stay outside until I get permission from my commander."

"As you can see, the sister is very cold," Borislav said. The policeman impatiently glanced at both of them, but Borislav persisted, "She can't stay much longer in this cold weather. I must take her inside now."

"Very well, Captain," the policeman said, "go ahead. But be quiet about it. Don't tell anyone that I let you in."

When Stanislava and Borislav got back to their seats, Borislav took off his military overcoat and put it over her shoulders. "Now you will be warmer."

"You are very kind. But aren't you cold now?" She pulled the coat tightly around her.

"No, I'm fine. I have hot Serbian blood in my veins."

Borislav paused for a moment. "Sister Stanislava," he asked, "are you going to stay in a convent forever?"

She hesitated, sighed, and looked at the floor. In her heart, she found Borislav irresistible, but her mind was filled with many sad thoughts. Her love for God was never in doubt, but she wasn't sure that all her life would be spent in the convent. She wanted to meet people, to be around people, not just her parents and their sheep.

Lifting her head, Stanislava finally said, "Truly, I don't know. My father wants me to learn to read and write so I can help him with the sheep and his tobacco business. But I don't want to stay forever in the mountains with my parents. In my village, I don't know many people who write and read. Neither of my parents do. But still, someday, I must go back and live with them, help them." Borislav moved to the seat beside her and put his arm around her shoulders to comfort her. Stanislava felt she wanted to be held, but she knew it was not right and gently pushed his arm away.

Despite the turbulance on the train and the cold weather, something magnetic passed between them.

Finally everyone returned to the train. No one knew what really had happened concerning the saboteurs. Tired and worried, the passengers were more concerned about reaching their destinations on time. The train slowly started to descend from the mountains.

Borislav got up for a moment and tried to look through the window. "I don't see any lights anywhere." He turned around and looked at Stanislava. "Soon we will arrive in Mostar, and I don't even know your last name."

Stanislava smiled. "In the convent we were taught to go by 'Sister' and our first name."

"But I would like to write to you. I need to know your full name."

"My last name is Pavkovic...but it is forbidden for me to receive letters except from my family. And most of them don't know how to write!"

Borislav persisted. "I would really like to keep in touch with you."

The conductor passed the compartment, opening doors and announcing that they would be at the station soon. The train stopped. As Stanislava stepped onto the platform, she gazed at Borislav, who was about to say something. The sound of the train's whistle cut his words off, a shrill noise echoing through the station as the train slowly moved. The smoke from the steam engine separated them for a moment, then vanished as the train drew farther from her. She could not hear him, but saw him wave goodbye. As he moved off into the distance, she raised both hands to wave and felt her Bible hit her foot.

Before Borislav returned to the academy, he fulfilled his promise to Stanislava and wrote a letter to her at the convent. It was the first of many letters.

CHAPTER 3

SMUGGLING TOBACCO

hen Stanislava arrived at the Mostar train station, she was lucky to meet an older couple named Sharic who were also going to Raketno. She was very happy to have someone to travel with. As they got acquainted, Stanislava learned that the Sharics' son would be waiting for them at Posusje.

"Do you have any one waiting for you, Chasna Sestro?" the man asked.

"No, I don't. I have received a message that my mother is ill and needs to see me."

The Sharics spoke at the same time. "Oh, you are welcome to come with us. Our son is bringing an extra donkey for our baggage."

The bus terminal was across the street from the station. Since the train from Sarejevo was late, the bus was already full. When they stepped on the bus, the tall, burly bus driver greeted them with a cigarette in the side of his mouth and the strong smell of slivovica. When bus driver started to drive out of the terminal, he skidded left and right in the snow. The passengers panicked and a man from the back of the bus yelled. "Hey! Watch out, we have women here. Are you drunk?"

"Zavezi usta—shut your mouth," the driver shouted back.

"Sit down. Don't worry. I have been on this route millions of times."

Another man on the bus, a postman, said, "I know the driver. I've been on this route every day with him. He is a good driver."

The snow was deep on the ground, and the bus was constantly skidding as it climbed up the steep hills. After several terrifying hours of sliding and skidding, they finally arrived safely at Posusje.

At the bus station, the Sharics' son suggested they should have something to eat and warm themselves before the long journey to Rakitno. The four of them stopped at a little kafana under the huge hill. The kafana was built in a cave. Inside, lambs were roasting on a huge fireplace. They had some hot lamb and vegetable soup.

It was late and they ate quickly, knowing that they must continue a long journey on rough terrain.

"You can ride with me," the woman said, "we are both light."

"You are so kind, and I shall have you in my prayers," Stanislava said.

They hopped on the donkeys for the six kilometer ride over the snow-covered mountain. Even though night had fallen, they could still see the narrow trail, just big enough for a donkey to pass, because the snow reflected the moonlight.

After the long ride, Stanislava was glad to arrive safely at the familiar stone house with smoke coming out of the chimney. She invited the Sharics to come with her to meet her parents, but they were tired and wanted to continue to their own home.

When Stanislava came close to the house, her heart started to beat fast and, in her excitment, she wanted to scream.

Instead, she kicked her feet in the air and fell on the crunchy snow. On the ground, she crawled on her knees and tried to peek though the window beside the door, but it was covered with ice crystals. She scratched the ice and removed the icicles so she could see, but steam from inside the house made it impossible.

Stanislava banged with her fist on the big heavy door; for a moment she didn't hear any response. She knocked again. Then she heard her father's deep tenor voice. "Who is it?" he asked. Again, her heart started to beat very fast.

"It is me, Father. Stana."

"Stano!" he called. "Is it really you?"

"Yes, Father! It is me, Stana."

The big old doors squeaked open, and her father emerged with a puzzled face. "How did you get here, my child?"

"I traveled with an older couple; they were visiting someone in Sarajevo. Their name is Sharic."

Andjelka pushed by Djurin and threw her arms around Stanislava, hugging and kissing her.

"Come on in, my child, you must be tired." her mother said.

"Yes, yes, she is tired and cold. Let's go in." Djurin urged as he shut the heavy door behind them.

"Stano, did you run away?" Djurin asked. "How did they let you out of the convent?"

"But...Father, I'm confused," Stanislava said. "What do you mean I ran away? Did you not send a message for me to come home? I received a message that Mama was very ill, and that I needed to come immediately."

Puzzled, Djurin looked at Andjelka. "Sarusa, you know..." He paused. "A week ago, when Ivo and I talked, he said to me,

'I miss Stanislava. I wish she would be here when I am visiting you.'" Djurin mumbled something, then said, "Now, I am sure! Ivo sent that message to you. And now he is gone."

With tears in her eyes, Andjelka hugged Stanislava and patted her shoulder. "My child, you are here now," she said, "and we love you. Oh, Stanislava, how we missed you so much and wanted to see you. Especially Ivo. He has always been fond of you, and I am sorry he isn't here."

"I wonder how he looks now, Mama," Stanislava sighed. "I had a dream about all of you, that something was happening. My heart desired for all of our family to be together again, like we used to be."

Crumpling her apron, Andjelka interrupted. "Stanislava, I love you, but I better go and prepare something for us to eat."

"Where are Mirko and Jozo? And Lucia?" Stanislava asked her father.

"They are visiting with their friends in the village," Djurin said. "Stanislava, why don't you go by the fireplace, talk to your mother, and get warm. I must finish what I started earlier."

Stanislava joined her mother, leaned over the old stone fireplace, and watched her stirring pura, corn meal, in the big copper pot hanging on a chain inside the chimney.

"Father looks so tired and worried," Stanislava whispered. "Has he been ill?"

"No, Stano, but he is worrying about food for all of us and the donkeys and sheep. This is a bad, cold winter."

Stanislava heard a heavy pounding noise from the attic and smiled. "Father is still chopping his tobacco, Mama. I can smell the sweet aroma."

When Djurin came down from the attic, he said, "Andjelka, I'm hungry and I am sure that Stanislava is hungry also. Let us eat soon." From one big bowl, the three of them ate the pura mixed with soft young cheese and kajmak–sweet butter that Andjelka had made.

"Stanislava," Djurin said after they had finished the dinner, "you must go to bed early. I am taking you with me to help deliver tobacco over the three mountains. You will need your warmest clothes; we have a long journey."

Andjelka knew that Stanislava didn't have any clothes that would fit her. "Don't worry," she said. "I have some extra warm sweaters, skirts, and shawls that you can wear."

Stanislava was very tired.

"Go to sleep, my child." Andjelka said. "I have fixed bedding for you in this corner. Last year I knitted a soft blanket from new wool. You will sleep sweet." Stanislava kissed her mother and put her hand on her face. "I will always pray for your well being."

She went to the corner of the large room were they all slept together, the only heated room in the whole house. She fell asleep on the mattress and the pillow her mother had stuffed with freshly cut hay.

* * *

The rooster's crowing announced the dawn. Stanislava was dressed, not in her nun's habit, but in her mother's clothing. With a kiss and blessing, Andjelka handed her a bag filled with pogacha, pita bread, and some goat cheese. As Stanislava came out of the house, her father shouted, "It's going to be a long journey, bring an extra mehur [flask made from a goat's stomach] of water to drink."

Two mules and a donkey were loaded, each side with a sack full of tobacco. Djurin and Stanislava traveled through the rocky terrain of the big mountains for two days and two nights. Since the mules were overloaded, they took turns walking and riding. Djurin knew every check point where gendarmes at the border hid, waiting to catch smugglers crossing the border into the neighboring territory.

They were very tired; the mules and donkey also needed a rest. Djurin had an old friend from World War I who lived not too far from where they were. They could see in the distance candles burning and fire sparks scattering from the chimney top. When they banged on the door, a man half the size of Djurin, with a gold tooth and a happy face, hugged Djurin and invited them in. There was no extra bed available in the house, but they were welcome to spend the night in the stall sleeping on the hay. They rested a few hours and left just before dawn to cross the last big mountain before reaching their destination.

In the crisp January air, frosty snow flakes dusted Djurin's long heavy mustache and eyebrows, and Stanislava's dark hair and the babushka. When the snow stopped, the sun came out and glanced through the valley. The sunlight reflecting on the edges of the frosty mountains looked like large silver diamonds.

Between the mountain and the valley they saw smoke behind large rocks and some wood that was still barely burning. Both were very happy to rest for a moment and warm their hands and frozen feet.

In the mountain passages, Djurin heard the sounds of horses snorting. He suspected that it was the border patrol, but he and Stanislava had to go that route or turn back.

Suddenly, they were surrounded by several gendarmes on horses. When the leader questioned him about who he was and where he was going, Djurin was silent.

"You're pretty loaded with those mules," the leader said

as his men began to search the sacks. "What are you carrying?"

"I had promised a couple of my old friends, to share some tobacco that I have grown. Also, to trade for food."

"This is a lot to share with just your friends. You must come with us."

The gendarmes tied Djurin's donkeys to the horses, and made Djurin and Stanislava walk behind them. They were taken to a small town called Imotski. Along the way, the gendarmes interrogated and insulted them. When they arrived at the head quarters, the gendarmes immediately confiscated the tobacco and animals.

When Djurin and Stanislava were brought into the gendarmes' quarters, several guards were standing and warming their hands over a wood-burning stove. One of the guards laughed sarcastically. "Aha, another smuggler. And what a beauty!" One of them pinched Stanislava's bottom and brushed his hand over her face; another pulled her hair down.

Djurin jumped and started punching everyone, shouting at them to leave his daughter alone. The guards fought back, but could not control Djurin because he was such an extraordinarily strong man. After struggling for a while, one of them surprised Djurin by coming from the back and hitting him with a piece of wood. While he was unconscious, they tied him down and returned to intimidating Stanislava.

Moments later, their commander Jovan Krzic came in. All the guards stood at attention and saluted him. Jovan was a tall, handsome, rather slim man and spoke gently, but with command in his voice. He ordered one of the guards to untie Djurin and bring him to his office, but left Stanislava alone with the guards by the stove.

Again she was a toy for them. They continued touching

and kissing her, pinching her bottom. She was emotionally torn and in tears, begging them to leave her alone.

Overhearing her cries from his office, Jovan came back, took her hand, and pulled her next to him. "That is enough," he commanded angrily. "Leave her alone. She is *my* prisoner." Jovan took Stanislava to his quarters. All the way there, Stanislava tried to free her hand from his.

"Please let me go. I beg you. Don't hurt me."

Jovan unlocked the door to his room and pushed her inside. As he was closing the door, he said, "You are really beautiful, and you are mine. I want to kiss you. Just once, now." He grabbed her and tried to kiss her, but she fought him back.

"Please, don't, don't. I am Chasna Sestra."

"Oh, you are a 'holy sister'—and a virgin. Oh, God! Come close to me. Kiss me, kiss me. I have kissed Muslim and Serbian girls, but I have never kissed a Catholic girl." As Jovan tried kiss her again, Stanislava turned her head and bit his hand so hard that she tore the skin and it started bleeding. When Jovan saw the blood on his hand, he slapped her face and pushed her to his bed.

"Do not move. Stay there." He grabbed a towel from a wash basin and glared at Stanislava as he wrapped his hand. She turned her head down and, through her tears, said, "I'm very sorry. I'm scared."

Jovan rushed out of the room, locking Stanislava in the room.

* * *

The next day, Djurin, who had been imprisoned in a small room in the basement, was released. He protested aggressively to all the garndarmes, demanding that Stanislava be released also. He barged into Jovan's office.

"Commander Jovan," Djurin said, "You must let my daughter go back home with me. Do you realize she is a Chasna Sestra? Please let her go back to her convent."

Jovan hit the desk with his fist. "I am in love with your daughter," he said. "I will keep her for myself."

Djurin raise his hands and kneeled down. "I beg of you," he said through the tears. "Let her go. Her mother will die if I return without her."

"Out. I'm tired."

Djurin turned away. He was powerless; all he could do was wait and hope for Stanislava's release.

The next morning, Stanislava found a way to escape. She climbed over the balcony from Jovan's room, crawled through someone else's window, and jumped on a small tree at the back entrance. As she slid down the tree, she heard a whispering sound, "psst, psst." Her father was waiting. Stanislava ran into her father's arms; he grabbed her hand and they ran as fast as they could.

Shortly, they were safely out of the town; no one followed them. Without animals or food, they had only each other. As they walked, Djurin noticed that Stanislava's blouse was torn, and that there were bruises on her neck and arms. He looked at her with sympathy but, as a father, he was too embarrassed to ask any questions. Stanislava cried and cried on their journey back. Djurin tried to comfort and assure her, but at the same time he was grinding his teeth, cursing, and mumbling to himself.

It was a long trip by foot, almost impossible, but they had to go back home. Their shoes were worn out and their feet were numb from the snow. Djurin kept his anger inside, cursing the gendarmes. Even though Stanislava was hungry and her stomach growled, she kept silent and prayed all the way home.

Djurin was too proud to stop at his friend's house to tell him what had happened. Instead, they stopped and asked for help at the homes of strangers along the way. They found people who were good to them. People gave them rags to wrap around their feet, hot milk to drink, and pogacha to eat.

Finally they reached home, but both became very sick with bad colds. Their colds quickly passed, but the bad experience was carved in their minds for the rest of their lives. Stanislava hid her face and avoided direct eye contact with everyone. She felt that her dignity was stripped away, and the best place to heal her mind and body would be the convent.

CHAPTER 4

SECRET OF THE CONVENT

The day Stanislava returned to the convent she was immediately called to report to the office of the Mother Superior. When Stanislava entered the office and saw the Mother Superior's face, she sensed that something was wrong and stood still by the door.

"Come closer, come closer, sister Stanislava," the Mother Superior waved with her hand. "Tell me about your trip." Stanislava slowly moved toward the Mother Superior's desk, not knowing where to begin. She was just about to say something, but was interrupted by the Mother Superior. "Faster, faster, Sister Stanislava. We have an important matter to discuss."

When Stanislava came closer, she noticed a couple of opened letters addressed to her lying on the desk. Thoughts of Borislav and the promise he had made went through Stanislava's mind.

"Did you know, Sister Stanislava, *that* is a sin?" said the Mother Superior, motioning to the letters on her desk. "Do you know that I broke the rules of the convent when I let you go? I took the risk because you were one of the most devoted worshipers and hard-working nuns in the entire cloister. And now... I am shocked."

The Mother Superior picked up one of the letters and read aloud, "'Dear Stanislava...' Oh, how dare he! He does not even say Sister Stanislava. Then he says, 'I will never forget the gentle touch of your hands...' What in the world is he talking about, Sister Stanislava?"

Stanislava's voice shook. "I... I assure you that Captain Borislav ... He is a nice and gentle man."

"To have any relationships with earthly man." The Mother Superior could barely control her anger. "Even by written letter, is a sin. You must love Jesus only."

Stanislava was silent.

"Go now and immediately repeat one hundred 'Hail Marys' to do penance for your sinful thoughts."

Stanislava knelt, kissed the hand of the Mother Superior, and left for the chapel. She spent several hours at the altar saying special prayers in front of a large statue of the Holy Mother of Jesus.

"Oh, Holy mother of Jesus, please pray for me," Stanislava repeated over and over, louder and louder. Suddenly, she felt someone's hand on her shoulder. Stanislava looked up and saw Sister Ilona, one of the older sisters.

"Come, Sister Stanislava," she said as she smiled and touched Stanislava's face, "Let's go out in the garden and have a breath of fresh air. You must not cry. Remember that Jesus loves us, and he always forgives us if we ask."

Sister Ilona gave Stanislava her hand and helped her to get up. They walked through the garden, still covered with wet snow. As they walked, Sister Ilona looked at Stanislava's face several times and wanted to ask something. Stanislava sensed Sister Ilona's curiosity.

"I haven't done anything wrong," she said still looking

down to the ground. "Not willingly," and began to cry.

"Ssh, ssh," Sister Ilona whispered. "Don't let Mother Superior see you crying, or she will know something is wrong for sure and call you back to her office."

"I don't mean to cry, but there is a big rock in my chest, and I want to talk to..."

The church bell rang for the evening meal.

"Let's go inside," Sister Ilona said.

From all different directions, the sisters walked briskly toward the main hall.

* * *

At the Military Academy, nothing went right for Borislav. The image of Stanislava's face was always in front of his eyes. Everywhere he went, his eyes looked for Stanislava. Even though studying for his final was extremely important, Borislav postponed it. He had to search for her and see her once more.

Borislav was not sure where to look. He searched several convents around Mostar, did not find her, but he continued to search. As he was searching, he wondered, "If I find her, what would I tell her? I love you? Wait for me until I get out from the Academy and... then what...? Am I ready for a wife? Perhaps if I could just see her face once more, my instincts will tell me."

Borislav's Serbian determination to follow his faith and his instinct spurred him on. His short leave permit was about to expire, but he was determined to go to one more convent near Mostar.

When he arrived at the small town of Ljubuski, he asked where the convent was and was told it was just a couple kilometers to the right side of the main road to the Adriatic coast. Borislav decided to have something to eat at the little kafana and look for a horse and buggy to ride.

By coincidence, he met two men who delivered threads, material for habits, needles, soaps, and brooms to the nuns in the convent. Borislav told the men that his young sister had run away from Serbia to be a nun. He would not want her to know that he was searching for her, he told them, he just wanted to see her from a distance.

The two men suggested that he swap his uniform for their civilian clothing. Borislav accepted the idea, disguised himself, and traveled with the one of the men to the convent.

Just before they arrived at the convent, the buggy driver advised Borislav to sit quietly and observe. "The Mother Superior is very smart and sharp, and she does not like strange men."

As soon as they arrived, all of the nuns came out to look at the goods. Borislav's heart was beating fast, but he told himself, "I'm a man and a soldier, not a weak sissy."

One older nun walked slowly around the buggy, looked at the horses, and said, "You bought yourself a new young horse, I see. He is a beauty." The nun touched the horse's head bravely, and smoothed his hair with her hand, and slowly moving towards the buggy she looked intently at Borislav. Quickly removing the big, oversized country hat which the man had lent him, Borislav smiled, and said, "Dobar dan – Good day Sister, forgive me for not removeing my hat sooner."

"Excuse me, Mother Superior," the driver interrupted. "This young man is my new help in the store. I am teaching him and showing him the roads I have taken."

The Mother Superior bowed her head down. "I thought you were the new young priest we have been expecting, but your striking black hair and Serbian accent are telling me something else."

Borislav was going to speak, but the driver kicked his foot. "He is not supposed to talk too much during training."

When the driver had unloaded the boxes of goods and was about to leave, Borislav asked him if he would stall for time.

The Mother Superior stood on the steps in front of the large doorway. Behind her were a couple of sisters—and one of them was Stanislava. Like the others, she poked her head to the side to see what was going on. Borislav jumped down from the buggy.

Pretending to look for his wallet, Borislav glanced at Stanislava. She looked hard at him, put her hand first on her heart then on her mouth. Borislav knew that she was afraid he would speak to her in front of the Mother Superior.

The driver reminded Borislav that he must return to his business. Borislav jumped back up into the buggy and waved to all of them. No one waved back—except Stanislava, secretly moved her hand as she ran back into the convent.

His wish to see Stanislava fulfilled, Borislav would write her another letter as soon as he got back.

* * *

Several months passed. Stanislava noticed that she was getting heavier. Confused and scared, she didn't know who to turn to or what to do. She was late for her classes and her work in the garden. Her frequent prayers and obvious visits to the altar were noticed by the other nuns. They knew something was wrong, but kept it to themselves. Several of the nuns even approached Stanislava and asked if anything was wrong.

At the convent eating hall, the cook Mariana noticed that Stanislava craved food. Mariana was an older woman who had lived and worked in the convent for many years. She was known as Happy Face Mariana, and she was full of practical wisdom. One day after lunch, she took Stanislava aside.

"Sister Stanislava, I have known you for a long time. You have always eaten like a bird, and now I notice that your appetite has increased." Then, she quietly whispered, "If I can be of any help to you, please call on me. I will be your best friend."

Stanislava looked at Mariana, took a deep breath, and left.

As time passed, Stanislava's behavior became impossible to hide. When the nuns prayed in the mornings and evenings, Stanislava was the last to kneel and last to rise. A sadness was outlining and overpowering her beautiful oval face. Stanislava felt there was no one at the convent beside Mariana the cook whom she could really trust with her secret.

One afternoon before dinner, Stanislava went to the kitchen to see Mariana. At the time, Mariana, was peeling potatoes.

"I knew you would come to me," she said. "I am glad you are here."

"Oh, Mariana, In God's name.." Stanislava burst into tears. "Mariana... My stomach is getting bigger...and its hard. Even my habit cannot hide it any longer." Mariana hugged her.

"I don't know how to ask you, Sister Stanislava," Mariana said, "but I have to be open with you. I think you will have a baby. You have all the symptoms I had when I was young. You are pale in the face, you eat more, and you are getting fuller. You must tell me. How did it happen and when?"

Stanislava cried in Mariana's arms like a little lost child, than lifted her head. "I just cannot tell you now. Perhaps some day. I can't talk to anyone about it. What shall I do?"

Mariana lifted her apron and wiped Stanislava's face,

then she took her hand, saying. "Come with me to the room where I live. No one ever goes there. When the time comes for the baby's arrival, you can hide there."

"Dear Mariana, thank you for comforting me and being my friend when I need one."

Stanislava left Mariana's kitchen with the feeling that the heavy rock had been removed from her chest.

* * *

It was midnight in late October. Stanislava was restless and could not fall asleep. She remembered what Mariana asked her, if she knew the time when it happend. Mariana had told her it took nine months for a baby to grow in a mother's stomach.

She counted back nine months. January! In spite of the bad memories of that cold January, Stanislava rested for a few minutes with the beautiful memories of Borislav and the train ride to Mostar.

Suddenly she woke up with a pain in her stomach. Inside her stomach was a lot of tumbling. Stanislava felt that it was time for the baby to come. Scared to be alone in her little room, she quickly wrapped herself with a shawl. The pain was unbearable, but she bit her lips as she stuffed her bed with anything she could find and covered it with a blanket to camouflage her absence.

Slowly, she opened the door, peeked left and right, and walked quickly toward the kitchen.

There was a sharp pain again, then she felt warm liquid coming down her legs. Very confused, Stanislava, suffering with tremendous pain, made it to the kitchen door. Knocking things around her, she made it to Mariana's room and pressed against the door. "Mariana, please help me, I think the baby is coming out." Mariana opened the door and said, "Come quickly, my child." Mariana put her hands around Stanislava to help her lay down on the bed. "I must leave you for a few minutes. Don't be afraid, I will be watching you."

Mariana rushed to the kitchen, stuffed her mouth with a piece of old bread and wrapped a scarf around her head and jaw, pretending to have a toothache. As she prepared a kettle of hot water and boiled kitchen towels on the stove, Mariana heard someone banging on the kitchen door.

Mariana started to scream and mumble aloud, "Oh, my tooth!"

At the door stood Sister Ilona. "Oh, you and your teeth. Why don't you pull them all out, so we can sleep around here."

In the long hall several nuns in their night robes asked what had happened. "Nothing, nothing really. Just Mariana and her toothache again," Sister Ilona explained.

Stanislava pressed her back hard against the wall to release the pain. Mariana stood by the door holding hot towels and water.

At 2:30 in the morning, Mariana pulled the baby out. "Lucky for you it is a baby girl, Stanislava." Then she cut the umbilical cord, bathed the baby in warm water, and lay her in Stanislava's arms to be fed. Stanislava put her arm around the baby and gently touched her nose.

Exhausted, Stanislava fell asleep. Mariana sat on the corner of the bed, then fell asleep herself.

When a rooster announced the coming of dawn, Stanislava worried what she should do. "Mariana, Mariana, wake up. I hear the sound of horses through the window. I think it is time for the milk man to deliver milk for the convent." Looking at her baby, she forgot her problems for a moment. "Mariana, I just remembered my father once said that when any of his five daughters got married, to name the first child, if it was a girl, Radojka."

"Is that what you want to name her?"

"Yes."

And so the secret of the convent was named "Radojka." After midnight, even though the sounds of the screams had been heard, no one suspected that a newborn had arrived in the convent. A healthy baby girl had been born to Stanislava without the help of a doctor or midwife, except Mariana.

At this point, Stanislava's love for her new born daughter was stronger than anything else in her life. Baby Radojka stayed in Mariana's room while Stanislava went back to her quarters and played sick for a couple days so she could rest. She went back and forth from her room to the little room behind the kitchen to feed the baby.

Whatever was expected of nuns at the convent—attending early mass, nun's prayers, evening prayers, and work duties—she did, but she also managed to feed little Radojka. For several weeks the baby remained in the room behind the kitchen. Radojka was a very quiet, healthy, and good baby.

Everything went well until one day when the Mother Superior heard the baby cry. She ran down the hallway, looking left and right. "I thought I heard sounds of a baby crying."

"No, no, we didn't hear anything," the sisters replied. Behind her back, they laughed. "I think she's a little bit...God forbid...lunatic."

Again, the Mother Superior heard a baby crying. She followed the sounds all the way to the kitchen.

"Mariana, I'm sure I heard baby sounds coming from this

direction." Mariana nervously stirred the food in her pan making a lot of noise.

"Mariana," the Mother Superior declared, "you are hiding something." She pushed Mariana aside and went straight to the back room. When she opened the door she was confronted with the incredible sight of a nun breast feeding a baby. The Mother Superior fainted.

After recovering from her initial shock, the Mother Superior developed a soft heart for Stanislava and her little Radojka. She delayed making a decision to excommunicate Stanislava for a while until she had consulted with the authorities. In the meantime, everyone in the convent loved the baby and took turns visiting and bringing gifts.

The baby was almost a month old when the decision was made to excommunicate Stanislava from the church, and she was told she could not stay any longer in the convent.

CHAPTER 5

EXCOMMUNICATION
FROM THE CONVENT

xcommunicated! Standing by the window in her small room, Stanislava watched the snow and rain coming down. The thought of the winter ahead, who to turn to and where to go, sent chills down her spine.

Stanislava's thoughts were interrupted as Mariana entered the room. "I want to give you this." she said, unfolding something in arms. "I have knitted this sweater and skirt for you. You will need a change of clothes."

"Thank you, Mariana. You are so good me."

"Don't thank me, Sister Stanislava."

"No, no. Not 'Sister' anymore, just Stanislava."

"You will always be Sister Stanislava to me."

"Mariana, I'm not a nun any more. I'm disgraced." And she started to cry. "But I love my baby."

"God will watch over you." Mariana said and took Stanislava's hands. "Oh, your hands are like ice; you must put something warm on. Let me help you pack. Quickly, before they come for you, hide one of your nun's habits in the basket."

"But I am not permitted to wear it anymore."

"No one will know. Wear it on the train and the bus so you will be treated with respect. Now," Mariana continued, "when people ask about the baby, tell them it was left by a young girl at the doorstep of the convent and that you are taking it to the authorities in Mostar. To survive from today on, you must always think of yourself and the baby first."

"Mariana, I will always respect your wisdom and never forget what you have done for the baby and me."

From the wardrobe, Stanislava pulled out one of her nun's habits, wrapped it in a cloth, and put it at the bottom of a large woven-straw basket. Then she packed her other belongings and the baby clothes that the nuns had knitted. Mariana dressed baby Radojka and held her close for a few moments. "Here is your Mama," she said with tears, handing her to Stanislava. "Be a good baby."

Sister Ilona came with a pouch in her hands. "We will be leaving shortly. Are you ready?"

"Yes," Stanislava said as she placed the baby Radojka in the basket and covered her with a shawl.

"Here is the money the Mother Superior agreed to give you for your travel and food. She also told me to give you back these letters that belong to you."

"The letters? I can have them?" She put the letters in the basket.

Stanislava was taken by a horse-drawn buggy to the train station. After her escorts left, Stanislava (as Mariana had suggested) went to the public bathroom and changed into the nun's habit before she bought her train ticket.

For a while Stanislava traveled with the noise of chickens and other farm animals in the third class compartment. She was almost overcome by the unbearable smell of the peasants carrying eggs, cheese, ducks, and geese to sell at the city market. She kept her baby Radojka covered in the large basket, leaving just enough of an opening around the face for her to breath.

When the conductor started taking people's tickets, he noticed something moving in the basket next to Stanislava.

"Sister, are you also taking chickens to mark— Ah, a baby." The conductor leaned over and pulled the cover. "Oh, what a pretty baby. Which one of you is the mother?"

Stanislava remembered what Mariana had told her, but in her heart she felt like saying, "It is my baby, *my* baby." Quickly, she replied. "I am in charge of taking this baby to the court house authorities. It was left at the doorsteps of our convent." The conductor was very sympathetic and gave her permission to move to the first class compartment.

The conductor helped Stanislava to the next car. Alone, she pulled Borislav's letters from the basket. "What is going to happen to me?" she asked herself. Her thoughts were interrupted by the train whistle. She stood by the window and watched as the train stopped at one station after another, observing the people getting on and off.

Stanislava found the latrine at the end of the railroad car, locked herself in and breast fed the baby.

On her way back to her seat, the train was slowing down and people were passing her closer to the exit door. Stanislava felt like everyone was looking at her, knowing the baby was her's.

A man entered her compartment and sat opposite her, reading the Serbian paper *Politika*. As Stanislava rearranged her basket to put the baby to sleep, the fringes of the shawl caught on the basket and pulled it to the floor.

Laying the baby on the seat, she bent for the basket and bumped heads with the man, who had dropped his newspaper to help. As they both apologized, Stanislava almost fainted.

"Captain Borislav... It is you!"

"Sister Stanislava!" Borislav clasped his hands to his chest. "I can't believe it! I have been searching for you everywhere. Did my guardian angel talk to your's? It cannot be just luck or coincidence."

"It is coincidence," she replied. "Since our first meeting, many things have happened in my life. My guardian angel took a snooze."

"Oh, what do you mean?" Borislav asked as he raised his left eyebrow.

"I cannot talk about it now, perhaps another time."

"Did you not get my letters?"

"No." Stanislava hesitated. "The Mother Superior has them. If you remember, the only letters we can receive are from family."

"I'm so sorry you didn't get them."

As they were picking things up from the floor, Stanislava quickly pointed with her hand towards the baby and told Borislav what she had told the train conductor—that the baby was found at the convent door.

"Left by the door? Oh, how sad," Borislav said, pulling the shawl from the baby's face. "Such a pretty baby." While Borislav looked at the baby, Stanislava quickly searched for the letters and hid them in the bottom of the basket.

To avoid any more questions, she asked, "Captain Borislav, what are you doing in civilian clothes?"

"I am out of the Military academy, but will stay in the reserves. My new assignment is in Nis; I have been appointed to be mayor of the city."

"Mayor of the city? What does that mean?"

"That means just like a father who is responsible for his

family and his home. From the many who applied for the position, I was the one who was selected."

"You will be a rich man and have a wife and many children."

"Yes, I would like to have a wife, but not many children, only two." Borislav leaned over and touched her hand. "Could you ever marry?"

Stanislava bowed her head. "Captain Borislav, you are such a strong man with such strong ideas and desires." Slowly, she pulled her hands back, clasped them firmly together, and looked Borislav in the eyes. "In all these years I have spent in the convent, I have never had a thought of anything else but church and Jesus. But recently, many different thoughts have gone through my mind. Yes, I wonder how it would be to become someone's wife and have a family of my own."

"If it ever happens that you decide to leave the convent and become someone's wife, I beg you to be mine."

In her mind, Stanislava wanted to say, "Yes, I will go with you," and tell him all about had happened since the day they had first met. Instead, she picked up her bible. "Only God knows what time will bring."

* * *

In their hours together, which made the feelings they had developed from their first trip even stronger, Borislav repeated his desire see Stanislava. He gave her his address in Nis and asked her to come to see him.

As the train slowed down, the conductor announced the station: "Mostar! Mostar!"

Stanislava held in her tears; her hands were shaking and she felt her legs tremble as she packed. When she heard the name "Mostar" she suddenly realized how impossible her situation was. Her family was not expecting her with a baby; her father would not accept what had happened. She could imagine her father's anger, his face red and twisted, shouting at her, striking her. But there was no other place she could go.

She grabbed her belongings and, holding Borislav's address in her hands, said, "Dovidjenja for now, but not goodby."

"Dovidjenja, Stanislava," said Borislav. "I will never forget you, and I will always remember our trip on the train together. Please remember me in your thoughts."

Stanislava thought she saw tears in his eyes.

"My feelings are telling me that we will be seeing each other again very soon," he said.

With Borislav's help, she stepped off the train. The conductor blew his whistle, announced his usual "All aboard," and the train slowly moved away. For a few moment's Stanislava stared at the locomotive's strong burst of steam. The smoke blew in many directions before it disappeared in the cold November sky.

Stanislava carried her basket with the baby to the train station's restaurant. The first thing she did was go to the washroom and change from her nun's habit to the blouse and skirt Mariana had given her. Then she fed baby Radojka. When she returned, she ordered some cheese and bread, and tried to decide what to do next.

Her first thought was to go home to her parents, but the thought filled Stanislava with fear. Her father was a proud man and would rather die than have his family name ruined.

She did not know anyone to turn to, until she remembered Jovan, the officer in charge of the gendarmes at Imotski. Despite the horrible night she had spent with Jovan, she remembered he had saved her from even greater harm at the hands of the other gendarmes. She also remembered what Jovan had told her when he first took her to his office, that he lived with his mother in Mostar by the historic bridge, the Kriva Cuprija (crooked bridge), and if she ever came to Mostar he wanted her to stay with him. Or, she thought, perhaps she could go to a hospital in Mostar where nuns were welcome to work. But what about the baby? Where could she keep her? She had spent the last of her money in the restaurant.

Stanislava wandered the cobblestone streets, looking for work. She was very hungry, the baby had to be fed. A decision had to be made fast. She went into a nearby restaurant and asked for work. To her surprise, she was accepted.

Stanislava and her baby shared a small room with the woman who owned the restaurant, a widow with two small children of her own. They all slept together.

Stanislava cooked, cleaned, and served customers at the restaurant until she decided to go to her home in Raketno. Even though she was fiercely afraid of her father, Stanislava wanted to show her baby Radojka to the whole world.

"I want to go home to Raketno," she finally told the woman. "Have I earned enough money for the bus ride?"

CHAPTER 6

STANISLAVA AT THE BUS TERMINAL

arly the next day after a sleepless night, Stanislava walked several long blocks from the restaurant where she worked to the bus terminal. As Stanislava pushed through the crowd, the handle of the basket broke and baby Radojka fell to the ground, crying but unhurt. Stanislava picked her up, kissing and hugging her until she stopped crying.

"Which bus is going to Posusje? Can someone help me, please?" Stanislava asked the people around her. Everyone was in such a hurry, they gave her the wrong directions. Finally, she found a courteous bus driver.

"Excuse me please, I have been asking everyone about my bus, and no one could show me the right one."

"Where are you going, mlada – (young woman)?" he asked.

"I'm going to Posusje then to Raketno."

"I have bad news for you," he said. "The bus to Posusje just left. However, another one will arrive in a couple hours."

Stanislava went back into the terminal to wait for the next bus. The hours passed quickly. When the bus to Posusje arrived, Stanislava and her little baby Radojka were the first on board.

The bumpy bus ride over the narrow roads on the high mountain was unbearable for Stanislava, especially when two buses passed each other. From her seat next to the window, she could see the valley far down below. It was scary, scary enough to forget how she would face her father, and who could take her to Raketno from Posusje.

The bus driver broke the silence. "In a few minutes we will be arriving at Posusje," he said.

Since Stanislava was sitting all the way in the back of the bus, she had plenty of time to get ready. Everyone was pushing to get off. Stanislava sadly looked through the window at the people outside. Everyone had someone waiting for them. "Except for me," she thought. She searched the faces, hoping to see a familiar one. "Oh, my God! My mother, I see my mother," she said to herself. "How did she know?"

Stanislava held the baby close to the window, waved to her mother, and pointed to the baby's face. "Mama, look, my baby!" Andjelka looked left and right, then slowly, secretly waved back. Next to Andjelka was Stanislava's little brother Jozo and behind them, tied to a tree, were two donkeys that belonged to her father. Andjelka looked very sad and tired, but young Jozo jumped up and down excitedly.

When Stanislava stepped off the bus, the baby started crying and she tried to hush her. At the same time, Andjelka came towards her with Jozo. "Stanislava, whose baby is that?" she whispered. "A woman from our village told us that she saw you with a baby at the bus terminal in Mostar. I could not believe it. Oh, Stanislava, what are we going to do? It is terrible. And your father knows. Tell me, whose baby is it?"

"Mama, I will tell you later. I don't have anyone else to turn to, only you." Tears formed in Stanislava's eyes. "The baby is mine, Mama." Andjelka cried with her as if someone had died. Little Jozo was confused, could not understand why both women were crying, and he cried with them.

The two of them hugged for a long time. "Mama, I want you to hold my baby. If you love me, you will love her too."

Stanislava watched her mother gently touching the baby's face and kissing the baby's hands. "Do you know," Andjelka said, "She looks almost like Jozo."

"I named her Radojka. I remember, when I was a little girl, Father once said, 'Whoever marries first and has a little girl, name her Radojka.'"

"Your father would love the baby but... It is shocking for him. He refuses to have you in his home. I am afraid ... he might be violent."

"What are we going to do, Mama?"

"Do you remember the church in Duvno?

"Yes, Mama."

"An older woman lives there alone. When she was young, she came to Duvno with her husband, who died. They were both from Mostar. She works in the church and lives in a house across the street. I will ask her if you could stay with her for a while. I am sure she will take you in because she loves to help people. It will only be for a short time, until your father calls for you."

Stanislava hopped on one donkey and her mother on the other with Jozo. It was a very cold and windy day, and a light snow was falling. As they travelled through the mountains, they unexpectedly ran into an old friend of Djurin's who was going in to Posusje with his wife. "Andjelka," they stopped and asked, "How are your children?"

"Fine."

Djurin's friend looked at Stanislava who had her head wrapped with a shawl. "Andjelka, that young lady looks just like your daughter who is a nun in a convent."

"Oh, no, no she is much bigger than her. She is my cousin's daughter from the Adriatic coast." Andjelka tried to avoid any further conversation and hurried to pass them.

The man shook his head. "Boga mi, so help me God," he said, suspiciously. "She looks just like her."

They continued their journey over the mountain and passed within sight of their home in Rakitno. Stanislava turned her head away. When they got to Duvno, Andjelka, with Jozo behind her, lead in the direction of the church. Andjelka told Stanislava to stay with Jozo while she went in and talked with the woman. After a few minutes, Andjelka came to the door with a tall, skinny woman and asked Stanislava to come in.

The woman, who was very warm and kind, welcomed Stanislava. "Stanislava will be fine with me," she told Andjelka. "You go ahead, go home with your little Jozo."

When Andjelka arrived home, Djurin was at the door waiting with a mean look on his face. "I have told you many times," he shouted, "You should never go alone with those donkeys." He pushed her against the door and mumbled that he already knew where she had been. Then he grabbed her. "Tell me, Andjekla. What did you find out? Is the baby really hers?"

Andjelka begged Djurin not to be angry with Stanislava. "She's a good girl. It is not her fault."

Djurin walked back and forth across the room, talking to himself. "I wanted her to be a nun. She was the best one of my five girls. Now, she's ruined herself and embarrassed my name. Oh, my God, how could this happen to her? When did it happen? Who did this to her? I want to kill him. Who did this?"

Andjekla answered him quietly. "You want to know who is responsible. Then I will tell you. But you must listen. Djurin, do you remember when you took Stanislava to smuggle tobacco with you? Stanislava came home to see *me*. And you ... you shouldn't have taken her with you. Oh, my Djurin, you must admit it is *your* fault."

* * *

It was the Sunday before Christmas, and the church bells rang, calling people to the morning service. Stanislava's room had barely enough space for her to move around. In one corner was a little wood stove with a fire constantly burning to keep the room warm. Under the window was a small cot made of four stumps and a couple of boards. It was barely wide enough for one person, but Stanislava and her baby managed to sleep on it.

Stanislava looked through the narrow little window and watched the people all bundled up coming to the church. She remembered the days when she was a young girl and her family walked the couple of kilometers from Rakitno to the church. All of her brothers and sisters walked with her mother behind Djurin.

Now, she saw her mother with her little sister Lucia and her brothers, but not her father. After the mass, Andjelka came alone to her room and brought milk, cheese, and pogacha.

"Mama, I want to go home with you. I am sitting alone in this room with the baby. Day and night there is no one to talk to. Can I go home today? It is almost Christmas. It would be nice to be together."

Andjelka sat on the bed and held her head with both hands and looked down at the floor. "Oh, my Stanislava, your father is still very angry–even with himself."

"Mama, I have to get out of this room."

"The children are waiting for me outside," Andjelka said.

"I must go." Andjelka kissed Stanislava and the baby goodbye. "Forgive me, Stanislava my child, your father is the head of the house, and the decision is his."

It was a heavy, cold winter, and Andjelka couldn't come to see Stanislava. There was no alternative for Stanislava but to stay and wait. During the long solitary days, she remembered what Jovan had told her, that he had loved her at first sight and would keep her forever, if she wanted to. At the same time, memories of Borislav came back to her of how he looked at baby Radojka and how he touched her hand.

Every day she looked out through her window, watching people passing by, hoping to see her mother. But she didn't come. The snow had melted. She watched the buds on the poplar trees in front of the church open to small leaves. Stanislava began to be very impatient. She felt the time had come, and a decision had to be made.

One day Stanislava talked with the woman she was staying with and asked her for advice. The woman said, "The best thing for you, Stanislava, is to go to Mostar. It is a city, and there would be more opportunities for you there. The hospital in Mostar might need nurses."

"I will go to Mostar," Stanislava thought to herself. "At least I have two alternatives there."

Stanislava sent a message to her mother, saying that she was leaving to go to Mostar. Remembering Mariana's words–"you must always think of yourself and the baby first"–she again packed her nun's habit.

* * *

When Stanislava arrived back in Mostar, she went directly to look for Jovan's house. She found the house as he had described it, facing the historic Kriva Chuprija. When Stanislava knocked at the door, a woman dressed in an old traditional Muslim dimije and with a veil on her face opened the door. Stanislava saw the mean look in her eyes and was afraid to be near her, but she asked, "Does Jovan Krzic live here? I'd like to see him. He might remember me. I want to show him a baby."

"What baby?" the woman asked. "Who's baby? Jovan's? Go away, young woman," she said angrily. "He doesn't have any babies."

Stanislava felt that the woman was not telling the truth and persisted. "So he does live here!" Stanislava asked her again. "I want to see him, now. I need to talk to him. Please, I am desperate. He told me to..."

Jovan's mother slammed the door shut. Stanislava leaned against the door and cried. With little Radojka still sleeping in her arms, she sank to the cobblestone-street, hoping that Jovan would come. For a few moments Stanislava closed her eyes and thought about her past in the Oshtric mountains and how nice it would be if little Radojka could see them.

Her short, sweet dream was distracted by the wind blowing a lace curtain in and out from the window next to the door. A woman's voice came from behind the curtain, "Go away, young woman. Ssh, go, go."

Exhausted, not wanting to argue, Stanislava walked away, clutching the basket and talking to her baby. "Don't you worry, sweet little Radojka, we will find a nice home somewhere. God will lead us."

She walked aimlessly for a few blocks, then stopped to rest at a little ice cream and baklava shop next to the bridge. She got acquainted with the owner and asked if he knew of anyone who would take her in for a while.

"Yes," the owner said, "There is a very nice woman who

comes for a coffee and baklava. She is a widow and lives alone. She once had a daughter and a grandchild, but lost them. Her name is Ilka. You will like her. Go see her and talk to her."

The man directed her back to the Kriva Chuprija and said. "There's the old mill right on the Radulja river next to the Kriva Chuprija. She lives next to the mill in a old two-story stone house surrounded with orange, lipa, lilac, and fig trees."

Stanislava followed the smell of the fig trees and crossed the Kriva Chuprija. She came to the gate of Ilka's house and saw a woman feeding pigeons from the second story window. "Gospodja Ilka," she called. "Can I come to see you?"

The woman called back, "Come on in, my child, come on in," with a warmth in her voice. Already, Stanislava felt as if she had known her for a long time. As she climbed up the old wooden steps, she smelled the aroma of Turkish coffee. Entering the doorway, Stanislava was surprised to see that the whole second floor was one huge room with several beds and a wooden stove. A beautiful, plump woman with a cigarette in her mouth stood by the open window, still feeding the doves and pigeons. She welcomed Stanislava in and offered her coffee.

"Gospodja Ilka..."

"No, no, just call me Ilka." the woman said.

"I am Stanislava, and this is my baby Radojka."

Ilka gave her and the baby a big hug. "I know why you are here," Ilka said. "God has sent you to me."

So Stanislava and Radojka had a new home.

* * *

After a couple of days, Stanislava told Ilka, "Please watch baby Radojka for me. I am going to look for work so I can pay you and have food for us."

Several days later, Stanislava was employed as a sister in the hospital. Before leaving the house to work in the hospital, she always changed into her nun's habit; that was the only way she could work there. Ilka took good care of baby Radojka, as if she were her real mother. She bathed her, fed her, and sang to her.

On the second week of Stanislava's night duty in the hospital, the orderlies, as usual, played mischievous games with the new sister. They sent her to the basement to get something. As Stanislava ran down the steps, she saw a man leaning against the wall. When she accidently bumped into him, she politely said "Excuse me."

The man rolled down the steps. She hurried down to help him, but when she touched him, he felt ice cold. He was dead. She screamed and ran back upstairs. The orderlies laughed and explained to her that it was a christening for the new nuns.

Everything went well for Stanislava until one morning just before dawn. She was returning home from the hospital, and she felt someone following her. At the house entrance, she turned her head and saw an orderly from the hospital. He shouted at her, "I know all about you. If you were a real sister, you would be living at a convent, not here." Stanislava ran in the house.

The next day she was called into the main administrator's office. She was questioned about her background, about what convent she came from, and was told she must prove it with some kind of document. Stanislava was in a panic, but kept quiet. The next day, dressed in a skirt and blouse, she returned to the administrator's office and told them the truth.

The oldest nun, who was in charge of the sisters, was not

very happy to hear Stanislava's story and immediately asked the administrators to let her go. Showing her father's temper, Stanislava answered so loudly the whole hospital could hear: "Yes, I committed a great sin, but unwillingly. It would have been a greater sin, if I had aborted the baby." Then she briskly left the administrator's office.

On the way to the house she cried out loud and asked God, "Oh, dear heavenly Father, please forgive me and give me the strength I need to adjust to this new life."

That night she wrote a letter to Borislav. In the letter she asked if the invitation he had extended when they last met on the train was still open. She also told him the truth about the baby and her excommunication from the church.

"I am looking forward to having a new life, if you still want me," she wrote. "The only person I think can give me a good life is you, and I have thought of you very often. I remember what you told me about your majestic Serbian tradition, the festive weddings that would last for days. Even now I can hear your voice, with its strength and sincerity, when you said, 'If it ever happens that you decide to leave the convent and become someone's wife, I beg you to be mine.' I couldn't allow myself to hear those words then. But now I can. Here I am coming with nothing in my hands except my baby Radojka.
Stanislava
PS. Dear Borislav, I forgot to tell you that I have seen the letters you wrote. The letters were given to me on the day of my excommunication from the convent. I will keep your letters forever."

As soon as he received the letter, Borislav replied that he was so excited about her wanting to come to Serbia that he couldn't wait. He told her they would live in the two-story villa-like house that he had inherited from his parents in the center of Nis. "My dearest Stanislava," he wrote back, "I can call you that now. The house is freshly painted, and there is a private room for the baby. Don't worry, we will be married as soon as you arrive. Everything is being arranged."

Although Stanislava had made the decision to move on with her life, she hated to leave Ilka. She had grown to love Ilka like her own mother, and she did not know how to tell her she would be leaving. When she finally told Ilka about Borislav, that he would make a good father for Radojka and that she was going to Nis to marry him, Ilka sadly accepted the news.

As usual, Ilka spoke with the cigarette still in her mouth. She took a long pause, walked to the window, started to feed her doves, then burst into tears. "Stanislava, you just came into my life, and now you are going away. But I know in my heart," Ilka continued, "that we will see each other again." Then they embraced. Stanislava held her so tight than she started to cry, "You know what, Ilka? I will never forget you. You have been my best friend."

"Stanislava, since you are going to see your loved one and its going to be a big affair, you need a city dress."

Ilka took Stanislava's measurements, then went to a store to buy the material. The dress Ilka made was a midcalf-long black silk with white polka dots and a white collar.

When Stanislava left for Nis with her baby Radojka in her arms, she wore her new dress.

CHAPTER 7

ARRIVAL IN NIS

or two days, from sunrise to almost sunset, traveling by buses and trains, Stanislava finally arrived in Nis. When the train pulled into the station and slowed down, she immediately spotted Borislav among the crowd. He was holding a large bouquet.

Excited and scared, Stanislava thought: "Oh my God, where am I going? To a strange city and people I have never met before." Just before she stepped off the platform, she remembered the promise Borislav had made to her in his last letter. "When we get married, Stanislava," he had written, "I will show you and little Radojka the best of life, a heaven on earth."

When she saw his warm, welcoming smile, she felt good about herself and the decision she had made, but felt a tremble of excitement all over her body. With Rodojka in her arms, Stanislava hurried towards Borislav. She wanted to fall into his arms and stay there forever, but she told herself: "Wait, it is too soon."

"Since you can't hold both the flowers and the baby," Borislav laughed, "I will keep the flowers until we find a carriage."

As they left the station in the horse-drawn carriage,

Borislav sat across from Stanislava and watched both of them with love in his eyes. "I'm so happy, there are no words for it, just happy," he said. He stretched his hands, touched Stanislava's face, leaned over, and kissed her on both eyes. Then he touched the baby. "Little baby, zdravo (hello)," he said as he looked at her. "I will be a good tata to you."

Stanislava watched the flowers shaking as the carriage rode over the cobblestone streets. "They are beautiful," she said. "Thank you." She smiled. "Borislav, I feel safe with you."

Borislav signaled the driver. "Please stop, stop," he shouted. "Here is the house. To the right, the house with the columns."

Stanislava was amazed at how big the house was. The two story mediterranean house was painted a light beige coral and had a red brick tile roof. At the sides of a large entrance door were two balconies, which were supported by the marble columns and two large statues. The house itself was surrounded with gardens. Standing in front of this grandeur, her eyes wide open and surprise on her face, Stanislava crossed herself.

"This is something like in the biblical books I have seen in the convent, the palaces and castles in faraway lands," she said. "How many of your family members live here with you?"

"No one," Borislav said as he stared at the house and sighed. "Yes, once it was a happy house with my parents and my brothers and sister. Since my parents are deceased, the house is empty."

Borislav pointed to the lipa trees on the street in front of the house. The last gleams of sun peeked through hundreds of little pale-yellow flowers hanging between two long leaves. "I watched those trees grow," he said.

Stanislava closed her eyes for a moment. "Yes, yes, I recognize the aroma. Mostar also has lipa trees."

As Borislav opened the door, they were greeted by the housekeeper, a white-haired, older woman. She extended her hands toward Stanislava and offered to take little Radojka to the baby's room. The table was set, the housekeeper told them, and dinner would soon be served. She brought a tray with a jar of homemade slatko (grapes sauteed in honey and sugar), two glasses of water, and a third, empty glass to put dirty spoons in. Each of them ate a spoonful of slatko and put their spoons in the empty glass. "Stanislava, this is your first lesson in Serbian tradition," Borislav explained. "Whenever someone comes to anyone's home, they are offered slotko."

As they walked through the house, Stanislava said, "It is quite different from the convent and my father's house." She smiled. "Oh, Borislav, I am so happy." She turned a couple of times like she was dancing. "It is so beautiful," she sighed. "It has such a serenity and ..." She did not know what else to say.

"Elegance?" Borislav suggested.

"What does that mean?"

After he had explained, she said. "Yes, that is the right word. The convent had a serenity, but in this house there is serenity and elegance."

Seeing her radiant face full of happiness, Borislav whispered solemnly. "I want you to stay happy and smile for me always."

As they walked around the house, Stanislava smelled the fresh paint. "The house smells so clean."

"I had the house freshly painted," Borislav said, "Which we usually do every spring."

The first room Borislav showed her was the baby's room which he had decorated especially for Radojka. As they entered, he said, "Shh, let's whisper. Baby Radojka is asleep."

Stanislava noticed the pink walls and the sheer draperies over the windows that faced the gardens and a gazebo. "It's so high," she whispered as she looked down. "I'm glad Radojka isn't walking yet. Oh, a little bed."

"It's called a baby crib," Borislav said. "All of us slept in it as babies." Then he smiled. "Except my parents."

Stanislava came closer and watched Radojka asleep in the crib. When she touched the crib, it started to rock. "It's moving!"

"It's made to do that."

Then Borislav showed her another bedroom. "This is where you will sleep until the wedding," he said. "But let me show you this." Borislav opened the door of a large armoire full of beautiful silk blouses and dresses in many colors.

"Whose clothes are these?" she asked.

"They are my gift to you, Stanislava. I bought them for you."

"Borislav, I don't know what do with them. I am not used to having so much. As a young girl I only had one skirt and two blouses that my mother made for me. And in the convent I only had a couple changes of habits."

"But, Stanislava, as the wife of a mayor you will need to look your best and up to date with the fashion. We will be entertaining and be entertained."

"Oh! Entertaining? Elegance?" Stanislava struggled with the words in her Hercegovina dialect. "My head is full of your surprises and beautiful things. No one in my life has ever done this for me."

"Stanislava, you are like a child. You have so much to

learn, and I am willing to teach you. Now, come with me." He took her hand and showed her the other rooms through the house. "This is the room where I sleep. The night of our wedding, you will join me here."

Shyly, Stanislava put her head down. "It is too quick and too much is happening in one year. I need time to adjust to everything...and to you." Then she looked at Borislav and touched his hand. "I know you will understand."

After dinner they talked until the late hours. Borislav noticed that Stanislava was sleepy and tired. She asked if she could be excused. Borislav kissed her forehead and replied, "I understand, you must be very tired. It was a long journey." As she got up from the table, Stanislava heard little Radojka crying and quickly went to see her. She lifted her up from the crib, kissed her, hugged her, then took her to her room where they both fell asleep on the bed.

The next morning at the dining room table, as they were eating breakfast, Borislav said, "I wanted to bring you belu kafu (Turkish coffee with hot milk), but I did not know if you drink kafu ili caj (coffee or tea)."

"Whatever you like and whatever your tradition is, I will like also."

"We can't always stick to tradition. Yesterday I came alone to the station to greet you, which is not a Serbian tradition. The tradition is that when someone is arriving or departing from a long distance, the whole family and friends will greet them. Since we are not married yet, I could not bring anyone. Also, no one knows about Radojka and the difference in our religions." He continued and explained that under Eastern Orthodox law, which is Slavic, the woman took the husband's name, as in any religion. Also, if she were not the same religion, she had to change to her husband's religion before they married.

"I understand," Stanislava said softly. "If we had been married, or if I had been Eastern Orthodox instead of Catholic, you would have brought your friends and relatives to meet me."

"Yes. Stanislava, I don't want you to worry about anything now or ever. There are good people and bad people in this world," he said. "We will try to choose and have good people for our friends."

"I don't need anyone now except you and my baby."

CHAPTER 8

WEDDING IN NIS

oon after Stanislava's arrival, the news began to spread around Nis that the mayor had a wife and child. When Borislav found out what was being said, he warned Stanislava, "Remember, if anyone should ask anything about us, tell them we were married two years ago in Mostar at the court, but not in the church."

One evening after dinner, Borislav suggested to Stanislava that they should have coffee and dessert in the gazebo. "Stanislava, on the train when we met, if I recall, I did not tell you very much about my parents. Now, I would like to inform you a little bit more. My mother, Juliana, was very quiet and well read. She wore soft, long skirts and lace blouses. I always remember her long dark hair and the mornings when she spent hours braiding it. My mother was a first cousin to King Alexander Karagorgevich. She died shortly after my father's murder."

"Borislav, it must be hard for you to talk about your parents. Especially, your father." Stanislava said, as she leaned over his shoulder and touched him. "You don't have to talk about it."

"No, I'm fine. I was close to my father, even though he was very strict with us when we were children. He was a man of opposites," Borislav smiled. "After all, his name was Strasimir. In

Slavic, *Stras* is a strong desire for life and *Mir* is peace. My father was a leader in the Eastern Orthodox church. He was invited to preach at a church on the Bulgarian border at the city of Chitluk. The young revolutionaries from Bulgaria didn't like his dedication to Serbian Christianity. He was taken out from the church, and his head was cut off." Borislav lit his cigarette, got up and walked around the gazebo.

"It must have been a terrible loss for you... And your mother, your brothers and sisters."

"Yes, it was." Borislav swallowed the smoke from the cigarette, exhaled through his nose, then took a deep breath and said. "That was the reason my mother died." He stared at the sky. "The members of my father's church built and dedicated a spomenik, a large bronze monument, to his memory. The monument was in the image of my father, with long hair and beard, holding the Holy Bible under his arm. It is in the gardens behind the church. People still go there to drink the mineral water and, for good luck, throw small silver coins in the fountain below the monument."

"Borislav, I feel cold. All that you are telling me gives me chills."

"I am sorry. Would you like for me to continue another time?"

"Perhaps you should," Stanislava said. "I would like to hear about your brothers and sister."

As they walked toward the house, Borislav had his arms around Stanislava and told her about his two brothers and his sister. "I have two brothers," he said. "My older brother, George, and a younger brother, Miodrag. Both of them are full-time military officers. George is a general and very close to the King's dynasty. He is married, has one young daughter, and lives in

Belgrade – Dedinje which is very close to the King's palace. Miodrag, who is a lieutenant in the army, is also married and lives here in Nis."

"You also said you had a sister."

"Oh, yes, yes... it is very sad. When I was in the military academy, she died giving birth to a child, a boy named Srbislav. Miodrag and I are raising him between us." Borislav smiled than said, "Now, little Radojka will have an older brother."

"Do you see the little boy often?"

"Yes, quite often. In a couple of weeks it will be our turn." Borislav said.

In the weeks that followed, Borislav arranged appointments for Stanislava with beauty salons and bridal dress boutiques. Dressing in elegant city dresses and looking in long mirrors was an unusual and pleasant experience for her. For the first time in her life, she was being pampered. In the convent, all she had were a pair of habits and a small hand mirror Mariana had given her.

Borislav had many social commitments, he was eager to prepare Stanislava for her role as a mayor's wife. Stanislava had a lot to learn, but she was eager and learned fast. Borislav hired a tutor to teach her etiquette and manners, emphasizing dining room etiquette and how to greet and introduce dignitaries.

Teaching her how to dance he reserved for himself. Every evening Borislav gave Stanislava dancing lessons in the large main entrance hallway, which had a smooth parquet floor and a high ceiling. Step by step she was learning, but she didn't take it into her heart. She learned to dance because Borislav insisted, but she never wanted to go to public dances, believing they were the devil's game. She was still very naive about her new life, so different from her life as a nun in the convent.

One evening after dinner Borislav and Stanislava relaxed in the gazebo. Soft music from the gramophone was coming through the open window. After a few moments of sitting and enjoying the music, Borislav broke the silence. "Give me your hand, my love." he said. "Come, my dear Stanislava, show me what I have taught you."

He gently pulled her closer to him. "This is a variation of the tango. Only with me can you dance this closely. The dance was created for lovers, where their bodies are touching and their lips are close together—like this." As Borislav kissed her, Stanislava closed her eyes and felt her whole body tremble with a strange beautiful feeling she had never felt before. Suddenly, she pulled back.

"What is wrong?" Borislav asked. "Stanislava, look at me." He lifted her chin and saw the tears in her eyes. "Am I doing something wrong?"

"No, no. It is just me." The music had stopped. Stanislava looked toward the window, then she whispered. "Borislav, look over there. That woman, your housekeeper, is watching us."

"Oh, don't worry. She is very nice."

"Gospodin Borislav, would you like me to crank the gramophone?"

"Please do."

When the sound of music came alive again, Stanislava took at deep breath, smiled, and grabbed Borislav's hand. "I am happy with you, and I will forget the past. Let's dance."

* * *

The night before she and Radojka were to be re-christened, Stanislava spent several hours kneeling and praying, asking for forgiveness. "Dear God, please forgive me for what I must do to become Borislav's wife. I hope it is not a sin to change my religion. I will always believe in You, Dear God, and be a good human being."

Early the next morning, Stanislava struggled to dress little Radojka. It took a long time to put the white christening dress on because she had never dressed Radojka in a dress before. She had always wrapped her in the large bandage-like wrappings which, according to the old beliefs, kept the baby's legs straight and the spine healthy. When Borislav knocked on the door to see if Stanislava was ready, he took a deep breath and said, "How beautiful you both look! I'm so proud of you. We must take photographs immediately."

Anxiously, Borislav rushed Stanislava and baby Radojka to the photographer to record what he had seen, then he took them to a Serbian church where they were christened and received Serbian names. The names they chose were Draginja for Stanislava and Radmila for Radojka. To Stanislava's Croatian relatives and friends, however, they remained Stanislava and Radojka.

During the ceremony the incense was so strong that Stanislava coughed all the way through. But little Radojka kicked her feet joyfully as she watched the popa swinging the candilo, the silver cup holding the incense, and blessing them.

After the christening, while they walked down the steep church steps, Stanislava played with crossing herself using three fingers instead of her whole hand. Borislav suppressed a laugh and helped her to cross herself correctly, saying, "Now, you are a Serbian, my dearest Draginja."

A week after the christening, Borislav arranged and set a day for their wedding. Usually, Serbian weddings are very festive and last several days. The father of the groom announces the wedding personally by making visits to the family and friends with a large chuturica, a carved and decorated wood bottle full of slivovica (Plum Brandy). Very seldom does anyone refuse an invitation to the wedding, because the women of the bride's family prepare the most exotic foods and pastries. The best wines and brandies are also provided.

The night before the wedding, the bride's and groom's families have a dinner together. The day of the wedding, the tradition is to serve roasted young pigs and different gibanica and pitas (cheese and meat pastries). Live singers, violinists and accordion players would entertain the guests with wedding songs.

Since everyone had been told that they were married two years ago, Borislav's and Stanislava's wedding was quiet and small. The only people present were their wedding witnesses, two kuma (best men) who were well-known businessmen and worked for mayors office. After the small wedding ceremony in a church, the four of them went to an elegant hotel and celebrated. One of the best men surprised them by bringing an accordion player and two violinists. The four of them drank, ate and sang the old Serbian songs.

It was almost midnight, when the musicians took their first break. Both of the best men got up, hugged and kissed Borislav and Stanislava. As they were ready to leave, one of the best men clapped his hands, a signal to the waiter to bring more red wine and four clean wine glasses. After the waiter had filled the glasses, the man who had ordered the wine lifted his glass and said, "Ziveli mladenci, to the health of the newlyweds." Then he drank to the bottom of his glass, threw the glass to the floor (in the Serbian tradition) and again toasted. "Nazdravlje." They hugged and kissed Borislav and Stanislava, then they left.

Again, the music started to play. Borislav put his arm around Stanislava's shoulders, joyfully admiring and complimenting her, and told her how beautiful she looked. He squinted his eyes (as usual when he was happy) and whispered, "I love you, I love you from here to the sky." Then he took her hand from her lap with both his hands and kissed it. Stanislava slowly pulled her hand away, touched his eyes, smiled and said, "Oh, Borislav, I love you too up, up all the way to the heavens."

One of the violinists, with bushy, curly hair and a thick black mustache, came close to their table and played romantic Hungarian tunes.

Borislav leaned over Stanislava and whispered, "My beautiful wife, my heart is beating fast from happiness and wants to jump out. Let's go to our home." Borislav snapped the fingers for the waiter to come.

"Is it more wine, you wish, Sir Mayor," the waiter replied.

"No. But, find me a two-horse fijaker (covered carriage) to take us home, and do not tell the kochijas (carriage driver) that I am the mayor."

"Uredu, Gospodine, (alright, sir)," the waiter answered.

CHAPTER 9

FOREIGN TRAVEL

As the mayor of Nis, Borislav was invited to many social activities, but he avoided them for a few months until Stanislava got adjusted to her new life and little Radojka got older.

One evening just before dinner, Stanislava was sitting in the gazebo concentrating on writing and pronouncing the Serbian alphabet. From the house, she heard little Radojka scream, "Mama, tata fall down." In a panic, Stanislava ran into the house and saw Borislav standing upside down on his hands and leaning against the wall, smiling. "I'm practicing," he said, "for the tournament." Then he started walking across the room on his hands. Little Radojka hid quickly behind Stanislava's skirt, crying.

"You scared us, Borislav. I thought you had been hurt."

"I'm fine," he huffed and puffed as he made his way across the floor.

The housekeeper came into the room and announced, "Gospodjo Bulic is here with your nephew."

"Is that Miodrag's wife?"

"Yes, her name is Vera." Borislav answered as he flipped back onto his feet. "She's a piano soloist and a little stiff, but you will like Srbislav."

At that moment, Srbislav rushed in and hugged Borislav. "Oh, Uncle Bulke, I missed you." Right behind him came Vera. She was dressed elegantly, but even her wavy, short brown hair did not soften her sharp features.

"Izvinite (excuse me)," she said to Borislav as she gave Srbislav's suitcase to the housekeeper, "but I must go back to practice my piano. Miodrag will come for Srbislav in a few weeks."

"Srbislav," Borislav said. "This is your new teta (aunt), Teta Draginja. Go ahead and give her a kiss."

Stanislava opened her arms to hug Srbislav and was surprised when he stood in front of her, grabbed her hand, and kissed it.

"It is a Serbian tradition," Borislav explained, "for children to kiss the hand of their elders when they are introduced."

"Welcome to Nis," Vera said, shaking Stanislava's hand loosely. "Perhaps we will see you at the opera this fall. I hope you like Mozart." She said in a squeaky, sarcastic voice, then left.

After the door closed, Stanislava asked Borislav, "Is Mozart a member of your family or a friend?"

Borislav laughed. "My poor Stanislava, I have so much to teach you. Mozart is a famous composer. And I will take you to the opera next, when you will *hear* Mozart's music, not see him."

The weeks of Srbislav's visit passed quickly. Even though Srbislav was older, Radojka enjoyed him being in the house. She laughed when she saw him copy Borislav and try to walk on his hands. Little Srbislav was a handsome little boy with huge brown eyes and dark black hair. Stanislava loved him for his kindness and well mannered behavior. He was fascinated with photograph books.

The day when Miodrag came to pick up Srbislav, it was raining, thundering, and the sky was black. The housekeeper announced to Borislav that his brother had arrived. Borislav asked Stanislava to come along and greet him. As they came downstairs, Stanislava saw a tall, slim man with thick glasses. Soaking wet in his uniform, Miodrag was brushing a few wet lipa leaves off his epaulets. "He does not look like you at all," she whispered to Borislav, "You are much better looking."

Borislav squeezed Stanislava's hand. "You will like him. He is very nice, soft hearted... hmm, but arrogant."

By the time the three of them had tea, the hard rain had stopped. While the two brothers talked, Stanislava went and brought the children downstairs. Srbislav was in tears because Radojka had taken his hat. "Teta Dragninja, I would hit her, but she is too little and I do not want to hurt her. Please tell her to give me my hat back."

Stanislava put her hand on Srbislav's head, gently fluffed his hair, and said with a smile, "Oh, do not be angry at little Radojka, that means she wants you to stay with us."

On the way out, little Srbislav waved with his hat and said, "When do you want me back? I hope ...soon."

* * *

For their first social engagement, Borislav took Stanislava to the opera. At the intermission, Borislav introduced her to some of his friends and acquaintances. They remarked how much she looked like the film actress Greta Garbo. Stanislava, very shy and self-conscious of a small space between her teeth, hesitated to smile.

Borislav, so proud of Stanislava, was eager to show her to everyone and to take her almost everywhere. She even went to

watch him in his favorite sports activity: at that time it was popular among Borislav's friends to walk upside down on their hands
with their heads down to test their athletic endurance. This
particular sport was only for men, and women did not like to
attend.

In the fall, on their first trip together, Borislav took
Stanislava and Radojka to Belgrade to visit his brother George
and his family. When they arrived in Belgrade, they went directly
to Dedinije, five miles from the center of the city where the ar-
istocracy lived.

Among all the beautiful villas in Dedinije, the two-story
villa in which George and his family lived was one of the largest.
It was so large that Stanislava was surprised to learn that only a
family of three and their house servants lived there.

When Borislav and Stanislava arrived at George's door, a
young lieutenant, the general's aide, appeared and asked who
they were looking for. Borislav introduced himself, saying he was
General Bulic's brother. "I will announce your presence," the
lieutenant said as he invited them inside.

A few moments later, George's wife, Jelena, came to
Borislav and hugged him. "It is so good to see you," she said. "It
has been a long time since your last visit."

Borislav quickly introduced Stanislava and Radojka. "This
is my wife and little daughter."

"So this is the Catholic girl from the mountains of the
Hercegovina. Vera wrote to me from Nis. Otherwise, we might
never have known."

"She is not Catholic anymore. She is a confirmed
Serbian, and she is learning quickly to become a good one."

Stanislava sensed that Jelena was not a very warm person,
but still she was pleased when Jelena bent and kissed little

Radojka. Jelena turned to Borislav. "George is in the garden, reading," she said. "He will be in shortly."

George came to greet them and was very happy to see Borislav. He was a husky but well-built and handsome man with a well-groomed, short moustache and black hair. Very dignified and serious, he looked like a leader and portrayed well the role of general. After he greeted Stanislava, he said, with his strong, deep voice. "My dear, it was a pleasure meeting you. If you don't mind, I need to borrow Borislav for a few moments while you ladies are having coffee."

Borislav and George went to the library to talk.

"Most likely, they are going to discuss politics," Jelena said. "George is far too serious about the situation in the world. Especially the rumors about Hitler's desire to take over." Then she whispered. "George would be angry about my telling anyone."

"Jelena, I don't know anything about politics, and I don't like politics."

Borislav came out of the library with George and said, "Stanislava, we must go back to Nis tomorrow. Things have changed, we can't stay any longer in Belgrade."

That evening they dined on the large terrace facing the gardens. After dinner, for a short time, they laughed and listened to the soft music of Chopin coming from the radio.

Early in the morning they left for Nis.

* * *

Upon returning to Nis, Borislav's first assignment was to go to Hungary, to the city of Buda-Pest, and meet with their mayor. Borislav took Stanislava and little Radojka with him. Radojka was about a year and half old and hard to control. Everything she saw in the windows of the stores that looked like a baby doll or a puppy dog she wanted. As for Stanislava, she loved every moment spent with Borislav. Traveling to a different country and learning about traditions she had never known before excited her.

In the evening, at the hotel, Borislav hired a nanny for little Radojka. Borislav and Stanislava dined at an outdoor cafe and were serenaded by Hungarian gypsy violins. They enjoyed the colorful people and folklore, the scenery, and the romantic violin music.

Shortly after their return from Buda-Pest, Borislav received another very special invitation. "The mayor of Nis and his wife" were invited by the mayor of Vienna, Austria to attend a large masquerade ball. Dignitaries from many other European countries were invited.

Before they went on their trip to Vienna, Borislav taught Stanislava how to waltz. The waltz was the hardest dance she had ever learned, but slowly she mastered it.

They flew to Vienna on a private airplane which belonged to one of Borislav's Kum's. Before the masquerade ball, they had time to have a dress and coat made for Stanislava. The night of the masquerade ball, Stanislava was a little bit nervous, but she looked beautiful.

In all this time there was only one disappointment. When Stanislava was around the house she accidently kicked something under their bed that made a clinking sound. When she looked under the bed, she found a tambourine. She thought it was a present for Radojka and she gave it to her to play with. Then Borislav heard the noise and came down from his study. "Radojka, give it to tata. That is not for children to play with." Then Stanislava asked, "What is that?"

"This is a tambourine," Borislav explained. "It is an instrument that a gypsy dancer uses to produce a rhythm when she dances."

"But what is it doing here in our house?"

"Well, Stanislava," Borislav hesitated. "Listen to me carefully. I love you very much. But men are men. They like to be together sometimes and go places where women are not allowed. One evening after work, I was out with a few friends in a night club. There was a dancer there. I had a couple of drinks and kicked this tambourine from her hand and I brought it home to fix it. The gypsy said she was poor and could not afford the cost. Are you angry with me?"

"No, I am not angry. I know you love me."

Stanislava was naive and did not know enough to be angry.

Borislav's and Stanislava's love grew so strong they couldn't be without each other for even a day. The three of them were happy together, immersed in a plush community of high officials, diplomats, and international travel. They lived the good life of wealth, security, and happiness.

CHAPTER 10

BOMBARDIERS IN THE SKY OF NIS

One evening after dinner, Borislav stayed in his study almost until midnight. Stanislava was concerned and went downstairs. She tiptoed silently to the doorway and peeked through the opening. She saw Borislav standing up holding a piece of paper in his hand and staring at his uniform which was hanging in front of him on the bookcase.

"Borislav, is everything alright? It is so late. You need some sleep."

"How can anyone sleep, Draginja? The war is at our doorstep."

"Another war?"

"Yes, a war. The Germans are already in Poland, and we will be next. You see this letter? This is not an invitation to a dance or a ball. This is an invitation to fight against a madman, Hitler, whose intention and desire are to take over the whole world."

Stanislava embraced Borislav and started to cry. "My Borislav, are you going?"

"Yes."

"Must you go?"

"I am a soldier, an officer. I was taught to defend my

country and fight its enemies."

"It is going to be hard for us without you."

"I have to go, Draginja. I was in the military academy before I was assigned this civilian position. Everyone I know has been activated. At any moment I will have to report to a military command. Be strong, my love; be strong, Draginja. Take care of yourself and our little girl. I will keep in touch with you. You must stay here in Nis."

"Borislav, I love you. Even though I do not have anyone here, I will stay in this house and wait for you."

Borislav and Stanislava spent the rest of the night on the sofa in the study, talking and embracing.

"We have so little time left together," Borislav said. "Tomorrow morning, I want you get into your wedding gown. We are going to the photographer and have pictures made."

"But why?"

"For you to remember me by."

Borislav had called his two friends who had been the best men at their wedding. Stanislava was very sad. They sat down in chairs with the best men behind them. The photographer suggested a smile, but they refused.

One morning a couple of weeks later, a military messenger brought Borislav his orders to report immediately. Borislav was activated with the rank of captain. Later he was to be promoted to major and transferred to Zadar on the Adriatic coast.

* * *

Within a week after Borislav left, the housekeeper went back to join her family, and Stanislava and little Radojka were left alone in the house.

There were constant radio announcements of the German threats against Yugoslavia. German bombardiers were conducting bombing raids on military installations on the outskirts of the cities, warnings to the Royal army to capitulate before Yugoslavia was destroyed.

The radio instructed people to evacuate Nis as soon as possible. Sirens were whining on and on, alerting people to take shelter. Stanislava was frightened, but she remembered Borislav's instructions to take cover from shrapnel with pillows. She grabbed two large pillows and little Radojka's hand and ran to the study. She covered Radojka with her body and the pillows. She could hear bombs falling in the distance; they were extremely loud, sounding like a strong thunderstorm. As the bombardiers approached, Stanislava prayed to God to save her Radojka, if not her.

The bombing stopped. Everything was silent. Suddenly, she heard a knock on the door. Stanislava opened the door and there stood Borislav in his uniform. As he rushed to embrace her, Stanislava saw the tears in his eyes. Little Radojka held onto his leg and cried, "Tata, don't go away, ever."

"I can stay tonight," he whispered to Stanislava, "but I must leave for Zadar before dawn." The candle in the kitchen was still barely burning. "I see, Draginja, you followed my instructions. No lights, and the curtains are drawn."

"Borislav, I am scared. Are they going to bomb the city?"

"More than likely. There is no escape for us. The Royal family and the young king Petar II have already escaped to England."

After little Radojka was asleep, the two of them spent the night holding hands and staring into each other's eyes as if it were the last time. The next morning, while it was still dark, Borislav left for the front.

* * *

Early on an April morning in 1941 Stanislava's voice was shaky as she woke up her little Radojka. "Rada, Rada, we must hurry and find a safe place to hide. The radio just announced that Germany has declared war! Oh, what am I saying? You can't possible understand. Wake up, wake up, sweetheart."

Moments later, the whole earth was vibrating with what sounded like billions of bumblebees. Sirens were whining and whining, like hounds on a chase.

All Stanislava could think about was what Borislav had instructed her to do. She could hear his voice saying, "Go to the neighbor's house. It is stronger and newer. Or go to the cemetery where there are no tall buildings or old houses."

Their beautiful old house was not very safe, after all, even though it had served Borislav's family for a century. The neighbor's two-story house, which belonged to a retired philosophy professor with bad epilepsy and a family of four, would be safer.

Stanislava grabbed a bag of her personal valuables and Radojka's little hand. As she stepped out of the house, the bumblebee noise became louder and louder. Carrying Radojka in her arms, she ran to the neighbor's house. She knocked and knocked, and finally the maid came to greet them. Stepping into the long, open hallway entrance, Stanislava asked if they could stay in their basement shelter.

The maid ran down the steps and returned to say that the basement was already full and there was no room for anyone else.

Stanislava was in a panic. Furious, she ran past the maid to ask for herself. When she came down the steps, Stanislava could see there was still enough room for two more.

The people in the basement were drinking coffee, sitting in big chairs, talking like nothing was happening outside. Obviously, the professor and his friends heard of the declaration of war and the bombing attack before Stanislava did. They had the furniture set up just like the upstairs living quarters. She stared at them. "But there is still room here. Can we come in?"

"No," the professor replied with a cold voice, "we are too crowded as it is."

In tears, Stanislava shouted, "God will never forgive you!" She grabbed Radojka's arm and ran back upstairs. As she reached the entrance, the whole earth shook with an extremely loud noise. Stanislava refused to go out of the hallway; the maid stood next to her and whispered, "Shh, be quiet and stay here."

Bombs were hitting all around them. Stanislava cried and prayed and waited for the bombs to hit the building, holding Radojka tightly like it was good bye forever. That was an awful moment, waiting for death to come. They could almost sense in the air the scary feeling of something coming.

Suddenly, there was an enormous explosion; dust, bricks, glass, everything was flying around them.

She didn't dare move, everything was so quiet. Silence everywhere. She opened her eyes. Half an hour earlier, Stanislava and Radojka had been standing in the entrance of a hallway; now, everything was open. There were no walls, only the entrance and the corners of the professor's house remained standing. Pieces of furniture, just about to fall, hung from the second floor, barely holding on to the shattered frame of the house.

Radojka looked around, calling for her mother. "Mama, mama," she screamed, looking at her mother. "Are you alive?"

Stanislava moved slowly and replied, "Thank God, we are both alive."

They were sprinkled with blood and their clothes had been torn off by the blast. Their bodies were marked with scratches and bruises. Stanislava and the maid, who had also survived, looked back down the hallway. The stairs were gone, demolished.

Radojka heard Stanislava and the professor's maid scream. Stanislava immediately closed Radojka's eyes and said, "Don't look."

Down past the demolished stairs where the basement used to be, a big hole had opened up like a bloody green lake with pieces of human beings floating on the top. The professor, all of his family, and his friends were dead. The only survivors were Stanislava, little Radojka, and the professor's maid.

* * *

When Stanislava and Radojka returned to their home, it had survived almost undamaged. The roof of the gazebo was gone, and there were a lot of shrapnel holes on the sides of the house itself, but the house was still standing.

A couple of days passed without sirens and bombs, giving Stanislava and little Radojka a chance to recuperate from the shrapnel wounds. Then the radio warned of another bombing attack. The sirens were whining and whining again, and everyone was urged to immediately go to the shelters.

The whistling sounds of the bombs in the air didn't give them enough time to get to the main shelters. All they could do was run away from the big buildings. Stanislava was running on the main street, dragging Radojka and carrying a big duckfeather pillow. The street was crowded with people in panic. It was a race to survive, running from death. They were pushing each other towards a church and cemetery.

As the bombs fell left and right, Stanislava's only chance was to duck down behind an old gravestone and cover both their heads with the pillow. Stanislava felt an intense explosion, but a few minutes later, everything was quiet. The air was dusty and thick; they were both so covered with dust and sand they could barely breathe. She couldn't see anything, not even the church which had been next to them. She waited. The cloud created by the explosion gradually became thinner and thinner, and still she couldn't see anything. Suddenly she realized the church was gone, with all the people in it; it had been totally destroyed.

Amid the destruction with little Radojka safely at her side, Stanislava kneeled, kissed the ground, then lifted her hands up to heaven.

"Dear God, thank you for sparing our lives again."

CHAPTER 11

THE HODJA'S MIRACLE

ugoslavia was invaded in April 1941 and Belgrade fell in two weeks. Since the king and his monarchy had capitulated, the leadership of Yugoslavia had broken up under several branches of the military. Many people had taken the law into their own hands, fighting with and against the Germans.

The Serbian part of the Yugoslavian army splintered and many escaped to the hills in western Serbia and to Bosnia-Hecegovina, where they formed resistance groups called Chetnicks and Dobrovoljci, among others.

As in Serbia, groups formed in other regions of the country. The most hideous of these groups, endorsed by the Nazi and Italy's Fascists, was a Croatian extreme nationalist organization called the Ustase. Genocide and civil war followed between Slavic brethren—Serbs, Muslims, and Croats—as well as Jews and Gypsies.

Another group, which was to play a decisive role in World War II and post-war Yugoslavia, were the Communists under the leadership of Josip Broz Tito. Taking advantage of the fear caused by the civil war, the Communists recruited many men from different regions, backgrounds, and religions into a

Partizan Army made up of non-communist recruits but directed by Communist commanders and unit commissars. The Partisans also enhanced their popularity with an apparent "popular call" to defeat the Italians and Germans as "invaders," reminiscent of the days of fighting the Ottoman Turks.

No one could remain neutral; the Partisans, Ustase, Dobrovoljci and Chetniks were active everywhere. Stanislava's brothers were being pressured to join one group or another. Every military-age male was eventually forced to join a cause or face being shot dead by the "recruiter."

When the Germans invaded, Borislav was under the command of Brigadier General Radosavljevich, the Commander of the Adriatic Infantry Division of the Royal Yugoslav army in Zadar. They fought the Germans for a short time before the general and his troops were captured at Jajce.

* * *

When Stanislava heard the news on the radio that General Radosavljevich and his troops had been captured, she was desperate and depressed. She didn't know where to turn. There was really no one to help her, except Ilka in Mostar-Hercegovina or Andjelka's relatives in the Dalmatia region on the Adriatic coast.

Stanislava packed a few belongings and locked the house. She tried to catch a city bus, but they were packed with other refugees in the same situation. Tired, worn out, and dragging little Radojka behind her, Stanislava finally reached the closest train station and took a train back to Mostar.

Arriving in Mostar, Stanislava found a city which was surprisingly changed from the city she had lived in before. It was quiet; people didn't walk freely in the streets, and the coffee shops had new customers sitting under the umbrellas at the tables outside—Italian soldiers with guns.

Stanislava came to the front of Ilka's house and saw Ilka at the upstairs window, feeding the pigeons.

"Ilka, Ilka! Look, its us. Zdravo. Here is your little Radojka. We are back."

"Oh, moja Stanislava, hurry, hurry. Let me see that little girl of mine." As usual, Ilka spoke with the cigarette in her mouth. "Come, let's have some coffee while it is still hot. Didn't I tell you that we would see each other again. Thank God, you are alive."

"Yes, I am alive, Moja Ilka. I am surprised that we are alive. We have been through a very rough time where the dead and injured were lying on both sides."

"I missed you two," Ilka said. "Don't you ever leave again. What pretty curly hair!" she said as she put her fingers through Radojka's hair. "I know what, little one, I will nickname you Karolina because you have curly hair, just like Shirley Temple."

Radojka was curious. "Mama, mama, what is Shirley Temple?"

"She is the prettiest little film star in America," Ilka explained.

As night approached, the city's tranquility overcame Stanislava. She listened to the pigeons fluttering and the gentle sounds of the river at the mill. "Oh, moja Radojka," she said to her sleeping child, "It is so nice. There are no sirens."

It was late in the night and Stanislava couldn't sleep. She pulled the wedding photograph out of her purse, looked at it for a long time, then put it inside her blouse and pressed it against her heart. The wick in the kerosene lamp flickered. She looked for a piece of paper on which to write.

"Dear Borislav," she began, *"As I write, my heart is beating fast and shaking my whole body. The thought of you being captured—or worse—fills me with fear. I don't know if this will ever reach you, but, as always, I am following your instructions and will mail this to our house in Nis. I pray to God for you to be released soon. Radojka and I are safe with Ilka in Mostar. We miss you and I love you. Yours forever, Draginja."*

The next day Stanislava wrote another letter, this one to her father and mother saying that she would like to come with Radojka to visit. She knew that they could not write or read, but she was hoping they would find someone to read the letter and write an answer for them.

A few days later, Stanislava went to a photography studio to have a portrait made of her and Radojka. In her letter to her parents, she had promised them that she would send a photograph. After the photographs had been taken, she got acquainted with the owner of the studio.

Even though Borislav had arranged for Stanislava's and Radojka's financial security, Stanislava still felt the need to work and keep busy. When she came back to pick up her photographs, she liked them so much she expressed her desire to work at the studio and learn photography. The owner asked her to spend some time in the darkroom behind the studio to see how the photographs were made. "If you like the work," the woman said, "you can earn some money."

Soon, Stanislava was employed at the photography studio, greeting people, taking their pictures, and developing the negatives. Also, the owner occasionally used Stanislava and Radojka at her studio as photography models. She liked Stanislava's photogenic features, her high cheekbones and oval face, and Radojka's playful expressions.

Each day when Stanislava left for the studio, Radojka went upstairs to visit Ilka. In Ilka's room there were two large box windows that she could sit in. The old mill in front of the house could be seen from both windows, but Radojka's favorite view was from the window closer to the Radulja river. The mill's waterwheel, surrounded with fig trees and oleanders, turned constantly as the river flowed underneath it.

"Karolina, come here quickly." Ilka called. "Let's feed the pigeons. Stay still, give me your hand." She put corn kernels into Radojka's little hand. "Now, slowly sprinkle them on the window like this. Let the pigeons see the corn; and don't move. Freeze your hands, and the pigeons will come to you."

Ilka also taught Radojka how to call the doves and pigeons. It was fun watching them fly and land on the window in front of her.

While Stanislava worked, Radojka played with the neighborhood children around the mill and climbed the fig and plum trees. The air was filled with the smell of the lipa and fig trees which the people of Mostar believed was healing for the lungs.

Sometime in the late spring, Radojka got seriously ill. Ilka caught her eating green plums, but it was too late to stop her. Radojka was soon screaming and crying from stomach cramps. Ilka was worried about whether she should call a doctor, but decided to wait until Stanislava came home. In the meantime she massaged Radojka's stomach and gave her hot camomile tea. The tea didn't work, and Radojka started to have convulsions. Foam was coming from her mouth, and her eyes were turned to the side. Her little hands pointed toward her throat. She was getting worse.

When Stanislava arrived and saw Radojka laying stiff in

the bed, she started screaming, "Oh my God, Ilka! What's happened to my child?" Stanislava leaned over and kissed Radojka, touching her forehead. "She's cold! Ilka, Ilka, please help me, help us. She is all that I have."

"You stay here with Radojka. Don't get in a panic," Ilka said. "I have seen this happen before when children eat unripe plums. Calm down, Stanislava, everything is going to be all right. I'm going to run and get a doctor. You stay with her." The doctor that Ilka brought couldn't see what was wrong. "Keep her warm," he said. "This is a strange reaction. I don't know what it could be. It could be malaria. I've never seen such a thing." They called another doctor, and he couldn't do anything either.

For three days Radojka did not move; she was in the same position with her arms crossed on her chest and her hands clutching her throat. Ilka called a third doctor, a very old man and slightly deaf, who Ilka assumed knew much more than the others. When he leaned over Radojka, he couldn't hear her breathing. "I think she is dead," he said.

Stanislava kneeled next to Radojka on the ottoman, crying, kissing her, and shaking her. "You can't be dead. Wake up, please, please. Look at your Mama. I love you." Radojka did not move. Stanislava was in a terrible panic, crying and screaming.

Ilka quickly hugged her, "Stanislava, don't cry. I am going to get a Hodja, a Muslim preacher, and bring him here. Just over the bridge there is a mosque."

"Go, please go get him."

Ilka ran over the old bridge between the mill and the house. She banged on the huge door to the avlia, the courtyard surrounding the mosque. A man came out and immediately knew she was not Muslim because she was not dressed in a shalvare, the traditional Muslim costume.

"Woman, who are you looking for?"

"Please, I need to speak to the Hodja. I need him to come quickly. A child is dying."

The man was confused, mumbling something. Ilka pushed him aside and ran into the mosque. The Hodja was alone on his prayer rug, saying his evening prayers. He was a heavy-set, older man with a long, silver-grey beard, white bushy eyebrows, and a white turban.

Ilka hesitated to interrupt him, but she tapped him lightly on the shoulder and whispered. "Forgive me. Please, please, come with me to save the dear child's life. You must come." Then Ilka kneeled next to him and kissed the floor.

Quietly, the Hodja followed her. When the Hodja saw Radojka, he immediately demanded that Ilka bring him an axe and a pair of scissors. He took the heavy axe, which he was barely able to hold, sang loudly in Islamic "Allah, Allah," and prayed. He hit the ceiling beam three times with the axe. Then, with the scissors, he cut Radojka's dress and repeated "Allah, Allah."

As Stanislava and Ilka watched, they witnessed something unbelievable. Little Radojka began to stretch and move. Her hands, which had been choking her throat, slowly unclutched, and she started to breathe and cough. "Stanislava," Ilka whispered, "Thank God, she is coming back to life."

Both women hugged the Hodja, thanked him, kissed his feet, and offered to pay any amount of money, but he blessed them and refused. He looked at both women, stroked his beard, and pointed his finger to heaven. "Allah will reward me," he said.

* * *

Summer came. The Germans occupied most of Yugoslavia, including Belgrade and Nis, while the Italians, as collaborators with Germany, occupied the coastal regions inland as far as Mostar and Sarajevo. Most of the Royal Yugoslav army had been captured and shipped off to German prison camps.

Mostar had been spared the bombing raids of the initial invasion. However the city was not spared the excesses of the Ustase, who went on a killing spree all over Croatia and Bosnia-Hecegovina to an extent more zealous than the Nazi movement elsewhere in Europe.

For Stanislava, Ilka, and little Radojka, however, day-to-day life continued with its small joys and calamities. One afternoon in June, while Stanislava worked at the photography studio, Ilka had a friend come with a couple of small children. While Ilka had Turkish coffee and chatted with her friend, the children played joyfully outside.

Radojka and her little friends climbed all over the shrubs and trees. A few days earlier, Radojka had seen Ilka with a small knife cutting figs that afternoon, she decided to do the same. She sneaked in the house and came back out with a paring knife.

She was the first one to climb up the tree, cutting the figs and throwing them down to the children below. A few moments later, she fell to the ground on top of the knife. Ilka heard the other children calling; she ran from the house and saw Radojka bleeding at the base of the fig tree. As she looked at her, Ilka noticed that, although Radojka was bleeding a lot, the knife had barely cut the skin of her neck. Then she comforted her. "Don't cry, don't cry, Karolina. It is just a small cut. Ilka loves you."

When Stanislava came home that afternoon, little Radojka ran to her with a big white cloth around her neck. "Mama, Mama, look," she cried, "I cut off my neck."

CHAPTER 12

MIRKO'S DEATH

For Stanislava it was difficult to handle Radojka's second incident. She began to be frustrated and worried. There were too many things on her mind: the war, Borislav's capture, not knowing how to get in touch with him or whether he was alive or dead, and not hearing from her parents.

As soon as Radojka recuperated from her wound, Stanislava decided to go Raketno and see her family. She had not received a reply to the letter she had written her parents, but she decided take a chance and visit them anyway.

When she arrived at the doorstep of the stone house at Raketno, Stanislava did not recognize her mother. She saw a woman dressed all in black and a black babushka on her head. She was sweeping the floor and talking to herself.

"My mother Majko, moja?" Stanislava asked. "Is that you?"

Startled, Andjelka dropped the broom with a loud cry. "Yes, it is me, moja Stano," she said. They both ran into each other arms. Andjelka, embracing her daughter firmly, cried and cried on her shoulder. Radojka, not knowing what was happening, pulled at both women's skirts and cried, too.

Stanislava wondered why her mother was crying.

"Majko, majko, you are in black! Who died? Chacha? Lucia, Jozo, Mirko? What happened?"

Andjelka motioned with her hands, she couldn't talk. With tears in her throat, she whispered, "Mirko ... Mirko. He was killed." With a deep breath, Andjelka tried to explain. "A few moons back," she said, "soldiers came, dressed in some kind of uniform. They wanted Mirko to join them. They were beating him. And poor Mirko was begging them, 'No, no I must stay to help my father.' 'Are you a coward?' one of the soldiers said, 'What kind of man are you?' But Mirko continued to beg them. 'I will join when it is time for me to join.'" Andjelka struggled to talk through her tears. "Then they took me, your father, Mirko—even little Jozo and Lucia—to the barn. They pushed us down to the floor and told us to sit and shut up. They made us watch while they were killing him."

Stanislava was speechless, then suddenly burst into a loud cry. Both women again embraced each other, screamed, and cried together. Mirko, a very soft-spoken young man, had been barely eighteen years old.

Andjelka continued with a wet face. "He was so handsome and hard working. He helped your father with the sheep and goats and the potato garden. The rest of you left us. But his will was to stay with us and help." Andjelka's eyes shifted back to Stanislava, leaving her memory of Mirko to rest for awhile.

"My Stano," she said. "I have not seen you for a long time. And Radojka. Let me look at that little one. She is beautiful." She stroked Radojka's head. "Come with your Baka, let her comb your hair."

Soon, Djurin arrived on a donkey loaded with a couple of bags of new potatoes. His shoes and clothing were muddy from working in the vegetable garden. He looked at Stanislava, then at little Radojka at her side.

"So, Stano, finally you come to see us." Djurin did not smile, but he reached into one of the bags and pulled out a potato that, even with his large hands, he could barely hold in one hand.

"Have you ever seen a potato like this?" he said to Stanislava and threw it to her as he jumped down from the donkey. Even though he did not shake hands with Stanislava or hug her, she sensed that he had missed her. She gently put her arms around her father, put her head on his chest, and heard the strong beat of his heart.

"I'm sorry, Chacha," she said. "About Mirko ... and the grief I have caused." Stanislava, choking with tears in her throat, continued. "Oh, Chacha, I'm so sorry about Mirko. He will never be forgotten in our hearts."

Djurin's eyes were watery but stern. "We can't bring Mirko back. If we could, I would give anything for him."

Djurin bent down to little Radojka, lifted her up high, and said, "Come with me. Dida will show you something." He took her inside the house, sat her in front of him on a small three-legged stool by the fireplace, and said to her, "Now, little Radojka, you will hear the sound of the gusle and receive your first knowledge of the past."

Little Radojka stared at him for a long time, touched his long moustache, and listened without blinking. When he stopped playing and reciting, she said, "Please, Dida, play some more." Stanislava came quietly into the room, leaned against the door, and watched the two of them together. It was like a huge stone had been taken from her shoulders.

* * *

Stanislava enjoyed staying with her parents and helping her mother with the sheep and goats on Oshtric mountain. Stanislava wanted to tell her parents about her marriage to Borislav, and how happy she had been with him. But knowing her father well, she kept her personal life to herself and also instructed Radojka not to mention "tata" to anyone.

While Andjelka, Stanislava, and Lucia took care of the milk and cheese in the mountains, Djurin stayed with little Radojka and Jozo back at the house.

One afternoon when the bees returned to their hives, Djurin took Radojka upstairs to the attic. As he approached the bee hives, he said, "Radojka, don't move. Be still and watch." He spread his arms and started singing and mumbling some words. Suddenly, hundreds of bees landed on his arms and sang back to him. Djurin heard Radojka crying—the bees were stinging her. He quickly sang to the bees; they listened to his command and flew back to their bee hives.

Djurin took Radojka downstairs and pressed fresh tobacco and mud on her bites. As he comforted her, he explained, "Radojka, the bees know only me. Jozo doesn't go up there, because he is afraid of them, and they know. No one else goes to the attic, but me. You were a stranger to them. I am their master; they listen to me."

Later that day he said, "Before your grandmother and your mother return, we must bring some water for supper tonight. Let's go to the vrelo."

The vrelo was where the underground spring water came from the surrounding mountains. With Radojka and Jozo beside him, Djurin carried two large wooden buckets tied with a rope onto a long wooden stick which he carried on his shoulders.

When they arrived at the vrelo, Djurin filled the buckets with cold drinking water. He left the buckets beside the vrelo while they visited a nearby hot spring. Djurin took his shoes off, lit his pipe, and put his feet in the warm water. "Radojka, it is healthy for the feet. Come join Dida and Jozo. Dida comes here every day after work and soaks his feet."

Djurin, Radojka, and Jozo returned to the house and found Andjelka and Stanislava cooking lamb chorba. At the evening meal, Djurin demanded silence. Radojka broke the silence trying to get attention.

"Mama, Mama...." she called, tapping her spoon on Stanislava's hand.

"Sshhh! Your grandfather wants us to be quiet."

Radojka whispered. "I wish Tata was here with us to meet Dida."

"Shuti mala—quiet, little one," Djurin said.

Again, Radojka whispered, "Mama, tell me, do you miss Tata?"

Stanislava leaned over Radojka and said. "Yes, Radojka, I do miss him." Then she got up and faced her father. "Chacha, I would like to tell you something, but I don't know where to begin." She took a deep breath, looked at both of her parents and clasped her hands tightly together in front of her, then she began, "On my first visit home from the convent..." She looked at her father, and suddenly she was speechless. Then she turned, looked at her mother, and was able to continue. "I met this exceptionally nice man who is an officer in the Royal army. Also, upon my return from Raketno on my second visit, we met again on the train. We were married in his church. We lived very happily for three years."

Very upset, Djurin got up from the table and started shouting. "In his church! Did you forget that we are Roman Catholics? You are supposed to marry a man of our kind! Catholic, like you!" he said as he pounded with his fist on the table.

Jozo and Radojka, scared, quickly hid behind Stanislava and Andjelka, who clung to each other. Stanislava took courage and spoke again quietly but firmly. "Perhaps it would be better for me to go away from you again ... I don't want to be a burden to you."

"Where would you go? There is war everywhere. Where is that loving man of yours, now?"

"He is captured. He was protecting our country against the Germans."

"Stano, you listen to me now. Remember! You are Roman Catholic." Then he waved his finger and said. "Don't tell anyone here in Raketno that you are married to a Serbian, because I have told everyone, whoever asked about you, that you are married in Mostar to a man of our kind."

Stanislava realized that revolution was rising everywhere among the Croatian and Serbian brotherhood and that it would not be safe for her and Radojka to stay in Raketno. A city like Mostar, she felt, would be much safer, at least for a short time.

CHAPTER 13

THE GYPSY WOMAN

Two days after Stanislava returned to Mostar, Ilka gave her a new identification card with her maiden name on it which she got from a friend in the city hall who owed Ilka a favor. Since Ilka liked Stanislava and cared for her like her own daughter, she worried that Stanislava might get in trouble for being the wife of a Serbian officer who was fighting against the Germans and their Italian collaborators. If anyone found out she was married to a Serbian, a Ustase assassin could simply end her life in the middle of the night. She would be like thousands of others who had mysteriously died or disappeared, only to turn up along with all the other bodies floating down the Neretva.

Stanislava started to work again at the photography studio. As the occupation continued through the fall of 1941 and into the spring of 1942, the photography business dropped drastically for the local people. Even though the owner wanted to close her studio, she was forced to stay open to serve her new customers, the Italian and German soldiers. It was hard for Stanislava to photograph the enemy soldiers, especially when she thought of Borislav being captured, but she continued to work because the owner needed her.

It had been over a year since the bombing of Nis and Borislav's capture, and Stanislava had still not received a letter from him. Almost every week Stanislava would pull out the photograph of Borislav, look at it, and show it to Radojka. Occasionally, Radojka would ask, "Mama, when is tata coming back to us?" And Stanislava hated to answer, but she did. "I don't know, draga Radojka, but I hope it will be soon."

One afternoon late in the summer, just before Stanislava came home from work, Radojka sneaked out into the back yard without Ilka's permission. From the upstairs room Ilka heard a child screaming. Rushing to the window, she saw a gypsy woman grab Radojka and run out into the street. By the time Ilka got down the stairs, the gypsy had disappeared.

Ilka rushed into the street. "Radojka has been kidnapped by gypsies!" she yelled to the neighbors. "Please help me find her." No one heard Ilka's cries for help. Ilka ran down the street toward the photography studio.

When Stanislava saw Ilka running toward her all upset and crying, she immediately sensed that something had happened to Radojka. She screamed. "Oh, my God, what has happened to her!"

Breathless, Ilka tried to tell Stanislava what had happened. "Gypsies ... They have kidnapped our little girl. I was writing letters, and I didn't hear her sneaking out."

Stanislava screamed and burst into tears. "Moja slatka – my sweet Radojka! We have to find her!"

"Stanislava, we must go to the police," Ilka said. "I know they will find her."

They quickly went to the city police and told them what had happened. Stanislava, Ilka, and the police searched everywhere in the city. They searched every restaurant, every market place, and behind all the stores, everywhere the gypsies gathered. There was no trace of Radojka. It was late at night when they got home. They were very tired, but they couldn't sleep.

Early the next day they returned to the police station to find if they had any news of Radojka. One of the policemen who had been involved in the search talked with them briefly. "I am sorry," he said, "we haven't found her yet. We spotted a group of gypsies and we deported them, but they didn't have any children with them. But don't you worry, we will find her."

For Stanislava the days that followed were like a nightmare; she couldn't sleep or eat. Both women were very upset, but they continued their search. The days turned into nights very fast. Soon a month had passed, and they still had not found Radojka. But they did not give up.

* * *

Early one morning when Ilka was shopping at the pijaca, the open peasant market, she ran into an older woman from the neighborhood who knew about Radojka's kidnapping. The woman told her she had seen a large group of gypsy wagons camped on the outskirts of Mostar. "You should go there," she suggested to Ilka. "I saw a lot of children with them."

Ilka rushed back home and told Stanislava what she had heard. "Stanislava, let's hurry. I think we will find Radojka today."

Stanislava's eyes opened wide, and Ilka could see a trace of hope in them. They both walked all day to the outskirts of Mostar. Finally, they spotted the gypsy camp near the road around some old, deserted barracks. Stanislava and Ilka quietly hid behind bushes and watched for a while. They saw gypsies in front of their wagons and ponies tied to the back of the wagons.

Children were jumping barefoot over open fires. Stanislava and Ilka were both very sad; they didn't see Radojka anywhere.

"Ilka," Stanislava said, "let's wait a little longer. We might still see her because people are going in and out of the wagons."

Some of the gypsies danced and some of them played music. Close by in another wagon, Stanislava and Ilka saw one of the gypsy women dancing barefoot around the fire with a tambourine as others watched. She was instructing young girls how to dance. Whenever the gypsy woman turned over the tambourine to show the girls how to beg, the shiny metal cymbals sparkled with the reflected light from the fire.

One of the gypsy men, with a red scarf on his head and a patch over one eye, was pulling a pretty, girlish-looking woman around him. She had black curly hair. The gypsy man was grabbing her, trying to kiss her. He whispered something into her ear. She giggled, laughed, and teased him, then both of them walked toward the bushes where Stanislava and Ilka were hiding. The couple rolled over and over, kissing and making love. Neither Stanislava nor Ilka dared to move, even when the gypsy man got up and pissed in the bushes over their heads.

After the gypsy "pirate" and his woman left, Ilka spit towards the bushes, then lit a cigarette. "Those dirty gypsies," she whispered. "If I could, I would pull his eyes out."

Stanislava was stunned and sick in her stomach. Ilka, seeing Stanislava's pale face, lifted her up and said, "Let's go home and continue our search tomorrow."

It was dark. On the way home, Ilka and Stanislava were stopped by Italian and local police. "Stop, who is there? Stop or we will shoot."

"Please, please don't shoot," Ilka said. "We are two women looking for a lost child." When the police came closer, they asked for identification. Rudely, one of the soldiers yelled, "There is a curfew. Don't you know? You must follow our rules." After they checked their identification cards, they let them go.

* * *

Everyday and everywhere Stanislava and Ilka searched for little Radojka. Both women were exhausted and frustrated, but they wouldn't give up. They persistently continued their search out of the Mostar area.

They heard of a large resort hotel not far from the outskirts of Mostar where gypsy bands performed. They took a bus to the resort, arriving late in the afternoon. As they came close to the hotel, they saw many people sitting in the bashta at tables under colorful umbrellas. The smell in the air of lamb roasting on a burning grill was so enticing that Stanislava and Ilka stopped to eat. Sitting at the table, surrounded by many other people, they waited for any strolling gypsies to come by.

After an hour or two passed, several gypsies came up to the tables and begged for money. The first group of gypsies were women, followed by lots of young women and a few little girls. One little girl played an accordion for the people. Another little girl came with a tambourine and danced. The girl with the tambourine had curly hair and looked like Shirley Temple. For a moment, Stanislava thought she was Radojka, but she wasn't.

Stanislava and Ilka spent the night in the hotel. The next day they waited at the bashta to have one more chance to see if any more gypsies would come by the tables. Again they sat at a table, but much farther away from the commotion of people coming in and out of the terrace. Suddenly, Ilka grabbed Stanislava's arm.

"Stano, look!" she whispered, pointing to a little girl with curly brown hair and lots of rouge on her face. "The little girl in the gypsy costume!"

The little girl danced between the tables with her tambourine. People showered her with money. When the music stopped, she gathered the coins and paper off the floor and put it in her tambourine. The little girl passed near Stanislava and Ilka's table, they right away recognized little Radojka.

Stanislava jumped from the chair, grabbed the tambourine and little Radojka's hand, and the money from the tambourine fell to the ground.

"Sunce moje, my sunshine, my Radojka."

Radojka started to cry "Mama, Mama" and clung to her mother. Ilka, with happiness in her heart and tears in her eyes, stood behind and embraced them both.

While the gypsies were picking up the money from the ground, one of the gypsy women came behind Stanislava, cussing her and hitting her. "Give me that child back...."

"This is my child," Stanislava screamed, "and no one will ever take her away from me." She looked at Radojka and held her tightly to her chest. The gypsy woman grabbed Radojka's legs and pulled her away from Stanislava.

"I want her back," the gypsy said, "I taught her how to dance and to make money for me." Stanislava clutched Radojka so tightly, she screamed in pain.

A policeman came and asked, "What is happening here?" He looked back and forth at both women, then turned to Stanislava.

"Madam, what is happening? Would you explain to me?" he asked. Stanislava put Radojka down in front of her. Radojka held on to her skirt. When Stanislava tried to talk, the gypsy woman interrupted her. The policeman yelled to the gypsy, "Chuti, woman, the lady is talking." He looked down to little Radojka. "Little girl, tell me the truth. I am a policeman. Which one is your mother?"

The gypsy woman whispered in little Radojka's ear and pinched her arm: "Tell him I'm your mother. Say it! If you don't, I will take your eyes out."

Little Radojka was petrified. She spread her little hands and pointed toward both women. She looked at the gypsy woman, and quickly frowned like she was scared of something, then she turned toward Stanislava and gently smiled. Finally, she turned to the policeman. "I like both Mommies," she said, "but I want to go home with this Mommy." The policeman realized the truth and arrested the gypsy.

On the way back to Mostar, little Radojka told her mother and Ilka that the gypsy woman had taught her how to dance. She liked it much better than staying home alone with Ilka while her "mama" worked. She told them that some children, especially the little boys, were taught how to steal money from a man's wallet. Also, she said she could stay all night with them singing and dancing.

As little Radojka talked and talked about the gypsies, she fell asleep between Stanislava and Ilka. Stanislava looked at the little face all made up with rouge and, smiling, said to Ilka. "We have to keep a close eye on our little gypsy from now on."

CHAPTER 14

ON THE ADRIATIC COAST

After all the turmoil of 1941 and 1942—the bombings, Borislav's capture, Radojka being near death, Mirko's death, and Radojka's kidnapping—Stanislava decided to take Radojka away from Mostar to recuperate. During her visit with her parents, Stanislava had learned from her mother that she had a cousin on the Adriatic coast near the city of Split. She remembered the cousin's name, Maria Sharic, but she did not know her married name.

When Stanislava arrived in Split, she searched for her cousin. She didn't realize Split was such a big city and no one knew of her cousin's family. Since Split was an international port, ships from Italy filled the harbor. Armed Italian and German soldiers were all over the city pushing and arresting people.

For Stanislava, the best thing was to get out of the city. Remembering that Andjelka had told her that Maria's village was just outside of Split, Stanislava walked and walked along the main road next to sea, with Radojka dragging behind. On the road between the homes and the sea, she saw older men and women sitting in terraces covered with vines full of grapes to be harvested.

Exhausted, and hungry, they finally reached the outskirts of Split and stopped in a small restaurant. Every table at the restaurant was filled with soldiers, but Stanislava decided to go in anyway because Radojka was cranky and hungry. She walked straight to the kitchen where she found one woman who was the cook and waitress. Stanislava asked her for something to eat, even a piece of bread and water. The woman was extremely busy but as she passed her with plates of food in her hands, she winked at Stanislava, saying, "Go in the kitchen. Help yourself."

Stanislava looked into the cupboards, found some cornbread, then sat on the kitchen doorstep and shared the bread with Radojka. A few moments later, the woman returned. "There is not much left," she said, "only a little bit of potato chorba."

"Please, give us anything. We have not eaten all day." The woman handed her a ceramic bowl with the chorba and two spoons. Shortly after Radojka had eaten she fell asleep on the kitchen floor, and Stanislava put her purse under Radojka's head.

As the woman went in and out of the kitchen, Stanislava tried to catch her and ask about her cousin. "Would you know Maria Sharic?" Stanislava asked. "She is married to a man named Lazar, but I do not know his last name. Maria is from my mother's side of the family. We have not seen each other since we were children." Stanislava drifted into a day dream for a few seconds, but her thoughts were disrupted by the noise of a knife banging against a glass.

The restaurant woman apologized. "I have to run," she whispered. "I have to serve those animals out there." One of the soldiers, who was leaning against the kitchen door with a tooth-pick in his mouth, overheard her. Then he laughed and kicked the woman on her bottom. "Hurry, bring us something to eat. We are in a hurry."

The woman was in pain, but she had to serve the barbarian. When she returned to the kitchen, she crossed herself and said. "Thank God, the soldiers are gone. Do you see what we have to do?" Shaking her head, she continued. "To survive, we have to kiss their feet." The woman sat on the kitchen chair, took a deep breath. "This is the first time I've been able to sit since dawn. Forgive me for not hearing you earlier. Did you say you have a cousin? What was her name?"

"Maria Sharic," Stanislava repeated. "She is from Mostar and she married a Dalmatian man somewhere around here."

The woman immediately recalled the name. "Yes, I know Maria. Lazar, Maria's husband, used to go fishing with my husband just before the war started. You see that house, painted in blue; it is the third house facing the sea. That is where they live."

Stanislava and Radojka arrived at her cousin's house on a cove by the sea. The back of the house faced the mountains and the main road to Split. The front yard—full of oleanders, orange, lemon, and olive trees—faced the sea. There were ropes tied from one olive tree to another, on which a tall, pretty woman was hanging a basket of clothing to dry. Stanislava called, "Hallo, hallo, I was told my cousin Maria Sharic lives here."

The woman dropped the basket and looked with surprise at Stanislava. "I am Maria. Who are you?"

"I am Stanislava, I am your cousin. My mother is sister to your father."

"Oh, yes, I remember. When we were little we played together, and your father's bees stung me when we sneaked into the attic." As the woman talked, two children, a little older than

Radojka, came out. "Those are my children," Maria said. "My husband Lazar has gone to fight Germans and Italians somewhere in the mountains."

Maria and her family occupied the bottom floor of the house. Visitors were given the main room on the second floor with a balcony that also faced the sea.

For a few days, Stanislava and Radojka enjoyed the beautiful Adriatic sun and sat on the balcony watching the warships going by. Then one night their tranquility was disturbed by the sounds of high winds and strong surf. They were awaken from a deep sleep when the heavy shutters on the windows of their room started slamming back and forth. Radojka began to cry, and Stanislava got up to close the shutters.

As the storm grew stronger, Maria came upstairs with her children, and they all spent the night together. The waves from the Bura, the hurricane, had begun flooding the house below. The following day the sun came up very early as usual, and the Bura was over.

Necessary visits to Split's markets and stores were frightening. Stanislava witnessed horrible scenes of men being hung on the poles of street lights and executed in the middle of the square. She felt much safer staying at Maria's home.

* * *

In Stanislava's heart and soul, she felt that Borislav was still alive. She wrote another letter to let him know that she and Radojka were staying near Split. During the war, women and children were often messengers because the men were either hiding or fighting. Maria introduced Stanislava to an older woman who had some relatives in Nis and was traveling back and forth. The woman was instructed to deliver the letter to either of the wives of Borislav's best men.

The fall and the winter passed, and still there was not a word from Borislav. Stanislava again wrote to him, hoping to make contact.

In the early spring of 1943, as Stanislava walked with Radojka by the sea near Maria's house, she heard the voice of a young boy calling. "Teta, Teta—aunt, this is for you." He ran toward Stanislava and handed her a stained piece of paper folded several times. "Grandmother...grandmother told me to give this to you. The German soldiers took her away...They took her away to a prison because a long time ago she was married to a Jewish man."

Before Stanislava had a chance to say a word, the boy ran away. "Thank you," she yelled, but the boy had disappeared down the shore.

Afraid to unfold the dirty paper, she kissed it and held to her chest, knowing positively that it was from Borislav. But the fear of finding that something terrible had happened to him made her heart beat tremendously fast.

Even though the sand was wet from a previous rain, Stanislava sat down with Radojka in her lap and looked in her daughter's eyes. "Hold me hard," she said, "if I start to cry. Razumes moja mala—you understand, my little one?"

"Yes, my mama. Can I hold you now? Because I can see your eyes are full of tears already." Stanislava could not help it; she smiled and kissed her.

When Stanislava unfolded the stained paper, a dried flower from the lipa tree fell on the ground. She lifted Radojka up in the air and screamed with excitement, "He is alive, thank God. Borislav is alive. Tata is alive, moja Radojka."

"Dear Stanislava," the letter began, *"I have received your letters and have written to you, but I am not sure that my letters have reached you. In case they haven't, let tell you again what has happened.*

"I don't know if you heard or not, but I was captured by the Germans. When they were transferring us, someone threw a bomb in front of the truck, and several of us escaped. Many nights and days I traveled over the hills and mountains and finally reached Serbia. I have joined the Dobrovoljci, the military branch that previously belonged to the King's army, but I don't think I will stay long with them or join the others.

"The Germans," he continued, *"are still very strong and there is heavy fighting everywhere. The country of Southern Slavs, Yugoslavia, is left without a leader, and a revolution is in process.*

"Some of the King's generals have decided to organize their own leadership, and they elected one of their leading generals, Draza Mihalovic, to lead them against Germany. Russia took the opportunity of the weakness of our torn country and appointed a Yugoslav communist leader, Tito, who was trained in Russia, to lead the partisans—freedom fighters who also fought against the Germans.

"People are confused about who to join, because all four branches are against the Germans and for freedom; all claim they are the best for the people. In some situations people are forced to join one of the parties; if they don't, they are shot or executed in other ways.

"I don't believe that communism is healthy for Yugoslavia, but I don't want to fight against my brothers. Instead, I have been writing articles which explain what a deadly cancer communism is and how it must be stopped. I am distributing leaflets

from town to town and village to village."

He finished his letter by telling her that he was in hiding. *"Please come back to Nis, and contact Kuma Vera, our best man's wife. Periodically I keep in touch with her. In case something happens to Kuma Vera, look for messages from me under the stone on the left side of the gazebo. I miss you and Radmila very much and I need you now more than ever."*

—Borislav

Stanislava kissed the letter and cried from happiness. In her mind she already knew what she had to do next. She wrote a short letter to Ilka, telling her she would be going back to Nis to try to find Borislav. *"Please do not worry about us,"* she wrote, *"I will be back someday to pick up my other belongings. When you drink coffee and feed the pigeons, close your eyes and think of us.*

Our love to you, to the doves, pigeons and beautiful Mostar. Stanislava and your Karolina"

CHAPTER 15

THE MAN IN THE CHIMNEY

It was the middle of the winter when Stanislava took the train to Nis with Radojka. The train was full of German soldiers asking for identification. The train was so cold people were coughing and hiding in their collars. Each time the train stopped, Stanislava watched German soldiers push Yugoslavian prisoners into the train. Their clothes were torn and they looked tired and unshaven. One of the men was an officer who had dark features and looked so much like Borislav. For a moment, Stanislava almost called his name. The sight frightened Stanislava. Now, more than ever, she had to find Borislav.

Stanislava and Radojka arrived in Nis. They were hungry and tired, but there was no food to be found. Again, soldiers were everywhere. Almost all the stores and buildings were damaged in some way by the bombing. Pieces of shrapnel from the bombs littered the streets. Lots of buildings had been demolished. The city looked terribly torn, unrecognizable, and depressing.

From the train station, Stanislava and Radojka walked to the Kuma Vera's house to pick up messages from Borislav. As they came within sight of the entrance to the house, Stanislava saw two German soldiers coming out of the front door. Realizing what had happened, Stanislava turned around quietly and said to Radojka, "Just hold Mommy's hand and don't say anything."

Only a few blocks separated Kuma Vera's house from theirs. Stanislava ran to the gazebo and found a short note from Borislav under the stone.

"Dear Draginja," the note said, "It is much safer for you and Radmila to stay in one of the villages on the outskirts of Nis. The peasants always have plenty of food. But first you must go to Prokuplje and look for a family named Popovic. When you arrive there, someone will inform me. I will come to see you both. The Popovic family and their parents knew my father well; they were members of his church."

Immediately, Stanislava and Radojka went to the train station. Not more than an hour's train ride later, they arrived in Prokuplje. The surroundings were unbelievably pleasant. The little train station was sheltered by a pine forest with branches covered with white puffy snow. In the distance they could see hills covered with dark green pine forests and huge, snow-capped mountains. Nearby was Mt. Jastrebac, the site of a winter sports center.

At the train station Stanislava asked how to find the Popovic family. A station attendant pointed them to a group of men with a horse-drawn wagon and said, "He is fixing the horse's head cover." As they approached, the man turned around as if he were expecting them and said, "Madame, I am the next door neighbor of the Popovic family." Without raising the attention of the others, he whispered, "You have a choice: walk the two kilometers, or ride with my pigs and me."

Stanislava and Radojka climbed into the hay in the back of the wagon. Stanislava held Radojka's hand firmly. They did not say much to each other, just listened to the squeals and grunts of Mama Pig and her piglets, whose privacy had been disturbed.

When they arrived in front of the Popovic house, several neighbors' children came running towards the horses, throwing snow balls. The Popovic family came out. Stanislava introduced herself to them and they gave her a warm welcome. A tall, thin man with black hair and thick bushy eyebrows was the first to introduce himself: "I am Rajko," he said, "and this is my wife Zora." She was also tall and thin, a pretty woman but quiet.

Rajko and Zora were living with Rajko's parents, following a Serbian tradition that, when a son marries, he brings his bride to his father's house and they all live together. Rajko and Zora had two young sons and a little girl who was a couple years older than Radojka. As a family, the Popovic were well off, with their productive farm, a large house, and a barn full of livestock.

Stanislava also learned some bad news. Their oldest son, who was almost fifteen, had been influenced by his friends to join the Chetnicks.

He was a courier, which was a very dangerous assignment for only the most intelligent and skillful young boys. Couriers frequently had to circumvent battles and cross through enemy lines to get messages to other units. If caught by the Partisans or Germans, the Chetnick couriers were frequently tortured. The innocence of the young somehow made it easier to go through the lines and escape suspicion.

It was late; everyone was tired and went to their rooms to sleep. Stanislava and Radojka had the room closest to the barn. Just before they fell asleep they heard, through a slightly open window, the occasional snorting and sneezing of the cows and horses.

* * *

The next day was very busy in the Popovic house. Everyone had a duty to perform for the coming holy family day called
Slava, the Saint day. Once a year, each Serbian family celebrated
their own unique Saint with family and lots of friends. The
women of the house baked and cooked many Slavic dishes—
sarma, stuffed sour cabbage leaves with beef, pork, and lamb;
pastry with cheese and meat; all kinds of stroudles, baklava,
tortas; and zito, a whole wheat grain cooked and mixed with
pecan and walnuts. Outside on an open spit, the men prepared
and roasted a whole young crispy pig. This year's Slava was very
quiet, with just the immediate family.

On the second night, just past midnight, Stanislava was
awakened by noises outside her window. A few moments later,
she heard someone whisper her name. Frightened, she jumped
from the bed and hid behind the drapery. Again, someone
whispered her name. Stanislava poked her head through the
drapes and saw a man crawling through the window. "Draginja,
Draginja." Even though more than two years had passed since
she had seen Borislav, Stanislava immediately recognized
his voice.

As they embraced, he whispered, "Moje Sunce Slatko, I
missed you." Stanislava clung to him and would not let go, crying with happiness. "Please, Borislav, don't ever leave us again."

They were both bathed in tears. Stanislava shut the window, pulled the drapes, and lit a small kerosene lamp. She took
a long look at his face and thought to herself, "Oh my Boro, he
looks so tired."

"Are you well, Boro?"

"Yes, but I have had many sleepless nights and I am restless. Too many things on my mind. I worry about you and

Radmila, about what the next day will bring, if I'm going to see you again. I have duties to perform, but I'm torn in pieces. I don't know what is going to happen in our country; too many leaders."

Stanislava kissed him. "I'm sorry, I'm sorry. I don't know how to help you, but I'm sure God will be guiding you whatever happens. What is meant to be, will be. It is God's will."

They lay down on the floor. Silently they held each other for a long time. Borislav could barely keep his eyes open. "Draginja, talk to me. Don't let me fall asleep," he yawned— then immediately fell asleep.

Stanislava stroked his unshaved face and watched him, unable to sleep. She went back in her memories to when he was teaching her how to dance, how he looked so clean and freshly shaved in his officer's uniform. And now, my poor Borislav, he wear soiled peasant clothes.

She touched his cheek and whispered, "But now I love you even more."

He heard her voice and put his hand over hers.

"I hear you, Draginja, my love. Don't worry, Sunce Moje, the war will soon be over and all of us will be together again."

Borislav sat on the corner of the bed at their daughter's feet. He watched her as she slept.

"How she has changed...." He bent over and kissed her face, then uncurled her little fingers, took a dunja, a quince, from his pocket, and put it in her hand.

Radojka stirred in her sleep, then slowly opened her eyes and looked in her hand.

"Mama, dunja! dunja!"

"Sshh, Radojka....this is Tata. He has come to see us."

As Radojka squeezed the dunja in her little hand, she

Andgelka and Djurin Pavkovic'
Stanislava's parents from Raketno,
Bosnia-Hercegovina.

Strasimir and Juliana Bulic' from Nis, Serbia.
Borislav standing in front of father.

 Stanislava
and
Radojka

"NUN and the OFFICER"
Stanislava and Major
Borislav Bulic'.
Wedding picture with best men.

Borislav (l) with friends.

Borislav (l) with fellow officers.

Borislav (7th from r) with his unit commanded by General Radosavljevich (l front), Jajce 1941.

"Little Radojka".

Radojka and Stanislava.

Radojka and Miloje.

Radojka and Stanislava with Slobodan.

Miloje (l) as a junior
officer with friends.

Srbislav (c), Borislav's nephew. Olympic competition.

Stanislava and Miloje

Slobodan

THE FORMER
YUGOSLAVIA
PRIOR TO 1991

SLOVENIA

● MARIBOR

SENTILJ

● ZAGREB

CROATIA

BOSNIA-HERZCEGOVIA

● BEOGRAD

ZADAR

44°NORTH LATITUDE

SERBIA

● SARAJEVO

KRAGUJEVAC ●

SPLIT

● RAKETNO
● POSUSJE
● IMOTSKI

PROKUPLJE ● ● NIS

◆ MOSTAR

● MEDJUGORJE

ADRIATIC SEA

MONTENEGRO

├── SCALE 100 MILES ──┤

18° EAST LONGITUDE

MACEDONIA

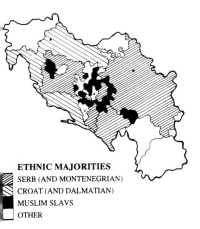

ETHNIC MAJORITIES
SERB (AND MONTENEGRIAN)
CROAT (AND DALMATIAN)
MUSLIM SLAVS
OTHER

GERMANY

CZECH

SLOVAKIA

UKRAIN

AUSTRIA

ITALY

HUNGARY

ROMANIA

YUGOSLAVIA

BULGARIA

ALBANIA

GREECE

TURKEY

Mostar—As we all remember it, before it was destroyed in 1993 during the civil war in Bosnia-Hercegovina.

remembered how he had given her dunja once before. She felt strange for a moment, then she smiled and hugged him: "Tata, are you going to stay here forever? I love you up to the sky."

"I love you too up to the sky. I cannot stay now, but I will be back soon. I promise."

He turned to Stanislava. "Draginja," he said, "the situation is very bad. Listen to me, and just do as I say. If anyone asks about your husband, you have to say he was taken to a German prison. That way, both of you will be safe."

Stanislava and Borislav embraced, then he quietly climbed through the window and was gone.

* * *

Early the next morning everyone sat around the table eating a traditional country breakfast known as kachamak, with kajmak, a cooked hot cornmeal with aged cream-butter served on top.

Stanislava was late for breakfast. She greeted them all with an apology and could not look in their faces. From across the table, Rajko's mother stared at Stanislava with a questioning look on her face. She came around the table, and tapped Stanislava on the shoulder. With her toothless smile she said, "Hope you slept well last night." Then she whispered in Stanislava's ear, "It was my duty to leave your bedroom window open."

"Zorice, come here," Rajko interrupted. He patted her gently on her bottom and said, "How about some Turkish coffee?"

Zora smiled at Rajko with her shiny gold front tooth, and playfully hit him on the head. "Dobro—great! Since today is Slava, I want all of you to know," Zora turned around and looked at every one. "I waited in line three hours for this coffee. It will be the best coffee."

Rajko got up from the table, holding a glass of slivovica, plum brandy, in his hand. "Zeveli, to health. A toast and hope that our first born son will be here." As he spoke, tears came to his eyes. "Let's keep our Slavic tradition and keep our family gathering on this day." He gulped the slivovica and sat down.

Early in the evening, just after sundown, everyone sat at the table, which was full of traditional Slava food. The sound of footsteps on the wooden kitchen floor got everyone's attention. Suddenly, silence. A tall, handsome young man, tired and unshaved, whispered "Sshh, close the curtains and lock the doors." Everyone jumped from their chairs and ran to hug him— the young man was Popovic's oldest son.

The Slava candle was still burning as they all returned to the table to finish the meal. Everyone was happy to see the young man who had risked his life to come home for Slava until loud voices interrupted their moments of joy.

"Open up, open up, or we will break the door!" Rajko peeked through the little hole in the door and saw several men with mixed uniforms and a red star on their hats.

"Partisans! Oh my God, Partisans!" he whispered and motioned to his son to hide. "Hide! Quickly, hide! Zora, put Tito's picture on the wall and hide Draza Mihailovic's picture." The young man hid in the chimney; he knew that if the partisans found him, they would kill him on the spot.

The men broke in through the door with their guns and shouted, "Where is he? We *know* he is somewhere in the house." One of the soldiers grabbed Rajko, hit him several times, and threw him on the floor. The partisan soldier shouted at him, "We know it's Slava day. Speak up, old man. Is your son here?

Where is your son?"

The men furiously searched the house, pushing everyone around and turning everything upside down. Stanislava was petrified, thinking that the partisans were looking for her and Borislav. She pulled the scarf from around her neck to cover her head like a babushka and rubbed her face with dirt from the fireplace to disguise herself as old peasant woman. She held Radojka in one arm and somebody's else child in the other, praying to God they would not question her.

In the fireplace, there were still traces of slow burning logs. Rajko and Zora could see that one heel of their son's foot was slipping down. Quickly, they stood with their backs to the fireplace, but one of the partisan soldiers pushed Rajko aside and saw the foot.

Zora screamed and fell to her knees. She begged the partisan to spare her son, but the soldiers pulled the young man down.

"They took me away," the boy plead, "I didn't want to go."

The father screamed, "He's young, please leave him alone."

One of the partisans hit the Rajko over the head with his rifle. Another cut Rajko's son's head off.

CHAPTER 16

CAPTURED BY PARTISANS

After the funeral, Stanislava and Radojka stayed with Rajko's family to help Zora temporarily overcome her sorrow for her lost son. Shortly after the funeral, Borislav returned to see Stanislava. It was very late when Borislav arrived, but even though he was tired he wanted to tell Stanislava all about his personal war against communism. "Where does the time go, Draginja," Borislav said. "It is almost the end of the war with the Germans. But the partisans are gaining strength, and it looks like the communists will take over. As you see, my Draginja, there is another war coming."

Stanislava glanced at the sleeping Radojka, and whispered, "My Boro, if the communists take over, what will they do to us?"

"Most likely execute us, or put us in prison. Who knows? I do not want to fight against my own brothers, but I strongly believe that communism is a deadly cancer. My Draginja, that is the reason I have traveled to so many different cities, towns, and villages—everywhere I could—to hand out the pamphlets I have written. Also, I cannot stay in one place for very long. I would be caught and recruited by either the Chetnicks or the Partisans."

"Borislav, I understand. It has been and will be very hard

for us. Where ever you go, I will follow."

For a while Stanislava tried to follow Borislav from town to town, from village to village, but it was very stressful and exhausting. A couple of months passed without a word from him, and Stanislava returned to stay with Rajko's family. Late one night, a young courier knocked on the door and asked for Stanislava personally. The courier told her that Borislav had been forced to join the Chetnicks and he would be in touch with her at the Nis address.

Stanislava returned to Nis to check the gazebo for any messages from Borislav. When she arrived, she saw German solders were going in and out of the house. She was frightened. She watched for awhile, until a woman came out who asked her if she could help. "This is my house," Stanislava told her, "I have just come back from visiting my parents."

The woman introduced herself as a German translator. "We are occupying the house for our offices," she said, rather coldly. "Nothing will be damaged or taken. One of our superior officers is a strict Catholic. When he saw rosaries and icons of the holy Mary, he was so impressed that he told everyone not to touch anything." The translator finished by telling Stanislava that she could not stay there. "You must find somewhere else to live," she said, then turned and walked away.

Desperate, hungry, and now homeless, Stanislava and Radojka sat on the doorstep and begged the Germans for some food. One of the officers who came to see the commotion spoke a little broken Serbo-Croatian. In civilian life he had been a medical doctor and he had been recruited into the army against his will. He told Stanislava how much he hated war, and how much he missed his wife and his little daughter. The German doctor then gave Stanislava some food and Radojka a couple of chocolates.

Stanislava asked if she could come back periodically and visit the gazebo, because Radojka liked to play there.

"I am sorry," he said, "but that is not possible. I am not in command here." Stanislava turned away and walked toward the train station, the only safe place to spend the night.

The next morning Stanislava decided to go to the Catholic church for help. There seemed no other alternative. Even though she had been excommunicated, she was more familiar with her own church than her adopted Serbian religion. Since Stanislava had hospital experience, the administrator hired her immediately because there were too many injured and sick people for the nuns to handle alone. Stanislava told the administrator that Radojka was at the age to start kindergarten. "Bring the child along," he said. "We will we do our best to help you."

The mother superior in charge of the nuns at the kindergarten told Stanislava there was no room. "We have so many orphans here," she said. "But, do not worry, we can always take one more child. Radojka will be safer here with us and have someone to play with."

The day Radojka started kindergarten in the cloister with the nuns, she cried and begged Stanislava. "I want to be with you all the time. I don't care where it is."

"Radojka, I work many nights and can't leave you alone. You will be much safer here. The rules of the cloister are that all the children must stay in the cloister together."

Stanislava left Radojka in the cloister with the nuns and found a one-room flat with a shower in a little house next to the train station she shared with a widowed older woman.

On Saint Nicholas Day of that year, 1943, Stanislava attended a Christmas party with the other mothers at the Catholic cloisters school. In a large room of the church was a nicely decorated table for all the children. On one side of the table were gifts and a statue of Saint Nicholas. On the other side, a person was dressed in a black suit with red ears and a long tail all of metal chain. Traditionally, good children would receive toys, chocolates, and baskets with dolls from Saint Nicholas; bad children would receive a long stocking filled with ashes from the devil.

When Stanislava saw Radojka receive the dreaded stocking full of ashes and burst into tears, she was very upset. According to the nuns, Radojka was wetting her bed because she was scared to go to the bathroom at night. Since it was a holiday, parents could take their children out of the cloisters for a few days. Stanislava took Radojka to her room by the train station. They were happy together again for a while. For a few nights, Radojka had fun watching the reflections of the trains on the wall and listening to the sounds they made.

* * *

Springtime in Nis, 1944, and the city was bare. The row of lipa trees had been run down by German tanks. Stanislava loved nature, the mountains, and the sea. She felt a need to walk in the evenings, to see the sky and the stars, to smell the evening air. But no one was supposed to be seen on the streets at all after dark.

Even for a woman who was exceptionally strong mentally and physically, it began to be impossible to cope. For Stanislava there was not much left in Nis. Just before her decision to leave Nis again, she heard the Voice of America on the radio announce that the Partisans, jointly with the Russians, Americans, and British, were winning the war against the Germans. The allies had been bombing the supply lines of the Germans to their North African Corps which passed through Zagreb, Beograd, and Nis en route to the Greek port of Solonica on the Mediterranean. In a matter of days, the announcer on the radio stated, the Germans would be capitulating.

Hearing this good news gave Stanislava hope again; she decided she would continue to stay in Nis and look for Borislav.

The German announcements on the radio became urgent. Repeatedly, the Germans told everyone to get out of their homes and leave the city immediately, using the major roads. Stanislava and Radojka joined the other people on the road going away from the city.

On the way to the outskirts of the city, the German soldiers hid behind the civilians, using them as shields against bombing and strafing by the allies. People were pushed by the German soldiers to move faster and faster. The young and old were tired and worn out. The road was full of tanks, trucks, and lots of people.

People were confused and in panic. This was the only highway that the German soldiers could use to get in and out of Nis. On both sides of the road were woods and corn fields.

Suddenly, a couple of fighter planes with guns banked over the road and started shooting. People were screaming and running everywhere. Stanislava grabbed Radojka's hand and the suitcase, then ran to the cornfield. She laid face down on the ground, covered Radojka with the suitcase, and prayed. A few moments later the planes were gone.

Stanislava kissed Radojka and pulled her to kneel and pray. "Thank God, we are alive and not hurt. Look, Radojka, our suitcase is full of scratches and holes. It saved our lives. Moja Radojka, we have been blessed and lucky. God has saved us again. You must not forget this, ever." Stanislava warned her daughter, "Radojka, just look at me always. Don't look left or right." People lay dead and injured around them. The cries of the injured people sounded like a million crows in the trees.

* * *

Shortly after the airplanes left, Stanislava heard the rumble of tanks and the sounds of rife shots. She saw the German soldiers with their hands up, marching in front of uniformed men with red stars on their hats. The men spoke a different language, not German and not Serbo-Croatian. An old man, laying injured next to Stanislava, said, "Those are Russians. and partisans."

She heard another tank full of soldiers cheering: "The war is over, the war is over. We have won the war." People started getting up; even those who were injured crawled to the road from the field.

Stanislava, holding Radojka's hand firmly, bent and kissed the old man next to her. She helped him to sit up, then tore a piece of her dress and wrapped his bleeding leg. Some of the people were kissing and cheering, some were screaming and crying over their dead loved ones. Once the cheering was over, those who could walk started back to Nis.

Stanislava and Radojka returned to the house to wait for Borislav, as she had a strong feeling he would come back there. The streets were empty; it looked like all the Germans were gone. People were listening to their radios, cheering: "War is over! War is over! The Germans have capitulated."

When they arrived at the house, the doors in the back and front were wide open. As Stanislava walked through the house, she noticed that the pictures of Borislav's parents were on the floor and the gold frames were missing. Also, the silver and gold goblets from the credenza. The beds were unmade, showing that the Germans had lived there. Stanislava opened the armoire; some of her clothes still remained at the bottom, and a couple of German overcoats were hanging inside. She grabbed the overcoats and threw them outside on the street.

She went to the gazebo and found a note from Borislav. She held it to her heart before she read it.

"Dear Draginja,

The war is over for some, but not for me. I still have to hide. The worse thing is that the Communists won the war. Today is Sunday. I will try to come on Wednesday late in the evening. Do not have any lights on, lock the doors from the inside, and listen for me. By midnight I should be there.

Love, Borislav"

Wednesday evening, when Stanislava and Radojka returned to the house, they smelled an unpleasant odor. Everything had been turned upside down as if somebody had been searching for something. The first thing Stanislava saw was writing in blood on the wall that said, "Down with the King and the Fascists." It was an obvious threat against Borislav and, maybe, his family.

Still, she had no choice but to stay and wait for Borislav, to warn him. Shaking, she pulled Radojka next to her. "We can't stay in the house, Rado, some bad people have been here. And they want to take your Tata away from us."

Stanislava and Radojka went to the gazebo and hid in the corner, watching the house from there. It was a full moon, and the night was chilly. It was close to midnight and Radojka was asleep on the floor next to Stanislava, when Stanislava saw the shadow of a man in a uniform and square hat approaching the house.

Stanislava woke Radojka and said, "There is a man there. I hope it is Tata. Stay here and keep very quiet." Then Stanislava heard a low whistle and a whisper. "Draginja?"

Cautiously and quietly, she ran on her toes towards Borislav, grabbed his hands, and said, "Hurry, we must not stay here."

Just then, Radojka ran from the gazebo. "Tata, tata."

"Ssh," Stanislava whispered. Borislav grabbed Radojka and lifted her up.

"Oh, you are so heavy and grown up," he whispered. They quickly ran over the broken brick remains of the professor's house, destroyed at the beginning of the war, and stayed behind the walls for a few minutes.

"Someone was writing in blood on the walls against the King and Fascists," Stanislava explained. "They knew it was our house. I think they were looking for you. I rented a little room by the train station. No one knows about it. It would be safer, at least for tonight."

The three of them hugged for a long time, then they went out on the street, briskly walking toward the train station. Suddenly, gun shots were heard. "Stop! Stop! Who is there?" Borislav did not breathe. He handed Radojka a bunch of papers. "Quickly. Put them in your underwear!"

When the Partisan soldiers came, they shoved Borislav. "You, Chetnick! I like to shoot you right now," one of the soldiers said as he held the gun against Borislav's head. Stanislava screamed and begged. "He's not a Chetnick. He's innocent. Dear God, have mercy. He's innocent."

Hanging onto his coat, Radojka screamed, "Let my tata

go. Please, let my tata go."

As the soldiers pulled Borislav away, he turned to Stanislava and said. "Good by, my love. Take care of yourself, and little Rada."

CHAPTER 17

SAD SATURDAY

tanislava and Radojka, sad and helpless, spent a restless night in tears. Daylight came fast. Early in the morning they went on the streets to find the prison to which Borislav had been taken. Stanislava asked everyone where the prisons were, but nobody paid attention to her.

The streets were full of invalids and people begging for food. Also, partisan and Russian soldiers were everywhere. Stanislava cried and begged the soldiers to tell her where the prisons were. She grabbed a passing soldier's arm and pleaded. "Please, please, tell me," she said, " My husband is in prison. I need to find him. He is a good man, he hasn't done anything wrong. Can anyone hear me?" She choked on tears, her handkerchief soaking wet. Radojka cried and did not know how to help her mother except by squeezing her Stanislava's hand and saying, "Mama, Mama, please do not cry."

"Whose prisoner is he?" one of the soldiers asked. "A German prisoner—or our prisoner?"

"*Your* people took him, people with the red star on their hats," Stanislava answered in a shaky voice. "I want to see him once more. Please help us."

The soldiers laughed and said. "If he is our enemy, he

should be in prison—and so should you, woman."

When Radojka heard what the soldiers said, she started to cry loudly. "Do not take my Mama away!" She buried her head in her mother's skirt and hugged her tightly. Stanislava, also frightened, grabbed Radojka and quickly walked away.

They spent the whole day searching the prisons, but no one could find Borislav's name or tell her anything about where to go.

The next day, returning to their big house to get some clothing, Stanislava found that the house was full of partisan and Russian soldiers. Remembering what the soldiers on the street had told her, she quickly turned away so no one would see her. But moments later, she turned right back, courageously entered the house, and started to tell all about Borislav and the house to the first soldier she ran into. Unluckily, the soldier was Russian and said, "Njet, ponimajem—I don't understand." A young soldier who was very kind overheard Stanislava and gave her directions about where to get information about Borislav.

The following morning, Stanislava found the building where the partisans and Russians had their headquarters and a large prison. The whole day passed by. Hungry, worn out, sent from one office to another, Stanislava was finally told by one of the officers that Borislav would be taken to Belgrade and tried with the other prisoners. Their house, land, and everything had been confiscated, except the sewing machine her father had given her on her last visit home.

* * *

There was nothing to keep Stanislava in Nis. Her strong desire was to see Borislav once more. She packed two suitcases with all they had, including Borislav's military overcoat which

Stanislava had kept in remembrance of their wedding, and went to Belgrade.

Stanislava had the addresses of Borislav's brother George and her older sister Dragica who had moved to Belgrade during the war. Dragica was married to a Russian immigrant, an engineer who designed and re-built bridges. Stanislava hadn't see her for several years.

When Stanislava arrived with Radojka at the door of her sister Dragica's house, she sensed immediately that she was not welcome. Apparently, Dragica had heard of Stanislava's marriage, but did not know all the details. Dragica looked angry and wanted to say something, but instead, she huffed and puffed.

As soon as Stanislava explained that she was married to an officer in the King's army who was imprisoned by the Communists, Dragica immediately asked them to leave her house. "You are married to a Fascist," she said. "I have two children. My husband is working for the new government. You will bring trouble to us. There is no room for you here."

Stanislava burst into tears. "You are my sister," she cried as she walked away. "You're my flesh and blood, why do you do this?"

"You will bring trouble to us. We have to survive."

* * *

Stanislava and Radojka, desperate for a place to stay, walked through the streets, hoping to find somewhere to sleep. After walking several blocks, they found an alley full of small shops and boutiques which was much warmer than the open street. This was where they slept on their first night in Belgrade. The next day they took the trolley-bus to her brother-in-law's villa in Dedinje. When she found the house, the doors were locked. An older woman in black approached Stanislava at the door.

"No one is there," the woman said. "The general's wife is in the hospital ill, and his daughter is married now and living in Zagreb."

"The general is my brother-in-law," Stanislava explained. "Did he come back from the German prison?"

The woman hesitated, then continued. "No... while the general was in prison, he lost his right leg. When the war ended, he was offered the choice of coming back home, but he chose to go to America instead. He was afraid that he would be executed by the communists."

Stanislava took a deep breath, "I don't know what to do," she said to the woman. "My husband is in prison. We don't have a place to sleep."

"I can offer you to stay with me a couple of days, but then we both have to move out. You see, my husband was executed," the woman said, "and I was notified by the new government to move out of my house."

"Where will you go?"

"I have a daughter who lives alone with her children in a small town. I will go to live with her."

Stanislava and Radojka stayed with the old woman for a couple of days, then slept in parks with their two suitcases. Many people who had lost their families and homes slept in the parks. Stanislava slept with one eye open, constantly on guard. For Radojka it was easier to sleep, as her head was always in her mother's lap.

Not far from the parks, in the center of Belgrade, was the Hotel Moscow. In the mornings they would sneak into the hotel, all dressed up as guests would be, to freshen up. Early in the morning was the best time to use the bathroom, because at that time of day only the cleaning people were there. After Stanislava told them of her situation, they sympathized with her and did not report her.

Getting in and out of the Hotel Moscow was easy, since they didn't look like hobos. They wore the same clothes for days, but they always freshened up their undergarments by washing them by hand. Everywhere they went, people respected them because they looked well-groomed and spoke with dignity and with reason.

After the days and days of humiliation—eating scraps from tables, sneaking in and out of the hotel, and sleeping in the parks—Stanislava decided to go to the market and sell everything she had in her suitcases.

She used most of the money to rent a room in an old building with walls full of shrapnel holes from the bombings. The building was close to the Kaleniceva Pijaca, one of the largest markets in Belgrade. The room had a small wood stove and a sink, and Stanislava and Radojka shared a hallway bathroom with several other families. From the balcony of their room, they could see the markets where farmers brought their homemade goods to sell, surrounded by small cafes filled with soldiers and a few civilians drinking Turkish coffee and slivovica.

Finally, Stanislava found the prison where Borislav was kept, but she was not permitted to see him. She was told that he was alive and well taken care of, but at the same time she heard from other sources that many prisoners had been shipped to Siberia to "reward" the Russians for helping the partisans defeat the Germans.

A few months passed, and Stanislava was behind in her

rent. She took the last suitcase and went back to the black market, where people were buying and re-selling. The money she made was enough for a short time, but now she had nothing left to sell except her sewing machine and Borislav's military overcoat, which she would never do.

* * *

When Stanislava heard that her sister-in-law, Jelena, was back from the hospital, she decided to go and see her. When Stanislava knocked, the door slowly squeaked open and a dignified, pale-faced woman, just barely walking, peeked out, covering her eyes from the light.

"Who are you? What do you want?" the woman asked.

Jelena did not recognize Stanislava, and for a moment Stanislava did not recognize her either. Jelena stared at Stanislava and Radojka as if she had lost her mind. Then she said, "You look like...like a... Borislav's wife." She squinted her eyes and scratched her forehead, as she tried to bring the memories back. "Oh, yes, you are Borislav's wife. And you, little girl, what was your name? You are so grown...," Jelena sighed. "Won't you come in? You know..." she could barely continue to talk, "I have been very ill. For four years I have lived alone and it is very difficult for me. My husband was a prisoner of war. You know, he is in America." She smiled. "He is happy now. But I am not." She coughed. Then, in a raspy voice, she asked, "What was your name?"

"Stanislava...ah, I mean, umh, Draginja."

"Oh yes, you are the Croatian girl from the mountains of Hercegovina."

Stanislava wanted to be angry, but she held it in. She thought: this woman is crazy. The Croatian girl from Hercegovina. Why would she even mention it?

As they walked through the house, Stanislava looked around. Everything was covered with sheets and smelled moldy. It was dark, and she could barely see anything. The air was still. Stanislava tried to pull the curtains back to open a window to get some air in. But Jelena said, "Oh no, no, don't. I have been this way four years. I like it this way."

"Mama," Radojka whispered. "Something smells bad. Let's get out of here." Grabbing her mother's hand, she whispered again. "Please, lets go."

Stanislava held her hand over her mouth and could not breathe. She felt she needed to get out immediately because they were both in desperate situations and helpless.

During the brief visit with Jelena, Stanislava had a chance to get George's address in America. She wrote to him and explained about Borislav and her situation, that she was on the street with a child and she needed help. A few months later, she received a package with clothing and a brief note from George. She sold the clothing and used the money to pay her rent and buy food.

* * *

Radojka would always remember it as Sad Saturday, a cold rainy day. She sat by the old wood stove listening to the wind whistle through the cracks of the old apartment house.

"What are those strange whistling sounds in the wind?" she asked her mother. Stanislava always had quick answers full of wisdom.

"Those wind sounds are from restless, unclaimed souls," she replied. "When someone dies and is not buried with a church ceremony, their souls become restless, homeless."

Saturday was a cooking day and a day to visit her father in prison not far from their temporary room. Watching her mother cook and smelling her aromatic foods was always Radojka's greatest satisfaction.

This particular Saturday Stanislava prepared one of Borislav's favorite dishes, "papricash." They just had a little taste of it because meat was very hard to find, even for people who had plenty of money. They had waited in line for two hours to get two hundred grams, about half a pound, for two people.

"Your father has been in prison for almost a year," Stanislava explained to Radojka "Very undernourished. He needs good healthy food and energy to survive the severe trials and interrogations there. So why don't we give him our portion to give him strength?"

It is a Yugoslavian tradition to have a drink of slivovica before meals; also, it was good to re-build energy. Several times Stanislava had hidden slivovica in the food she took to Borislav. She put a little bottle, about 2-3 ounces, on the bottom of the papricash, which was topped with peppers, tomatoes, and onions, all sauteed. Next to the dish, she put another little bottle visible to the prison guard so he would take that one away.

For some time, Stanislava had exchanged secret notes with Borislav in prison. In his last couple of notes, he wrote that he was not receiving any food, just dry bread and water. He asked her to bring him a package with whatever food she could spare and his military overcoat.

She was not allowed to see him, but the guard took the package and overcoat. That same day she saw a huge, abnormally fat snake long across the road. It was simply lying there in front of her. Stanislava always believed that, if she crossed herself, any type of evil would not harm her but would go way. The snake moved slowly to the other side of the road.

Stanislava felt cold and sad as she remembered her encounter with the snake. She felt something strange was going to happen, but she didn't know what. The morning went by, and they were ready to walk to the prison and take Borislav his package and food before lunch. They walked about 3-4 kilometers to the prison. After showing their visitor's permit, they were allowed to pass through the barbed-wire gates into the waiting room where the families of the other prisoners were also present. As usual, the families were getting acquainted and exchanging messages or news. The news from the underground sources was bad. Stanislava heard that some people would be executed and some, at the request of the Russians, would be sent to the labor camps in Siberia.

At twelve o'clock, the time the guards normally began to inspect the packages, a large militia man entered the waiting room and yelled, "Cutite—shut up." Suddenly, dead silence overcame everyone. As if he were telling them to jump into a frozen lake, the militia man commanded all the adults to get up and follow him to another area. The children were to remain in the waiting room alone.

The older children helped the very young, but still, the young ones cried. They sat together like they were all from the same family. Moments later, the cries and screams of women were heard in the distance.

The children with petrified—still, ice-cold bodies waiting for another command. They dared not move; the air was so still that a fly could have been heard buzzing around. Their hands were sweaty; they could all hear each other's hearts beating. Little hands would not let go of other hands, the little blanket, or the baby doll.

The deadly silence was finally interrupted by the sounds of hundreds of guns firing—to Radojka, it sounded like the guns of hungry game hunters—in the misty fall day of sad Saturday.

Stanislava and the other adults returned after witnessing the massacre of their loved ones. Stanislava ran to her daughter screaming, "Oh my Radojka, what's left? What we will do without him?" She was carrying Borislav's bloody military overcoat with epaulets and his other belongings, including the last package of papricash.

Borislav's last request had been to be executed in his military uniform, the uniform of the King's army. Just before the guns fired, Stanislava heard, "Long live the King."

Returning to their temporary nest, Stanislava and Radojka spent the rest of the day crying and embracing each other.

CHAPTER 18

RADOJKA IN ORPHANAGE

orislav's death was unbearable. For days, Stanislava could not sleep or eat. Knowing that Radojka needed her, she tried her best not show the grief, but instead she kept it inside of her. Stanislava tried to heal, but in her heart scars were left forever. Her love for Borislav was so strong she would have done anything to bring him back or avenge his death, even though revenge was against her religious beliefs.

For several weeks, Stanislava survived by working odd jobs and selling things on the black market. One day at noon, she was on her way home from the market when a strange woman approached her. The woman tapped her on the shoulder and said, "Excuse me, are you the wife of Major Bulic?"

Stanislava stopped cold. She put her hand on her heart to stop the rapid beating, took a deep breath, and said to the strange woman, "How do you know him? Why do you ask me?"

"Don't be scared, I am a friend. My name is Mileva. My husband was executed on the same day as your husband."

They strolled down the street and talked discreetly. Mileva offered to treat Stanislava to coffee at a kafana. As they sat and talked, Mileva looked around, then whispered to her, "I want you to join our underground organization."

"Your organization? What organization?" Stanislava raised her voice.

"Ssh, tiho, tiho, quiet. Somebody might be listening." Mileva continued whispering. "We are the widows and families of the people who have been executed by the communists. We meet once a week."

"I have a little girl," Stanislava said. "What would happen to her if they kill me?"

"We all have children. We are like a family. Believe me, it is safe." Mileva sprinkled tobacco from a pouch on a piece of newspaper and rolled a cigarette. "Umm, there is nothing like good tobacco from Hercegovina."

"Hercegovina? That is were I'm from."

Mileva lit the cigarette, inhaled deeply, and let the smoke out through her nostrils. "One puff is good enough." She handed the cigarette to Stanislava. "Pushite? Do you smoke?"

"No, no, hvala—thanks. I don't smoke."

Mileva crushed the tip of the cigarette in the ashtray. "I'd better save this for later. We are having a meeting tomorrow night. I want you to come. By the way, what is your first name? You never told me."

"Draginja."

"I'm sure, Draginja, that you loved your husband. You must fight for his beliefs, if you loved him."

"I still love him," Stanislava said. "I will never forget him. His beliefs are my beliefs. Yes, I will come."

The first underground meeting was in someone's basement. When she arrived, Mileva greeted Stanislava and introduced her to the others. Immediately she noticed the written message on the pamphlets which one man who was handing out. On those pamphlets was Borislav's message to the human race: "Communism is a cancer. Fight it!"

* * *

Stanislava continued to attend the underground meetings. She also handed out the pamphlets which Borislav had written, the pamphlets he had died for. One day, on the way from the open market, Stanislava did some trading with the farmers and at the same time secretly handed out the anti-communist pamphlets. Radojka was left alone on those evenings. Whenever Radojka asked her mother where she was going, Stanislava always said she was working.

Late one evening several days before New Year's Eve, Stanislava returned home from an underground meeting and collapsed on the floor. She was covered with blood, had a broken nose and two black eyes.

Radojka was in a panic. There was no one to call for help. Stanislava whispered in a low voice, "Radojka, my love, help me. Get a towel, warm water, and wash my face."

As Radojka knelt on the floor and blotted the blood from her mother's face, she cried. "Mama, Mama, open your eyes? Talk to me. Don't die. Please, don't leave me alone."

"Radojka, someone knew ... about the meeting. They informed on us. You can't trust anyone."

"What meeting, Mama?"

"Some men came... They were hitting everyone. Arresting people. I was lucky. I ran."

"Would those men come and get you again? What would I do?"

"Radojka, if we are ever separated...you mustn't tell your real name. Your father was a high ranking officer ... for the king. He fought against the communists."

Radojka helped Stanislava to crawl to her bed, and they held each other in their arms. They comforted and cried together all night.

It seemed like they had not even slept one hour, when they heard men's voices calling at the door, "Open up or we will break in!" Stanislava and Radojka didn't even breathe. Again, one of the voices called, "We are here to arrest you! Open up or we will break in!" At that moment, the men kicked the door in. They were the UDBA, secret police, and looked very ugly dressed in long black leather coats.

"Get dressed," one of them said. "You must come with us for questioning." The UDBA took them to the same building where Borislav had been imprisoned.

When Stanislava arrived she was greeted by a nicer man who took her and Radojka to his big office and gave them hot burek— meat and cheese pastry—yogurt, and, for Radojka, chocolate.

The man asked Stanislava for the names of her friends and the people who had attended the underground meetings, but she simply refused to give any information. The man, who had been so nice at first, got up from his chair and started to yell, "You must give me their names. Do you hear me, you Fascist wife?" He pulled her chin up. "Look at me? Do you know who I am? I can put you in jail forever."

Radojka cried and pleaded, "Molim vas—if you please, chico, leave my mother alone. Don't put her in prison, please."

Stanislava in tears, with a shaky voice, said, "How dare you ask me to collaborate with you! You have shot my husband, confiscated our home and all our belongings. Go ahead, kill me if you wish."

"That would be too easy." The man turned back to his

desk, called someone on the phone, and talked for a few minutes in a low voice. Moments later, a rough-looking woman walked in. "Drugarice – Comrade! Take her child away." When Stanislava heard what the man said, she jumped from her chair and kneeled in front of him. "Please, leave me my child. She is all I have." The woman grabbed Radojka and started dragging her on the floor toward the door. Radojka resisted, biting the woman's hand.

"Mama, Mama," she screamed, "don't let her take me away." Stanislava tried to stopped the woman, but the man held her back. As Radojka was pulled out the door, the last thing she saw was the man hitting her mother on the face.

* * *

Radojka was taken to an orphanage by bus, where a woman stood by the door writing down the children's names in a large book. When Radojka's turn came, she remembered what her mother had told her the night they were taken by the UDBA: "Never tell the communists your real name." Desperately, Radojka tried to think of a name that she could give.

"What is your name?" the woman repeated sternly, jerking Radojka's hair.

"My name, my name is....Stanislava."

Radojka was moved from one orphanage to another. It was awful to be without her mother and constantly moving, but Radojka got used to it because there were so many other children in the same situation. The orphanage was full of children whose parents were in a prison or dead, and most of them didn't know their last names.

The large room where they slept was very cold, and the plaster on the walls was peeling. There was one light bulb in the center of the room. Each child was given a single green blanket, a bottom sheet, and a mattress. Once a week they took baths in hot water; the rest of the week, even though it was winter, everyone was forced to wash in cold water.

One night, when the lights were off and they had been told to sleep, one of the other children came and took Radojka's blanket. "Someone took my blanket," she called out in the dark. Suddenly, the light turned on. In a husky voice, one of the women guards shouted. "Who is talking? Get back to sleep. Chuti."

The blanket was returned before dawn, but that night Radojka got a severe cold which turned into pneumonia, and she almost died.

The orphanage was a mixture of boys and girls from the age of five to the early teens. Some of the younger boys were not very clean. Because they attended the classroom with lots of children together, ate together, and sat close together in the big dining hall, almost everyone got lice.

The barber came and shaved the hair from the boys' heads, and the girls had their hair cut very short and kerosene poured on it. Some of the girls had lots of lice which couldn't be removed with kerosene. They also had their heads shaved. Those girls wore babushkas most of the time to cover their bald heads.

In the evenings after dinner, there was time given to the children to visit with each other. They took this time to exchange stories about their families. One of the older boys had nightmares about his father, a Partisan who had been killed by the German soldiers just before the war ended. The boy told the children how he, his older sister, and his mother found his father hanging from a tree in their backyard. The boy escaped into the woods, leaving his sister and mother behind.

As Radojka listened to the boy's story, she thought about her mother and her throat choked with tears; it was terrible to be separated from her mother. Every night, Radojka thought of her mother and remembered what she had taught her about survival.

Radojka attended classes at the orphanage school. Almost all of the children whose parents were anticommunist and in prison flunked the orphanage school that year. Even though Radojka was naturally very smart and gifted, the memory of her father's execution made her hate the communist teachers and she was also flunked.

At the orphanage all the children had to work and were assigned duties after school hours. They worked in the kitchens, fields, gardens, and building sites. Even though exhausted from the classes and her kitchen duties, Radojka fulfilled the will of her mother and prayed every night. As she kneeled to say her prayers, some of the children laughed at her. Always in her prayers she prayed to God to see her mother again.

* * *

Sometimes the children would hang around by the high windows, which were hard to reach. They would climb on each other's backs to keep an eye on the front of the building entrance, where their families entered. It was forbidden to climb the walls, and those who were caught were separated for a day or two and put in a small room, alone or with another child.

One day in the late spring Radojka was caught and ordered to go into the single room alone. Radojka started to cry and begged the supervisor, "Please let my friend come with me."

The woman tapped Radojka on the head, "You have been a good kid all this time, except today. I will let your friend go with you."

Radojka missed the laughs and humor of the children. The small room was depressing, and there was not much to do except to climb the window again and look at the people outside.

The next day was a brighter day for Radojka; she was courageous and climbed on her friend's back to sit in the box of the window. Then, firmly holding the heavy metal bars with one hand, she helped her friend climb up. They both sat and watched the people through the bars.

When Radojka saw her mother talking to the guard by the orphanage gate, she was so excited, she almost fell from the window. "Mama," she shouted, "Mama, Mama." But her mother didn't hear her and walked away. Radojka couldn't understand why her mother didn't come and take her away that day.

When Radojka was back in the large room with the other children, she was happier. She quickly forgot the punishment and went back to the windows, hoping to see her mother. Stanislava was walking through the gate towards the building with other mothers, and Radojka spotted her. From the window, she shouted her mother's name. "Mama, it's me, Radojka. Look up in the window." Then she called out the Serbian name her mother was given when she married Borislav. "Draginja, look up. Please!" Stanislava looked up at the window, lifted her hands to the sky, and ran to the building.

Radojka stood by the door waiting to hear her mother's voice. The woman who had been nice to her showed up at the door with her mother. "Is that one your daughter?" she asked as Radojka ran to her mother, kissed her, hugged her. "Yes, I am her daughter."

The woman looked down in the book holding Stanislava's christening and marriage certificate. "But in this book you have a different name."

Radojka quickly said. "It is my fault. I gave my Mama's name."

The woman looked at Stanislava. "Drugarice... but your daughter's name is not on this certificate?"

Stanislava took a deep breath. "Sve je uredu—everything is all right," she said. "Stanislava was my name before I was married. And my daughter used my name. She is mine."

"I can't let her go." the woman said stubbornly. "Until you prove—"

Stanislava got up, threw her purse on the table, and shook everything out.

"Do you want me to call the militia?" the woman said.

"I am just trying to find the certificate to prove to you that she is my daughter." Stanislava found Radojka's christening certificate. The woman did not even look at the certificate. "Get up and go," she said." I believe you."

Stanislava quickly put everything back in her purse, thanked the woman, and left with Radojka before the woman could change her mind.

From the orphanage Stanislava and Radojka went straight back to the room where Stanislava lived alone. Radojka hated to go back to the same building with its restless, unsettled ghosts, but she was happy to be with her mother again.

Their first evening together, they sat and talked for a long time. They looked at each other and embraced and kissed.

"I didn't realize until now how much I missed you, my

Radojka."

"Mama, I missed you very much also."

"It is easier for you. You had other children with you to play and cry with. But I was alone. I spent twenty-five days in prison and cried and cried for you every night. After I was released, I needed some money to survive. I sold everything but the sewing machine and one dress for each of us. During the day I ran through the markets, bought and re-sold things just to survive. Do you know that I searched every orphanage for you?"

"I'm sorry, Mama, I'm sorry." Then she wiped her mother's tears and kissed the tears in her own little hand.

CHAPTER 19

DRAGINJA AND MILOJE

tanislava's resources were drying up. They were hungry and had no money for the rent due on the apartment. The time was very difficult; many, many days they went without breakfast or lunch or any food the whole day.

While Stanislava scrounged around in the black market, Radojka was in the third grade and liked the school, especially the classes where she learned the Russian language. One day Radojka came home from school very happy because her teacher had announced that her class was one of the best Russian language classes in the city. As the best class, they would have the privilege of seeing the Yugoslavian president Tito and the Russian president Stalin in person. They would have a position on the very front row in the street next to the rope where Tito, Stalin, their ministers, and bodyguards would parade. For that occasion they had to wear their Pionir class uniform, and make sure their red scarves were pressed and neat looking.

The next day, early in the morning, Stanislava took Radojka to school and followed the crowd towards the street. She watched from the side as Stalin greeted the children.

Radojka was infatuated by Stalin because he had a sweet

grandfather look with his thick moustache and well-groomed, bushy hair. When Stalin passed near the children, Radojka pushed forward and tugged his military coat. Stalin patted her on the head, and smiled.

When Radojka came home that afternoon, she told her mother what she had done.

"I saw everything," Stanislava replied as she spit on the floor, "Phew on those communists! Don't you ever forget your father was killed by their hands."

* * *

Since the war was over, President Tito asked the Russians to leave Yugoslavia because he was afraid that if they stayed too long they would take over. After the Russians left, Tito maintained strong relations with them, but also expanded his relations with other countries.

Later that fall, another dignitary came to visit Tito—his name was Haile Selassie. Again Radojka was in the front row next to the rope with the other children. The day before the parade, the teacher explained to the students that Haile Selassie was the king of Ethiopia and a holy man. Radojka was determined to be in front close to the rope and touch his robe, but when she saw his face, she crossed herself and pulled back. She thought he looked like a devil because she had never seen a black man before.

The excitement of the visit soon passed. Every day after school Radojka went straight to the apartment to prepare food before her mother came home. The easiest food for her to make was potato soup. Stanislava had taught her how to peel the potatoes, mix the floor for the gravy, put it all together, and cook it slowly.

Starting the fire in the old wood stove was the hardest thing for Radojka. As she struggled, in her mind she heard her mother's voice: "Watch the matches, keep them away from your face and hair, keep it inside of the stove when you are lighting it with the paper." Before Stanislava came home, Radojka had the soup ready and had swept the floor with a old broom that was much bigger than her.

A difficult time began for Stanislava and Radojka. Stanislava felt it was worse than under the German occupation. Waiting in long lines at the city hall to get food stamps or for bread and meat was exhausting, especially when their turn came to buy and the store clerk said, "We are out of everything. Come back another day."

Since the stamps were not enough, Stanislava had to find other sources to survive. She heard that the International Red Cross was helping people in need. From the Red Cross they received canned food, eggs, milk in the form of powder, and clothing. Stanislava sold the clothing on the black market to get money to buy food.

Dealing on the black market frustrated Stanislava. She took Radojka from school and they went for a short visit to the Adriatic to her cousin Maria. When they arrived at Maria's home, Maria appeared at the door step all in black. Her children were around her. The first thing Stanislava asked, "Is it Lazar?"

Maria nodded her head, then said. "Three men came, took him to the sea, and drowned him." She sighed. "You know, Stanislava, during the war he stayed with our small children, and didn't join any of the military groups. We were lucky for a long time. The children and I couldn't have made it without him. Now they are older, and we have to."

Stanislava stayed with Maria and helped her at home. It was both sad and pleasant to stay in the balcony where she had received and written letters to Borislav. Sitting on the balcony, she noticed the line of clothes still stretched between the olive trees. But this time there were no tiny children's clothes; they were all grown-up garments. Out on the sea there were ships with the red star and red flags.

After a couple of weeks, Stanislava and Radojka returned to Belgrade by train. Since they didn't have money for the tickets, they hid in the latrines when the conductor came by. On the train Stanislava met an older woman who was returning back to her home in Belgrade. As they got acquainted, she sympathized with Stanislava's situation and invited her to her home. The woman had lost all her family in the war, and she was more than glad to have Stanislava and Radojka stay with her for as long as they wanted to. "Even though I cannot feed you, I can at least give you a place to sleep."

* * *

The Hotel Moscow was one of the largest and most crowded hotels in Belgrade. People liked it because they could mingle, ask questions about the political situation, and not worry about being arrested. On the street they risked being shot.

Several times Stanislava and Radojka visited the Hotel Moscow and pretended to look for a friend. They had almost no money left, just enough for the waiters' tips but not to pay their bill for food. They had to eat and just walk away. The waiters were very understanding because they were also survivors.

Stanislava and Radojka were dressed up and sitting like ladies, but they were hungry; their stomachs were growling. They watched the people near them and waited for someone to leave some food on the table.

Finally a couple of men dressed in leather jackets, looking like budjas, big shots, left their plates half full. A newspaper left at the side of the plates made it look like they were coming back. Since the men didn't come back, Stanislava and Radojka moved quickly to fill their stomachs with the leftover breakfast pastries. Stanislava realized the men had left without paying, and she was worried that the waiter would charge her for the food. Luckily the shift had changed, and the new waiter assumed Stanislava had ordered the food and paid earlier.

Since the Hotel Moscow was large and crowded with many people, it was easy to eat "free" and escape unnoticed. They returned many times.

One day at noon, as Stanislava sat at a table with Radojka, she spotted food on the table next to her. As she was reaching for the scraps from the table, she heard a soft-spoken man's voice say, "May I join you and buy you lunch?"

Stanislava turned and saw a handsome, very thin man with large blue eyes, and a dark mustache sitting at the table behind her. Even though he was young, he had salt-and-pepper hair. He was dressed in the military riding breeches of the King's army and an English Air Force khaki shirt with epaulets.

"My name is Miloje Milinkovic," he said.

As they talked, Miloje told her about how he had been captured by the Germans and taken to a concentration camp where he got seriously ill with heart and lung disease. According to the Geneva convention, the Germans were supposed to release all sick officers, but they did not release him until just before the war ended. He was returned to Yugoslavia, literally speaking, half dead. Yet he was one of the lucky ones—he had returned. It was an interesting and happy coincidence that

Miloje had been an acquaintance of Borislav at the military academy just before the war started. Even though she liked listening to Miloje, Stanislava knew that Radojka were very tired and they needed to head back to their little room.

A few days passed. Radojka needed a pair of shoes, so they went out window-shopping. As they stood in front of the Bata Shoe Store, Stanislava saw a man's reflection behind her in the window. She recognized Miloje and was very happy to see him again. But Radojka was pulling Stanislava's hand and whispering, "Mama, I want those shoes. I want those shoes."

When Stanislava saw the price, she kissed Radojka and whispered back, "We can't get them today."

Radojka started crying, and Miloje said, "Don't cry. We will get those shoes for you now." To Stanislava, he said. "Please, may I buy those shoes for your daughter?"

"Da, Mama, Da, let chica buy it."

"Radojka," Stanislava whispered back. "That's not nice. I hardly know the man."

"I insist," Miloje interrupted. "I want to buy the shoes for your daughter." He looked at Radojka. "Give me your hand, and we will get you your shoes."

They went inside the store. When they came back out, Radojka was very happy, embracing her shoebox.

Together the three of them strolled all the way to Kalemegdan, a huge park on top of an ancient fortress filled with monuments to the famous poets and war heros of Yugoslavia. Miloje and Stanislava talked and talked as Radojka walked behind them. Before they arrived at Kalemegdan, they stopped in a small outside cafe, sat under the umbrellas, and ate lunch. Miloje suggested a visit to where the Sava River and Blue Danube met. They walked in the park and visited the large fortress the Serbs had built to defend the city against all intruders.

It was getting dark, Radojka was restless and tired. Stanislava thanked Miloje for the good time, the lunch, and the shoes. They agreed to meet again.

Miloje was a military adjutant lawyer and received an invalid pension plus a small supplement. He was a quiet man and a thinker. Miloje was also conceited; he knew he was handsome and spent a lot a time in front of the mirror combing his salt-and-pepper hair. When the war ended he was in his late thirties.

Stanislava grew to trust Miloje and began to like him. They both felt they needed each other and would be good for each other.

After a couple of months of their courtship, Miloje and Stanislava met at a small cafe. As they held hands and drank Turkish coffee, Miloje said "I have a sad news to tell you."

"Oh, no, you are married."

"No, no. Let me explain to you, Draginja. I am only in Belgrade trying to get my invalid pension from the new government. I have to go back to Kragujevac where my mother lives and where I have a house and land."

"But, it seems to me that we just met, and you have to go. How soon do you have to leave?"

"Today, tomorrow. Belgrade is too expensive for me. The sooner I leave, the better." He squeezed her hands. "Draginja, would you go with me to Kragujevac?" he asked. "We can get married here in Belgrade, if you want, or we can get married there."

To Stanislava it was good news because she wanted to have a home for herself and Radojka. "Miloje, we hardly know each other. You know it is hard for me to forget Borislav, but I like you very much, and I want to love someone. I think you will be good for me and my daughter."

"Then you will come with me?"

"Yes, but I think it would be better to get married in Belgrade."

The next day, they went to the court house to get married, and the following day they took a train to Kragujevac.

CHAPTER 20

KRAGUJEVAC

As the train arrived in Kragujevac, Stanislava noticed that all of the women, except the children, were wrapped in black. The only men on the streets were soldiers. At the road sides she saw graves, monuments, and large cemeteries everywhere. Near the station was a monument with a large sign that said: Germans are not welcome in the city of Kragujevac.

When Stanislava asked Miloje about the sign and why there were so many women in black, he explained sadly, "A very gruesome incident occurred here during the war. In retribution for the killing of one German officer, all the men and all the boys of high school age were executed in a single day. That incident has been recorded in the history books. The women of Kragujevac will be in black for a long time. They will have to raise their fatherless children themselves."

From the train station Miloje, Stanislava, and Radojka walked about 3 kilometers to a house in the small village of Groshnica on the outskirts of Kragujevac. The house was located on acres and acres of land full of plum trees. As they neared the house, Miloje pointed to the trees and said, "Every year I sell the plums from those trees to peasants who make their own slivovica."

When they arrived in front of the house they were greeted by Miloje's mother, a very pleasant older woman. She was also in black, in sorrow for her husband and her youngest son who had both been killed by the Germans. Miloje's mother had prepared homemade bean chorba cooked with bacon and smoked meats, which she served with hot cornbread.

His mother's house was too small for all of them to live together. Also because of his poor health, Miloje needed to be closer to doctors. So Miloje, Stanislava, and Radojka moved to Kragujevac where they rented an inexpensive, one-room efficiency directly across from the train station. The one large room was everything for them—a living room, a bedroom, and a kitchen with a faucet—except a bathroom. During the night, instead of going to the outhouse, they used the bedpan for emergencies.

The two narrow beds were put together for the three of them to sleep on. From the ceiling, Miloje and Stanislava hung a blanket on a rope to divide the two beds for "privacy." At night Radojka would hear unusual "sounds" coming from the newly-weds. Radojka couldn't sleep, and the next day would ask her mother if she was feeling alright. Stanislava would tell her she had a stomach ache.

Radojka felt neglected and left behind, watching her mother and Miloje holding each other's hands, touching and kissing as they walked through the parks. She felt that Miloje was taking her mother's love away from her.

* * *

In spite of her jealously, Radojka began to adjust to Miloje and even had fun listening to him tell stories when he had a drink or two. In the evenings after dinner, Miloje would talk about his experiences in the German camp.

On one occasion he told them how he worked for a German farmer who had a very fat daughter and tried to "match" them. Miloje refused the farmer's offer, and the farmer hated him for his coldness toward him and his daughter.

One Sunday, the farmer, dressed in a white shirt to go to church, invited all the prisoners who worked for him to be treated to Sunday lunch. But the farmer told Miloje, "You stay here and clean all that manure before we come back from the church." The daring Miloje got a full shovel of manure and threw it on the farmer's white shirt.

On another evening, Miloje entertained them by bragging about his courageous days in the military academy. One night under a full moon, he and his friend from the pilot training school got drunk. Stealing a plane from the training center, they flew under the Mostar bridge several times. They were written up in the newspaper and also suspended for a month.

* * *

Months passed. Being in one room was getting too crowded and hectic. Many times they went to bed with a cup of soup or tea as their only meal for the day. They were forced to learn quickly how to survive.

Because Miloje was an invalid pensioner, he and his family were promised a decent apartment, but he was told they had to wait for a few months. Miloje did not know anyone in the city government who could help to speed up the paperwork. Those who he went to school with or had been acquainted with before the war had all been killed.

While Miloje stayed at the apartment and Radojka went

to grade school, Stanislava went to the store and bought a large jar of face cream and another large jar of pure lard. She washed the lard many times in cold water, then mixed it with the face cream, and poured it into many little jars. Before dawn, Stanislava hitched a ride on the train and went to the country-side to sell the jars of face cream to the peasant women. Instead of money, she brought home rucksacks full of food, live chickens, eggs, bacon, butter, and smoked meats.

Living next to a busy train station was an advantage. Since wood for heating and cooking was expensive and hard to get, Radojka and other children hung around the train station with little baskets to pick up the coal that fell from the train cars.

On several occasions when a train stopped, Radojka climbed on top of the coal car, threw as much coal down to the ground as she could, then scooped it up and took it home. One time she was on top of the coal car and so busy grabbing as much as possible that she didn't feel the train begin to move. When she jumped from the moving train, she broke her ankle.

Not far from the room where they lived was a military camp secured by barbed wire. The children could hear the lunch bell ring and see the communist soldiers lining up for their lunch. The soldiers ate at benches not far from the wire fence. After they finished eating, the soldiers threw their left-over food into a large metal barrel next to their barracks. Several times Radojka and the other children crawled under the wires with buckets and stole the leftover food from the barrels.

Radojka's survival tactics became more dangerous when one of her friends taught her how to steal chickens from the military camp. She had to roll the soft part of a piece of bread in her palm, like a marble, attach a long string, and let the bread dry. Then she threw the bread under the fence and waited until a chicken pecked at it. When the chicken swallowed, Radojka quickly pulled the string towards her and got the chicken. This didn't work all the time, and was especially difficult with older and bigger chickens.

Bread was very hard to find, and the small portions provided by the stamps were not enough. Radojka and her friends quickly discovered a nearby bakery where, for several evenings, they watched through the window as the baker pulled the hot bread from the ovens and put it on the shelves.

The only way to get to the bread was to climb on each other's backs and go through the window. Even from a distance the smell of the hot bread was so tempting. They stole many loaves, each dark and warm and almost half as long as Radojka was tall.

Stealing the bread and giving it to people who were hungry was fun, until the day when Radojka and her friend were caught by two men who were waiting for them as they climbed out the window. The men grabbed them, took them inside the bakery, and called the militia.

The parents were warned that they would be imprisoned, instead of their children, if it happened again.

* * *

After a few months living in poverty by the train station, a happy day arrived for Stanislava, Miloje, and Radojka. Miloje came home with a piece of paper saying that they would be granted a two-bedroom apartment with a kitchen and indoor bathroom where they could stay until it was needed for another war veteran who had greater priority. The apartment was located on the second floor above a jewelry store in the center of the city. They moved in and accumulated a few pieces of furniture.

From her room Radojka enjoyed leaning on the deep front window and watching people promenade down the street, which is called a "korzo." From the window, Radojka could often overhear what the people were saying.

One day Stanislava said to Miloje, "Since the bus terminal is just around the corner, why don't we make the apartment into a bed and breakfast? Oh, it would make my dream come true."

"Who is going to wash the sheets?" Miloje asked. "Who is going to clean the toilet? Not me. But, Draginja, we only have one tub."

"You forget, Miloje, that I did not have the luxury of a tub for a long time. And neither did you. Let's help ourselves."

"And what if someone reported us?" Miloje asked.

"We do it secretly, quietly, minding our own business. I'll send Radojka to the bus terminal to look for the putnike, the passengers."

Stanislava took the best pieces of furniture and their own bed to the guest room, and they all slept on the floor. Then she taught Radojka how to go to the bus terminal and call in a loud voice, "Sobe za spavanje! Rooms for sleeping!"

The bed and breakfast was going well for them except that poor Stanislava carried a heavier burden than Miloje. She was the one who, leaning over the tub, washed the sheets and then ironed the sheets on the kitchen table. Radojka helped her mother by putting hot coals from the stove into the cast iron, then waving it with her hand to keep it hot and burning. Whenever they had someone spend the night, Stanislava got up early the next morning and prepared breakfast.

Then someone from a nearby bus terminal hotel reported Stanislava and Miloje, threatening them with the loss of the apartment if they continued. For a while they stopped accepting people. But when they ran short of food and money again, Stanislava sent Radojka to the bus terminal. This time, she had to whisper and be careful who she brought.

One rainy evening Radojka brought home a pregnant woman and her four little children. They were all dirty and ungroomed; the children had a dog and cat in their arms. In their faces, you could see the fear that their little animals would not be accepted. Radojka whispered to her mother, "They do not have money to pay for the room, but please, Mama, take them in. Her husband has left her and their house burned down." Stanislava saw the tears in Radojka's eyes. Touching her face, she said, "Dobro, Radojka, just one night."

Stanislava kept the woman and her children for a few days, then gave her some clothing and a little bit of money to take another bus to her destination. That was the last time Radojka brought people in from the bus terminal.

* * *

One night Miloje got very sick with a high fever and infected gums. It was late at night and the veteran's hospital was very far away from the apartment, approximately a couple of kilometers. Miloje was unable to walk because of the fever, and Stanislava had to carry him and drag him step-by-step to the hospital. She was exhausted, even though Miloje only weighed 110 pounds.

As soon as they arrived at the hospital, the military doctor took a look at Miloje's mouth, checked his fever, and said: "This man should not be moved tonight. He must stay here under a doctor's observation at least until tomorrow morning."

Stanislava spent a sleepless night sitting on a wooden bench next to Miloje's bed, comforting him. The fever was still high, even though the doctor had given him penicillin. The next day, as soon as the fever was gone, the doctors pulled out the teeth that were causing the infection.

When Stanislava and Miloje returned to the apartment, the very first thing Miloje did was open his mouth, look in the mirror, and start cursing: "Stupid communist doctors! Stanislava, do you know what they did to me? They took my back teeth out. They didn't even ask."

* * *

After a few days of tranquility, they received bad news: their apartment was to be given to a war hero who had a higher priority than Miloje. The notice said they had to move out as soon as possible.

Life had become frustrating for all three of them. Stanislava could see that Miloje was very lonesome. The men his age, with whom he could socialize, came from different parts of the country and they were all in the military. Every day he followed the same routine: he got a newspaper, read it, sat around the house, or went for a walk. Not having her bed and breakfast and seeing Miloje so restless made Stanislava uneasy.

Stanislava also worried about Radojka being unhappy in school. Radojka couldn't do her homework on time, and the teach was always criticizing her in front of the other students. One day when Radojka was sitting in the first bench in her math class taking a test, there was an earthquake. As the classroom desks started shaking, Radojka used the opportunity to revenge herself against the math teacher, who always gave her a hard time, by "accidently" spilling ink on the teacher's dress.

Radojka came home with ink all over her hands and her own dress, and told her mother what had happened. For the first time, Stanislava refused to comfort Radojka and took the teacher's side. "Take care of your own dress," she said. "Revenge is bad. Don't do this again."

That evening Miloje and Stanislava had a long talk, and they both agreed that a larger city like Belgrade would be better for both of them and for Radojka.

CHAPTER 21

BACK TO BELGRADE

A fter a couple of years spent in Kragujevac, moving to the extremely large city of Belgrade was a drastic change for the three of them. They knew it would not be easy, but perhaps it would be an opportunity to start a new life.

Stanislava knew that, living in Belgrade, she would have to cope with many bad memories, but she felt the change would be for the better because she knew the city and how to deal in the markets.

On the day they had to move, Miloje rented a freight car and also arranged for a horse and wagon to carry their belongings to the train station. The freight car they rented was used for livestock and was large enough to hold all their furniture and still have plenty of room for ten more people. They had only a few pieces of furniture: two small beds, a kitchen table, three chairs, and Stanislava's sewing machine.

As they finished loading, Miloje fainted. Stanislava quickly poured slivovica onto a linen cloth, put it under his nose, rubbed his forehead, and let him have a sip. When Miloje regained consciousness, he was embarrassed and tried to sit up, but he was too weak. Stanislava pulled him up on top of the mattress on Radojka's brass bed.

As the train moved away from the station, it started to rain. Heavy rain followed them all the way to Belgrade.

For most visitors to Belgrade, the first sight they see is the majestic white houses high on the hill and a large fort greeting the international trains. When the Turkish sultan occupied part of the Balkans, they named the city Beli Grad which means the "white city."

Arriving at dark, all they could see in the distance were the city lights. The window in the freight car was so small, only one person could see out at a time. Miloje slid the large door on the side of the car open, so all three of them could see out. Because of a heavy fog, visibility was poor, but the city lights stood out in the fog like lights on a Christmas tree.

For a moment their view was blocked. Another train with lighted windows full of people passed by them going in the other direction, then disappeared back into the fog.

They heard the conductor blow his whistle, announcing, "Belgrade!" Stanislava stepped down from the freight car first, then helped Radojka and Miloje who was feeling much better.

Miloje asked the conductor where they should unload the furniture and how long they had to stay. The conductor told him to go back into the freight car and wait. "Another locomotive will pull you to a track at the side of the station. You have the right to stay there for a couple of days and unload."

They stood in front of the freight car, watching and listening to people talking, accordions playing, and gypsies singing. Shadows of people were all around them, but they couldn't see their faces because of the fog and spurts of steam from the locomotive.

Miloje felt someone's hand on the side pocket of his

coat. "My wallet!" he shouted, "My wallet! Someone stole my wallet!" Since no one responded in the crowd, Miloje quickly walked to the train station militia office while Stanislava and Radojka stayed inside the freight car and watched the furniture.

The militia couldn't do anything for him, but since Miloje was an invalid pensioner, they believed him about the stolen wallet and gave him a temporary identification card and some money.

When Miloje returned, the locomotive was hooking up to the freight car. He waved them down and jumped in.

The locomotive moved them to the back of the train station onto a side track, but they were too tired to unpack. Since they had money from the militia for a hotel room and Stanislava had some money also, they decided to treat themselves to a night in a nearby hotel.

Within walking distance of the train station was the Hotel Belgrade. As they walked into the lobby there was a commotion. Lots of people surrounded a young soldier who was lying on the floor in convulsions, kicking, screaming, and rolling all over. Even though the war had been over about four years, he was using words like he was reliving the war. "Get that swaba," he shouted, grabbing his stomach like he had a severe cramp, "Ouch! Majko moja," he called, "Oh, God help me." Then suddenly he came to his senses, and someone helped him to get up.

Stanislava and Radojka were holding each other, as Miloje whispered and said, "Let's mind our own business, and go to sleep."

The hotel room had unusually high ceilings and tall windows facing the park. The room had two small beds with clean, snow white sheets, and one shower with a small wash basin and a toilet bowl. They all took turns.

They looked through the window—it was still drizzling rain, and there were people sleeping on the benches. They were not "homeless," but peasants with little money, or people who would not spend money for a room, saving it for food. That scene was not rare; there were always people sleeping on the benches in the park by the train station.

As Stanislava stood by the window and watched the people sitting and sleeping, memories of the times she and Radojka had spent in the parks went through her mind. She was sad for a moment, then she turned and looked at Radojka lying on the clean bed and Miloje with his mouth open snoring. She started to laugh. Putting her hand to her mouth and crossing herself, she thought "Thank God, better days are coming."

* * *

Early in the morning, they were awakened by the sounds of the squeaky wheels of the old city street cars changing tracks. Miloje got acquainted with the men in the lobby, who told him that since it was very expensive to live in the city, he should find a place on the outskirts of Belgrade. Several men he talked to recommended Rakovica. "There are a lot of small companies there," they said, "and a good school." They were sure he could find a part-time job to supplement his pension.

At noon they took a streetcar to Rakovica, which was about seven kilometers from Belgrade. Near the top of a hill overlooking the Rakovica train station they found an old country house occupied by older woman whose husband and son had been killed by Germans. She lived with her young daughter-in-law and a small grandchild. A huge, long room with plaster walls and a packed dirt floor was available to lease. It was large enough to be divided into three average-size rooms.

The only entrance to the house was from the back yard. Narrow steps, without a guard rail, led to a balcony with two doors next to each other. The left door was for the older woman with her family, and the right door was for Stanislava, Miloje, and Radojka. Since it was all open and there was no privacy, Stanislava hung a large Turkish cilim – a heavy, hand-woven rug between the two doors.

Again, all three of them shared a single room and slept in two narrow beds as they had in Kragujevac. Only in Rakovica, the room was much larger. In the summer the stove and kitchen table were moved to the balcony, which became the kitchen and sitting room. The outhouse was far back in the yard. At night, a German helmet that Miloje had found in a field was used as a bedpan.

Their room had two very large, old-fashioned, deep-set windows where Stanislava kept geraniums in pots. The windows faced a vegetable garden, and a third small window faced the balcony. One side of the balcony overlooked other homes with their gardens and, in the distance, the train station. Since the house was high up on a large hill, the view was beautiful.

Stanislava and Miloje were glad to have a home and once again behaved like newlyweds. Radojka walked to a school not too far from the house, and life seemed to have settled into a happy routine.

* * *

Because of her magnetism and wit, Stanislava was always surrounded by the neighborhood women. One very cold day in the middle of November just before Slava St. Gurgica, Radojka came home from school and was about to open the door, when she overhead the voices of the neighbor women. Peeking through the steamy window, she saw the women leaning inward toward Stanislava, who was holding a small cup close to her eyes and looking deep inside it.

Radojka moved closer to the door, trying to hear what was happening. One of the woman asked Stanislava, "Tell me, tell me—is she young or old? Do you see him with her?" Apparently, the woman's husband was cheating on her. Radojka was very cold and her knees were sore from kneeling down outside the window, so she decided to go inside.

She opened the door slowly, but the door squeaked. All of the women looked disappointed that she was there, as if they were children playing and she would take their toys. Stanislava stood up, indicating that it was getting late and she needed to prepare dinner.

The women were all about Stanislava's age and they were all smoking. Out of respect for her elders, Radojka was supposed to curtsy and kiss each woman's hand as they departed. But the thought of their smelly, cigarette-stained hands made her disappear quickly, offering to gather wood for the dying fire in the stove. As the women were leaving through the doorway, Radojka returned, her arms loaded with chopped wood.

For a long time, Radojka could not understand why those women smoked and drank that muddy Turkish coffee. "Tell me, Mama, what were those women doing with the coffee cups when I came in. Why were all the cups turned upside down?"

As Stanislava searched for the words to explain, she gathered the cups left by the women from the table and put them in a big pot filled with hot, soapy water at the side of the wood stove. "You are young and protected from all the bad that happens in this world today, as well as in days long ago. Wars, the suffering and surviving, made people find things to believe in.

People inherited traditions and habits after the Turkish occupation, like strong coffee and tobacco, and reading coffee grounds on the inside of small coffee cups. The Turks called it 'fildjan.'"

Stanislava saved one cup and pointed inside it as she talked. "Whoever sees the figures inside the cup is usually smart and has had strong experiences in life, both good and bad. When someone finishes their coffee, and the fildjan is empty, they turn the cup upside-down, let it set for a few minutes and think of the good things they want to know about. Love, happiness, the past, the present and the future. To bless the reading, the reader will make the sign of a cross with her hands over the cup.

"The reader will see in the coffee grounds parallel and vertical lines and different images, like animals and birds. Each line or figure inside the cup means something."

Radojka sat in the corner of the room on a bed close to the wood stove, not even blinking an eye as she listened to her mother. Their time alone was so precious to her. "Mama, did you learn fortune-telling in the convent? Did the church permit that?"

"Ah, no, no. In the convent, we learned the good things—to pray, to help sick and needy people." Stanislava looked up at a clock on shelf of the old credenza filled with pots and pans.

"Ah," she sighed. "We still have time to talk before Miloje returns. And we'd better start working on the Slava cake and decorations."

Stanislava handed a bowl to Radojka, filled with ingredients she had prepared earlier. "Here, Radojka, it's time for you to learn. Mix it and knead it."

After a few minutes of kneading, Radojka's hands were

very tired. She returned the ball of dough to her mother. "Mama, my hands are tired. You do this, and give me something else to help you do."

Stanislava smiled. "You are not ready to be a woman. Women are strong. I will finish this. Here is a small ball of dough for you to make figurines. Put some flour on the table. Sit there and mold the dough into little grapes, birds, and chickens for the Slava cake's decorations."

While Radojka worked, Stanislava got up to light a cigarette. She looked through the large window facing the train station. "Rado, pull the light bulb string down and shut the light out. The moon is so beautiful."

Radojka yawned. She was growing sleepy.

"It is ten o'clock," Stanislava said. "The Orient Express has just passed by." She could tell the exact time by the sounds and speed of each passing train. "Miloje should be coming on the next local train. It's never on time."

Radojka, worried that her mother was getting off the track with her story, was afraid she would not hear the rest of it before Miloje arrived.

"Mama, do you remember that once, long ago, you were helping an old woman who nobody else would help? You were changing her clothes and visiting her? Did she have anything to do with fortune telling? Was she the one who taught you?"

"Well," Stanislava began. "When you were a little girl during the war, we went to Mostar and spent some time with Ilka. I had lots of worries on my mind about experiences in my past, some seemed mystical and many had not been solved. Ilka was my most trusted friend, even though she was much older. She knew of a very old Turkish woman who was known as the best fortune teller and visionary in Europe. Her name was Aisha and she was 108 years old. Ilka also told me that, when Aisha was 11 years old, she was stolen from her wealthy parents by thieves, sold on the white slave market to the Turks and put in the Sultan's harem of forty wives. Since Aisha couldn't bear children, she was set free—out on the streets. Aisha was a beautiful girl who had green eyes and long curly hair; she was quickly spotted and kidnapped by gypsies. They trained her to dance and tell fortunes. She was very perceptive by nature.

"Aisha traveled all around the world with the gypsies. When she became older and could not dance anymore, the gypsies poked out one of her eyes and forced her to become one of their beggars. She was degraded and did not want to stay with the gypsies anymore, but with real people. Later, Aisha isolated herself from everyone and lived in a little shack near the Neretva River."

Stanislava began to cry as she continued her story, and Radojka listened, mesmerized. "Please, Mama, don't stop now! Tell me more."

"Well, there was not much more. After Ilka told me no one had visited Aisha for a long time, I decided to take some food and see if I could be of any help to her. Since it was a beautiful walk along the aqua blue Neretva River, I decided to freshen up my old memories and go the long way instead, over the steep Mostar bridge. On the way to her place were lots of little shacks made of flat stone and rocks, and used as a beach cabins. The shacks were not more than one tiny room and most had been all torn down by hoodlums. Aisha's was left undisturbed because the hoodlums were younger boys who were afraid to come close, believing a witch lived in it.

"Aisha's shack leaned against a big fig tree, its only support from the back side. The front almost touched the fast-flowing water of the Neretva.

"I had been told by Ilka that Aisha's shack would be watched and surrounded by young curiosity seekers who were told that was the shack where the witch lived. I took a deep breath and touched the door, slowly pushing it open. The door squeaked, as if it had never been opened before, and I entered, leaving the door open.

"The early morning sunshine found its way into Aisha's room through a hole in the ceiling. My heart started to beat very fast when I heard her whispering, raspy voice. 'Who is so daring to come and see me? Did Allah send you for me?' The skin on one of her eyes was sealed completely and her white hair was all greasy and tangled. She whispered again, 'Who is it?'

"I tried to take a breath, but the air was unbearable. I said, 'My name is Stanislava and I have brought some food for you, Aisha.' 'Stanislava, Stanislava,' she repeated. 'You are Catholic and you came to see an old Muslin woman like me?'

"'Yes, Great Aisha.' I said. 'I have heard you are very wise and I would like to learn some wisdom from you.' As I talked, I noticed spider nets hanging from the torn ceiling all around her bed. Whenever it rained, water dripped on her head."

"'Come, come my child.' Aisha said. 'Give me your hand. Let me know you since I can't see you.'

"As I put both of my hands over her's, chills went all over my entire body—Aisha's hands were like rakes. Then I said to myself, 'Stanislava, you have been through worse before.'"

"Oh, Mama, were you very scared?"

"No. Listen, did you hear the train whistle? That is Miloje's train. Moja Rado, Aisha taught me great wisdom that you cannot learn in schools. And, now, my wish for you is that you take all the wisdom I have to give you."

CHAPTER 22

MYSTERY MAN

Even though they had settled in their new home, everyone had to contribute in some way toward their survival. Miloje's monthly invalid pension was barely enough to buy milk, bread and potatoes in a small quantity. Stanislava again realized that she must go and hustle on the markets to help her family.

Radojka attended school, but she was unhappy. She did not have anyone to help her with home work. She walked a couple of kilometers to and from school, and prepared meals for her step-father and mother when they were both working. Most of Radojka's school friends were dressed better and had both parents.

Late one afternoon, Stanislava found Radojka sitting on the steps crying. "Rado, sunce moje," she said. Dropping everything to the ground, she scooped Radojka into her arms. "Rado moja, tell your majka why you are crying."

"All of the kids laughed at my shoes; they saw the hole when I walked. And my dress had a little patch on the sleeves." Radojka started to cry again. "And my report card is not the best," she continued through tears.

"Hajdemo unutra – lets go inside. I have something to

show you." Stanislava emptied her ruck sack on the bed. "Look what I brought for us." She opened several little packages wrapped in newspaper. One little package was greasy but smelled good, so Stanislava unwrapped it first. Almost in tears, she said, "I want to tell you that I had to negotiate for whole hour for this piece of smoked bacon. Give me a knife, Rado, I will slice a piece for us now, then I will show you something else I got."

Radojka was so exited that she forgot about her dress and the holes in her shoes, hugged her mother, and kissed her several times. "Mama moja, don't you ever die."

Chewing a piece of smoked bacon in her mouth, Stanislava could not wait to show Radojka what was in the other package. "Rado, close your eyes and touch."

"Hm...Something soft, a...apron, so I can help you more in the kitchen," Radojka said laughingly.

"No. Keep guessing. It is something for you, something you wanted for a long time." Stanislava handed the package to her.

Radojka impatiently tore the corner of the package and peeked through. "Oh, Mama, it is so beautiful, the colors. What is it? A dress?"

Stanislava smiled. "It is two meters of material for your new dress."

"Oh, moja Mama, you work so hard you should keep half for you."

"Don't you worry, moja Rado. As long as I am healthy and alive I will always find a way to help my family. Hand me those little pins and also the measuring meter. Tonight I will measure you and cut the fabric for your new dress."

"Mama, I am so happy when we can spend time alone

together like tonight. I wish Miloje would go more often to visit his mother."

"Rado, I have feeling that you do not like him."

"No, mama. I do not hate him, but somehow he is not easy to like. Besides, he is always touching you, and he never buys anything for me."

"Please, do not hate Miloje. He is a good man, but he does not have much money, and it is a hard time under communism."

"It has been a hard time before, under the German occupation you told me. When will we have a good time?"

"Oh, moja Rado, good times will never come to us for free. But if we create our own life and do the best we can, with God's will, good times will come when it is our turn."

"Mama, I am sorry for you. You always work so hard to help us survive. Why is God not helping us more?"

"Remember, Rado, all the bombing attacks we have been through that God has helped us to survive." Stanislava yawned, then looked at Radojka. "You are absolutely right, duso draga. I think we all work hard, but in a different way." She yawned again. "It is getting very late."

Stanislava looked around for the clock. "Hmm, he must have taken the clock with him to Kragujevac," she mumbled to herself, then she poked her head through the window and looked up. "It is about midnight—the moon is pretty high in the sky." Stanislava closed the window and opened the lace curtain to let the moonlight shine through. Radojka was already in bed. Tired and barely undressed, Stanislava collapsed in her bed. She put her hand on Radojka's head and said, "In a few more days, your school year is over and we will have more time together."

The two of them talked for a while even though they

could not see each other over the cilim, separating the two beds. There was a short silence.

"Mama?" Radojka pulled the cilim up and tapped Stanislava on the shoulder. "Mama, are you asleep?"

"Almost. But I will listen. You can talk."

"I know that I am a big girl now, but I still would like to come and snuggle with you like we used to do when you were married to tata."

"Oh, Radojka. What bothers you. The beds are so narrow. Dobro dodji—all right, come."

"Do you know, Mama, this is the first time we've slept together for a long, long time. I wish that I would never grow up and always be your little girl."

* * *

One day Stanislava received a letter from Ilka saying she had fallen down the steps of her house and wasn't doing well. Also in the letter was other news: "Come, Jovan is very ill and dying. He has requested to see you and Radojka."

There is an old Yugoslavian belief that, if someone who is dying has such a request, it means the person is asking for forgiveness, so he can die easily.

Stanislava read the short letter a couple of times and tried to figure out how to explain to Radojka about Jovan. Should she tell her now or wait until they arrived in Mostar?

Since Stanislava was planing to take a trip with Radojka to see her parents anyway, Ilka's letter made her plans firmer. Miloje never knew or asked anything about Stanislava's past life, except her marriage to Borislav. Stanislava tore Ilka's letter in small pieces and threw it away. She had told Miloje that she was taking Radojka to stay with her grand parents in Rakitno and spend some time with Ilka.

* * *

A couple of days later Stanislava and Radojka took the local train from Rakovica to the major train station in Belgrade where they transferred to the train for Mostar. Radojka was excited about her new little flower dress that Stanislava had made for her.

It was late in the evening. The conductor blew the usual signal and called the passengers to board the train by announcing the names of the major stops. Radojka snuggled on her mother's shoulder and fell asleep. Stanislava, an experienced traveler, hid her purse between them and put her small suitcase above. A couple of seats across from them a man smoked a pipe almost all night long. It was a cool summer night. Whenever someone opened a window, the smoke blew towards Stanislava and Radojka, but that was the only unpleasant part of the trip.

Everyone was asleep except Stanislava. Her mind was busy with lots of questions about how much she should tell Radojka about Jovan and her past.

Everyone began to take turns visiting the latrine, the women to comb their hair and put lipstick on. These were signs that a major city stop was near. A young man came by with his basket of pogacice, bread rolls and black coffee. Of the six or eight people in the train compartment, only one person could afford coffee and a biscuit. The others ate whatever they brought with them from their homes.

Close to Sarajevo, the train slowed down from tunnel to tunnel and over green hills. Again it climbed up, then curved around. Radojka opened the window and counted the train cars, then turned to Stanislava and asked, "Mama, come look with me. I can see the end of the train; it is absolutely beautiful."

"Moja Rado, I have been on this route so many times." Then Stanislava went into deep thought about how she had met Borislav. Radojka talked and talked, but Stanislava didn't hear her. The conductor entered the compartment and asked to see the tickets of the new passengers who had come in.

For Radojka looking through the window, the ride through the steep, scenic route was scary but very exciting at an elevation of 7000 feet. Close to Mostar the train full of passengers crossed the historic Partisan Jablanica bridge over the Neretva Valley gorge.

Close to Mostar, Radojka started to asked her mother about their visit to deda Djurin and baka Andjelka. "We don't have any gifts," she said.

"We will stop to see Ilka first—she might have some clothes, things she does not need."

"Mostar! Mostar!" the train conductor announced as he passed by their compartment. Stanislava and Radojka picked up their bags and stepped out of the train. It was early Sunday morning. As Stanislava stepped out, she took a deep breath, closed her eyes, and said, "Oh, my Rado, Rado. There is nothing in the world like the fresh smell of the lipa trees and figs." Then she continued, "Can you hear the church bells ringing? That is a reminder for people to go to Mass. Oh, look over there ... up high. There is the Hodja on the top of the Mosque. Listen, listen. He is calling 'Allah, Allah,' for his fellow Muslims to come to the mosque and pray."

Stanislava, all excited, started to sing, off-key, "Oh Mostare divni grade—Mostar, beautiful city ..."

"Mama, suti, people are listening," Radojka whispered.

"But I am happy that we are here again." Stanislava kissed

Radojka on the forehead. "Oh, you are so grown I don't have to bend down anymore when I kiss you. Rado, listen to me please, we must not forget our old tradition. Let's stop by the baklava sweet shop. Sometime ago they used to sell some fruits too. You know, Ilka likes oranges, those big Haifa oranges that come from Israel..."

Stanislava bought a couple of oranges for Ilka and one for Radojka. Radojka ate almost her whole orange, but left one slice for her mother.

As they started crossing the Kriva Cupria they saw the doves and pigeons sunning themselves on Ilka's upstairs windows. Radojka tried to whistle and call the pigeons the way Ilka had taught her. When they approached the garden gate, the pigeons had flown away and they could see Ilka at the window. They climbed the worn-down wooden steps, knocked on the door, pushed the door open—as always, it was unlocked—and walked in.

Ilka limped as she came towards them, choking with tears, her arms open. "O moja Stanislava, you have not changed at all, you are still most beautiful. And you, little Karolina, izvinite gospodjice, excuse me, miss. Turn around and let me look at you. My God, have you grown, you are almost as tall as your mama."

Later that day, Radojka took a walk around the old mill and sat on the bridge watching the river turn the mill wheel. Stanislava and Ilka were having a good chat with coffee, when Stanislava suddenly said, "I would love to smoke one cigarette with you, Ilka. You know, I started smoking a few years ago. Any good tobacco these days?"

Ilka's eyes opened wide, then she smiled, gently biting her lips and said "Yes, I have. Get the box under the ottoman.

There is some good tobacco there."

Stanislava pulled the box out and opened it. "Umm, this tobacco is so strong; it smells like my father's tobacco." She folded a couple of cigarettes in cigarette paper.

Ilka laughed. "Let me tell you about a woman who smoked too much and always gave her husband the best nourishing food and saved nothing for herself. Stanislava, do you remember Mate, the mill man? He had a good friend who always visited him. On one visit he saw a real pretty, well-built woman. Then he whispered to him, 'Mate,' he said, 'I am tired of my skinny wife. Can we throw her through the mill with my corn? I want to get rid of her.'

"Mate said, 'Well, bring her in. Since you are paying me good money and we are good friends. Why not?'

"A few days later, Mate's friend brought his wife and left her there. She was beautiful, with good bone structure, but she needed to gain weight. Mate felt so sorry for the pretty woman that, instead of fulfilling his friend's request, he helped her with everything she needed and fed her with the best food.

"Several months passed. She regained the weight she had lost. When Mate's friend came back for a visit, he assumed that Mate had done what he had asked. He didn't ask any questions. They sat and talked. Mate clapped his hands, and a woman entered the room. He asked her to bring some coffee. As she left, Mate's friend, who didn't recognize his wife, asked, 'Who is that beautiful girl, I would like to buy her.'

"'Well, since I have two, you can have her for a couple of bags of corn.' Mate's friend took the pretty woman home with him. From that day on, she fed him bones and ate the good food herself."

They both laughed, then Ilka said, "I am telling this,

Stanislava, because you are on the thin side, and you need to feed yourself first and take care of yourself more."

* * *

The next day, Stanislava took Radojka to see Jovan, telling her that he was an old friend who was sick. A street away from Ilka on the other side of the bridge was the old house that had been built in the Turkish style. They knocked on the big wooden doors with door knockers the size of a horseshoe. Very close to the door was an open window with a curtain moving in the wind. An older woman dressed in a Muslim veil poked her head through the curtain, gestured with her hand, and said, "Keep knocking. He is in there. I saw him earlier."

The doors opened. A very tired-looking man with a cane in his hand, who could barely walk, appeared and greeted them. He didn't smile. "So, this is the little girl," he said.

"Yes, this is my Radojka." Stanislava answered. "She's a teenager already."

They followed him through an enclosed cobblestone garden to a sitting room. While the two of them chatted, Radojka followed the narrow, curved steps to the upper rooms and looked around. Directly above the sitting room was a large room. All around, along the walls, were narrow ottomans covered with colorful Turkish cilims. In front of the ottomans were four low brass coffee tables. One of the tables had several fildjana—tiny cups without handles—with copper djezva a coffee server, ready to serve Turkish coffee.

Off that room was a long narrow balcony, overlooking the enclosed garden with lipas, fig trees, and oleanders against its walls. In the middle of the garden was a hand water pump.

Radojka heard Stanislava calling, "Radojka, come down.

We are leaving." As they parted, Stanislava asked Radojka to give Jovan a hug. Radojka wrinkled her nose and silently refused. Instead she curtsied and gave him her hand. As they were leaving, Stanislava turned her head once more and said to the man, "God be with you."

On the way back to Ilka's house, Stanislava was silent. "Mama," Radojka asked, "Who is that man? He looks awfully sick. Why did we come to see him?"

Stanislava stuttered. "He is ... he is just an old friend from the past."

"You look so pale, Mama, like you are getting sick. Mama, I have an unusual feeling that I was there before and played with the pump. And climbed the steps above. Is it a dream I had? I don't know. I am puzzled."

Stanislava did not say anything more about Jovan. "I have the same feeling," she answered, "that at some time I have been at a place before. It is not unusual for people to feel that way."

* * *

The next morning at the bus terminal Stanislava bought a new pipe for Djurin and a silk scarf for Andjelka. As the bus arrived at Posusje they were surprised to see Stanislava's older brother Ivo, who had driven in from Italy. There were tears and laughs at the same time; it had been many years since she had seen him. Since the road from Posusje to Raketno was still very narrow and rocky, Stanislava refused to go in Ivo's car. Instead, they hired a man with donkeys and rode to Raketno together.

During the journey, Ivo and Stanislava laughed and recalled their childhood in Raketno and on Ohstric Mountain. Radojka listened quietly and absorbed their family stories.

"Stano, you remember when our old man Djurin hit me

with his big hand and you cried and begged him not to hit me anymore? He was kind of harsh on us, wasn't he? I remember I lost my hearing for awhile after that."

"He always liked us girls, but he was more partial to the young ones—little Jozo, Lucia, and Grgo."

"Old Djurin: I wonder if he's changed any. Do you think he's still cutting his tobacco and playing with his bees? Our family is very hardworking and strong, we are survivors," he continued. "I wish could have taken the car to show him, take him for a ride in it."

It was a long ride and the donkeys needed a rest. Radojka watched Ivo and Stanislava hugging and weeping, still talking about their lives.

"Ivo," Stanislava asked, "Were you not thirteen or fourteen when you ran away from Djurin?"

"Yes, and since then I have done everything—good and bad. I worked in restaurants, washed the dishes in the back of the kitchen, worked on the beaches in Italy, slept in the parks—but I survived. Now I am a successful businessman."

"Ivo, you look great. I hope we can see each other more often. You and I always got along better than the others."

"I remember when you were a little girl," Ivo said, fondly, "and went down to the room next to the stall where our majka kept her milk and cheese. She had just put hot milk in the korito, the long wooden tub, to cool it for kajmak, when she caught you skimming the kajmak off the top with your little hands and eating it. You really got whipped that time, and you cried and cried. You ran to me, and I wiped your tears."

When they arrived at the house, they found Djurin outside working in his garden with Jozo; Grgo was standing near them, a young recruit with his shaved head and army uniform.

"Allo, allo," Ivo shouted. As usual, he spread his hands, rushed up to them and started singing, kissing, and hugging. Stanislava, following behind him, asked, "Where is Majka?"

Djurin turned his stern face, holding his shovel in his hands. "You rich city people," he said, "you already forgot that in the early summer your mother has to take the sheep and goats up to the mountain house. She and Lucia will not be back until August. They have lots of sheep to shear, wool to spin, and cheese to make for the winter."

Ivo, being the older of Djurin's children, asked lots of questions but didn't talk about himself. Grgo was on temporary leave from the army. Djurin demanded that, after his army service, he come back and help him with the livestock.

When they all entered the house, Djurin, as usual, had to be the one who lead the conversation. Everyone was quiet, waiting for him to begin. Instead of talking, Djurin surprised them by getting out his gusle, tying the strings, and starting to play. He spent the evening singing his favorite ballads of the war against the Turks and the Austro-Hungarians.

Before dawn the next day, Ivo, Stanislava, Radojka, and Jozo rode donkeys and a mule up through the sharp ridges of Oshtric Mountain to spend a day with Andjelka and Lucia. When they arrived, several sheep dogs barked at them. In the distance they could see Lucia and Andjelka wrapped with their kudelja, spinning their wool, and watching the sheep. The sun was about to set, and a cool breeze brought the smell of the hazelnut and herb trees. Ivo and Jozo unsaddled the donkeys and tied them to trees near the cabin. As she greeted each of them, Andjelka cried for a long time and reminded everyone that Mirko should not be forgotten.

Ivo and Jozo lit a fire in the fireplace. While Stanislava

and Lucia recaptured the past, Radojka listened. Andjelka prepared hot palenta on a skillet over the open fire. After the dinner, Stanislava and Radojka slept together on the only bed; the rest of them slept on piles of hay under homemade woolen blankets.

The morning came fast, and Andjelka was in tears again to see her children leaving, not knowing when they would be back again. She kissed and embraced each of her children good bye. As they got on the donkeys to go, Andjelka said to Radojka, "Don't forget your baka. Please come back as soon as you can."

CHAPTER 23

MIDNIGHT RESCUE

It was a cold November day 1950. Sveta Djurdjica Slava—family saint day was approaching. Stanislava was preparing kolache and a sweet bread cake, traditional food for Slava. She had separated some of the cake dough and left it on the side of the table. Miloje sat by the stove reading aloud to her from the *Politika* newspaper and laughing. "Ha. Look at this picture." He turned the page of the paper toward Stanislava. "Our president Tito, spending all the people's money on his elegant suits and his villas on Brioni while people are starving."

Stanislava, with flour in her hands, patted Miloje on the face. "Chuti, Miloje, chuti." She stroked his hair to the side. "Don't get into trouble. Now that I have you and Radojka, lets be happy."

"Don't worry, they can't touch me."

"I don't want to lose you."

Miloje got up and motioned with his head. "You work too hard. That can wait. Let's take a nap."

Moments later, Radojka appeared at the door and found them in the bed. Stanislava jumped from the bed, buttoning her blouse, but Miloje covered his head with the blanket.

"Radojka, you are back so early from school."

"Mama," Radojka's face was twitching with anger. "How embarrassing."

"But he is my husband."

"And ... He? Look at him." Radojka stammered as she pointed to Miloje. "Shame on him, too." She rushed out to the balcony, sat on the steps, and cried.

After a few minutes, Stanislava came out to the balcony and said. "Come inside, Rada, and eat something. I would like for you to help me with the decorations for the Slava cake."

The next day was Slava day. Stanislava wrapped the cake in a beautiful embroidered cloth, and gave it to Miloje and Radojka to take to the church and have it blessed. Radojka was still angry, and Miloje was still embarrassed. They walked in silence, except for Miloje's occasional nervous coughs.

* * *

Since Radojka had reached puberty, a most difficult time began for Stanislava. For Radojka, it was difficult to even be in the same room with her step-father and mother.

Remembering how Jesus had suffered and carried his cross, Stanislava reminded herself that all people on earth must carry their own before they can rejoice. Even though World War II had left lots of unhealed scars, it made Stanislava stronger. Always close to her daughter, Stanislava felt they were one body and soul. Radojka had suddenly grown from a skinny girl into a young woman, with interests outside her own home. If anything bad would happen to Radojka, it would be, like taking a rib from Stanislava's side.

One day at the market, Stanislava saw a peasant who was selling a button accordion. Since it was an excellent buy, Stanislava, trying to make Radojka happy, bought the accordion and brought it home for her. But the accordion was heavy and hard to handle. For awhile Radojka took lessons and she soon lost interest.

Radojka had a need for love and friends of her own age. She liked everyone in school, but was particularly close to one girl named Mima, who was tall, very pretty, and a year older than Radojka. Mima's mother was a Serbian, her father Hungarian.

Since Mima was a little older than Radojka, she knew where all the dances were being held. In many ways they were alike, as both loved dancing and music. Latin music was very popular; at the dance halls, the bands would play the samba and the rumba.

One night when Mima took Radojka to a dance hall where a high school band was playing, Radojka met the drummer for the band, Acim. Radojka was impressed by Acim's musical talent, but her love of dancing made her resist his demands that she sit in the corner and listen to him play.

Radojka had to dance. Even wearing her mother's shoes and a full-circle dress she received from the American Red Cross, Radojka was the best dancer on the floor. Music and dancing were in her blood; they were more important to her than anything else in the world.

One day Stanislava went to the school to take Radojka the sandwich she had forgotten and was very angry to discover that Radojka was not in school. Not able to accept the changes in Radojka, Stanislava punished her by not allowing her to go to dances. But Radojka always found ways to sneak out from the house anyway.

* * *

The spring came. Miloje was happy with his small pension, which he spent for the rent and food. But, still there was not enough money for shoes and clothes for Radojka. Stanislava continued to carry her heavy cross. To supplement the household income, she made trips to the small villages in the country around Belgrade to buy, sell, and trade anything she could. Buying fabric in bulk on the black market, Stanislava would cut it into small pieces and sell it for blouses.

One day, coming back home from the country on the local train, Stanislava sat near a young peasant woman who was in the last stages of labor. The young woman started screaming, "Oh joj, I think the baby is coming out! Please, call a doctor. Pull the handle, stop the train!"

But the conductor said, "We must continue because an express train is coming behind us."

There was no doctor immediately available, but Stanislava's past experience in hospitals was helpful. In her rucksack bag she had food and a bottle of slivovica. The sewing scissors she always carried with her, for cutting fabric and for protection, were handy. She used the slivovica to sterilize the scissors before cutting the baby's umbilical cord. Stanislava also cut the young woman's cotton slip and wrapped the baby in it.

Although it was Stanislava's train stop, she decided to stay on the train and help the young woman with her bags and the baby. The woman's parents and her young husband rewarded Stanislava with a small gold coin and a bundle of smoked sausages.

Upon returning home, Stanislava found no one there. Miloje was at the kafana having drinks and talking politics with the men there. Stanislava was worried and puzzled that Radojka was not at home. Where could she be? She found a note on the table, it was written in Serbian and she couldn't read it.

Stanislava went to the train station and talked to the switch man. Describing Radojka, Stanislava asked him if he had seen her.

"Yes, I have," he said. "She was with a tall gypsy girl. I know of her father. Isn't he a Hungarian gypsy?"

"Hmm, I didn't know that," Stanislava replied.

"They took the local train to Belgrade. Incidently, they painted their lips."

* * *

Radojka and Mima had been invited by freshman to a dance hall at the university in Belgrade, and were having so much fun they closed the dance hall.

Since they had missed the last street car, Mima and Radojka had to walk all the way home. The only way to find their way home was to follow the railroad tracks and to count the train stations. At the station just before Rakovica, Radojka and Mima decided to leave the tracks and turn on to the main road, which was much safer and not as isolated as the train tracks. There were homes and business buildings scattered along the road.

As they walked, they heard the someone following them. They took their high heels off and carried them in their hands, walking faster and faster. But whoever was following them was also coming closer. Suddenly they heard men's voices shouting: "Hey, Drugarice, wait for us. We would like to ask you something. We were at the same dance you were."

As the two young men caught up with Radojka and Mima, they said, "We have just come back from the army, and we would like to meet some young girls like you." Their heads were shaved, and one of them grabbed Radojka, saying "I saw you dancing earlier."

He tried to kiss her. In the meantime Mima ran away

from the other man, leaving Radojka alone. While the one man chased Mima, the one kissing Radojka pulled her blouse, then lifted her skirt up. Radojka felt panic, but told him she needed to go in the bathroom and that she would be right back.

Radojka remembered that she had seen some construction on the road and lots of workers; also there were barracks at the side of the road for their temporary living quarters. She walked slowly across the street toward the barracks yelling, "I will be right back." Then she ran to the first barracks and banged on the door, "Please, someone help me!"

Lights came on. Radojka looked around and saw many road workers sleeping on the floor. "There were two men out there. They tried to rape us. Get them." The workers jumped up, some of them with their clothes on, some in long johns. They grabbed their shovels, but the two young soldiers had disappeared.

Several of the workers escorted Radojka home. Close to the house, she thanked them and went on alone.

Stanislava was waiting at the door. She was angry with her daughter. "Only bad girls come in so late at night."

Radojka tried to explain why she was late, but Stanislava interrupted: "Radojka, you are too young to go to the city. And it is very embarrassing for your stepfather and me to have a daughter coming in so late at night. What will the neighbors say, what kind of girl are you? I don't want you to ever come late again. If you want to dance, you will come with us only."

CHAPTER 24

FIRST MEETING WITH JANKO

t was already the mid-fifties, and life was still difficult for many people. Waiting in long lines for bread and meat was much the same as it had been for the last ten years, but there was evidence that life was improving. Those who lived on the outskirts of the city could raise a pig, a goat and have several chickens. Everyone learned how to smoke their own pig meat and store it for the winter, the only way to preserve the meat without refrigeration.

Stanislava, Radojka, and Miloje continued to struggle. Each year before Easter, Stanislava would buy a mature chicken and one rooster. All the fresh eggs that the chicken laid, Stanislava would save and put into a large basket on top of some hay. The old chicken sat on top of the eggs for a couple of weeks; just before Easter, baby chicks arrived. When the chickens had grown a little larger than a pigeon, the male chicks were killed, roasted, and used for soup and papricash. The female chicks were kept to produce more eggs.

Everything was quiet until one day when Miloje came home from his daily visit to the post office and said, "Here is a letter from Borislav's family."

Stanislava noticed that the letter had been opened and

resealed. "Hum, someone has already read this letter."

"I did," Miloje answered. "I thought the letter was for me."

"Well, since you opened it, what did it say?"

"Why don't you read it yourself?" he said, knowing she couldn't read Cirilic. Stanislava held the letter to her heart and smiled. "It is okay. Radojka will read it for me."

Stanislava waved the letter over her head. "Oh, Radojka, we got a letter from Srbislav. Please read it quickly."

"Oh, from Srbislav! Let me see it, Mama."

"Dear Aunt Draginja," Radojka began, "I received your postcard and was happy to hear that you and Radmila are alive."

"But I have not written to him," Stanislava said.

Radojka smiled and looked her mother straight in the eyes. "I found his address in a box where you keep your photographs and addresses. I thought I would surprise you. I wrote to him and told him that you had remarried. I also invited him to come and visit us, since he is tata Borislav's nephew."

"Oh, Radojka, you are still full of mischief. I want to hear what Srbislav says. Read it."

"And he says 'As you may have heard, Aunt Milica got very ill after Uncle Miodrag's death in the German prison camp. Yesterday she was buried. Since you are the only family I have left, I want to stay in touch.'"

Stanislava started to cry. "Oh, how sweet. Yes, we are his family. Poor boy." She sniffled and poked Radojka in the arm. "Go ahead, read."

"'I would like to visit with you for a while,'" he says. "'I have just finished my one year of military obligation, and I have been accepted at the DIF Government's free faculty. Only the best athletes are accepted there.'"

"I am so proud of that boy," Stanislava said.

Miloje nervously cleared his throat. "How can he come here? Where can he sleep?"

"Oh, Miloje, don't be so selfish. He doesn't have anyone but us. It's a big city, expensive. Where can he go? This room is big enough for twenty more people. I will fix a blanket and pillow for him in a corner somewhere. He's young and healthy, he can sleep on the floor."

A week later Srbislav arrived at their door with a neighbor who had helped him find the house from the train station. Srbislav looked so much like Borislav! He was holding a small suitcase and had a guitar case under his arm. He quickly put everything down on the floor and hugged Stanislava. As she looked at him, she said, "You have grown so much, you are no longer the skinny little boy I remember."

"It has been a long time since we have seen each other," Srbislav said.

"As you can see," Stanislava pointed to the cilim and whispered, "we don't have much privacy. We share the balcony with a neighbor. Let's go into the room and talk."

While they talked, it got darker. Stanislava reached up and pulled the string from the ceiling and turned the light on. Srbislav looked surprised.

"You don't have a light switch here?" he asked, lifting his left eyebrow.

Something about his face made her pause, then she remembered. "Oh, my God, you know, Borislav used to lift his eyebrow like you just did."

* * *

It was fun to be with Srbislav. He was full of jokes, laughs, and life. His guitar was his best friend. When Stanislava, Radojka, and Miloje were together in the evenings, they listened to him playing jazz and American songs from the films he had seen. Srbislav played the guitar very well, but he was not the best singer.

The summer passed very quickly before it was time for Srbislav to move to the dorm at the University of DIF in Belgrade. From the day Srbislav arrived, he had brought lots of happiness, excitement, and changes to lonely Radojka. Even though they had been crowded in one room, it was sad to see him leave.

Although Srbislav was a newcomer to DIF University, the sports leaders in Belgrade quickly recognized his skills in gymnastics, especially pole vaulting. Later, Srbislav would participate in the European tournaments and the world Olympics, where he earned a medal for Yugoslavia.

Since Rakovica was on the outskirts of Belgrade, Srbislav visited Stanislava and Radojka often. In turn, they visited him and watched him in the local sports tournaments.

After Srbislav had a chance to get acquainted with the other athletes, he invited Radojka to several activities. Through him, Radojka was able to swim at the DIF swimming pool and attend basketball, ice hockey, and soccer games. He also invited her to the parties after the games, where she met the top sports players. In those days, tickets were only available to celebrities and to budjas, big shots with lots of money and connections.

Srbislav, noticing Radojka's excitement for the soccer games, was delighted to surprise her with two tickets. "How would you like to go with me and sit on the front row?"

"Really, on the front row? Radojka's doe eyes opened wide. "Me? I would sit with you on the very front row? Oh, Srbislav." With a kiss and a hug she thanked him.

As she sat on the front row with Srbislav on the day of the game, Radojka felt like a rooster in the middle of hundreds of hens. Surprisingly, she was confident in herself, feeling that she belonged in the front row sitting with the rich and famous. Srbislav glanced at Radojka and whispered, "I am so proud of you looking so pretty and sitting like a lady." She whispered back, smiling, "Someday, I will be rich and famous too."

Radojka's attention moved away from the crowd around her to the players on the field. When one of the soccer players kicked the ball right in front of her, her heart pounded. He was a handsome man with a square masculine face, wavy golden brown hair, and much taller than the others. She jumped up and screamed.

Realizing she was the only one standing, Srbislav quickly pulled her back down.

"Who is he?" Radojka whispered as she grabbed Srbislav's arm. "He's so good looking."

"His name is Janko Zvekanovic. Ah, he's too old for you. But he is one of the Red Star's best soccer players."

"I never thought I would be so close to a famous man. Before this moment, I've only heard his name on the radio when soccer games were on. Do you know him very well?"

"Not personally, but we all mingle together. You will have a chance to meet him—not today, but wait, another time."

Many sleepless nights passed—Radojka could not wait for Srbislav to introduce her to Janko. A couple of weeks later, her dream came true. After the Red Star won the game, everyone was on the field celebrating. Srbislav introduced Radojka to several of the players: Tosa Zivanovic, Bobek, and Janko.

It is a Yugoslavian custom for people to shake hands when they meet and when they leave. When it was Radojka's turn to shake the hand of her admired Janko, she was speechless. Her body turned to fire and trembled when she put her small hand in his. Their eyes met.

She stood for a moment, staring at her hand. When Srbislav asked if something was wrong, she said, "I will not wash my hand until I see him again."

Radojka came home with a big smile and quickly went to a mirror to brush her hair. Stanislava noticed Radojka's unusual behavior. "Radojka, did you meet a young man at the game?"

"Well, they were all handsome and kind of young, but I have forgotten their names. Srbislav and I had the best seat on the front row." She hesitated, biting her lip. "But, I remember one. His name is Janko. He kicked the ball right in front of me, and after the game Srbislav introduced me to him."

Later that night, Radojka was studying while Stanislava mended the sleeve on Miloje's jacket. As she stitched, Stanislava noticed Radojka staring into the distance instead of reading. She sensed that Radojka was in love. "You are so young, Radojka. Concentrate on your school work. There will be plenty of time for the young men. There is an old saying: for every hole there is a patch. That means that when the time is right, the right boy will come."

"Yes, Mama," Radojka answered and went back to her book.

* * *

Radojka's heart's desire was to see Janko again. Her mind was on Janko the whole summer and fall, even when she went places with her friend Mima. Several times she skipped school and went to the stadium alone to watch him practice. She wanted to talk to him, but she did not know how. One day she told Mima about Janko and asked her to go with her to the stadium to watch him practice. Mima was in shock. Janko was a famous man, how could Radojka have met him?

Radojka had written Janko a note asking if he would see an American film with her. She handed the note to Mima. "See that man there? That's Janko. Please give this note to him."

"But I'm scared, I can't do that," Mima replied.

Radojka grabbed the note, and ran to the field, but she suddenly became self-conscious.

"Are you looking for someone?" Janko asked.

"My name is..."

"I have met you before. You are Srbislav's sister."

"Yes, yes. Thank you for remembering. I have something for you," she said as she handed him the note.

When he had read the note, he put his arm around her shoulder. "You know, you are a pretty girl," he said, "but you are too young for me. You are still wet behind the ears, like a baby bird who is learning to fly."

Radojka's face was red, her whole body burning from excitement and embarrassment, but she was persistent in fulfilling her desire.

"Can't we just go to the movies?"

"Perhaps, someday. I have to get back on the field." He started to walk away, then turned back. In December we usually have a big party. If you'd like to come, ask Srbislav to bring you."

As she waved goodbye, she said to herself: "Yes, definitely in December, if not before."

Slowly, she walked back to Mima. "He wants to take me to the movies and dinner..."

"Radmila, I can't believe it. I saw you two talking. Can I come with you, too, sometimes?"

Radojka smiled. "I think Janko would prefer just two of us."

CHAPTER 25

HEJ BABA RIBA, HEJ BABA RIBA

Young people noticed the improvement in every day life, especially in terms of freedom. They wanted things their parents could not afford and found ways to get them. They spent money on zvaka (chewing gum), movies, and other items while older people spent money on food.

The new wave of western influence was welcomed by young people. American movies were sold out for months in advance, zvaka was bought before bread, as were blue jeans and nylon stockings. Also, American jazz had quickly become popular among the young people.

One of the best-liked movies, by all ages, was *Ball on the Water* with Esther Williams and Harry James. Everywhere people went, they could hear the tune from the movie. The sounds of *Ball on the Water* were heard in Radojka's school. Boys whistled the tune and snapped their fingers to the rhythm of Hej Baba Riba in the classrooms.

Even if their parents were in the communist party, teenagers were not interested in politics, only American movies and sports. They would give anything to dress in jeans and western clothing. Many of the youngsters bought jeans and nylon stockings from the consignment shop and resold them for much more.

The struggle continued for Stanislava, Radojka, and Miloje. Everyday, when they got up, Miloje wondered if the communist regime was going to stay or go. But no matter what happened politically, getting food was still a daily worry.

Radojka and Mima soon learned in the black market how to buy for less and sell for more. After school, they stood in the long lines in front of the movie theater across from the Moscow Hotel and bought tickets for cowboy movies. Later in the evening, they sold the tickets for much more than they had paid for them. To avoid getting caught by the militia, they stood in a corner and pretended they were waiting for someone. Mima and Radojka took turns whispering to people, "I have an extra ticket, would you like to buy it?" That was the only way for Radojka and many other young people could afford to get into the movies.

One day Radojka came home with a couple of free tickets for *Ball in the Water.* Radojka liked the movie so much, she wanted her mother to see it. "You have to see this movie," she said. "it is absolutely out of this world. You will love it. Please, Mama, let's go see it together."

"Oh, Rado, that's for young people. Besides, we need money for food. Can you sell them to someone else?"

"Mama, you need to get out of the house. You work so hard. You need something for your soul, not for your stomach always."

"Dobro, Rado, if you want me to come I will go with you. Do you think the young people will laugh at me?"

"No, Mama, when I saw the movie with Mima, there were lots of older people there."

Stanislava loved the movie, especially Harry James with his trumpet and his beautiful blue-green eyes. After seeing the movie the first time, Stanislava asked Radojka to get some more tickets so she could see it again. Even though it was expensive, they splurged.

After they had seen the movie for the last time, Stanislava and Radojka had couple of glasses red wine. Radojka was never allowed to drink straight wine in front of her mother and step-father, but could mix it with water. But that was a special evening for sentimental Stanislava, who liked to talk about Borislav. "Oh, my Rado," she said. "I will never forget his warm and gentle touch. No matter how busy he was, he always found the moment to touch my face and say 'Draginja, you are my love forever.' He had the most beautiful thick, dark brown hair and dark brown chocolate eyes. When he looked at me he lifted his left eyebrow and his eyes would talk for him. Oh, he was an unusual man, and I will not forget him as long as I live."

As Stanislava talked, tears came. "A few months before the war started I had a miscarriage at home. It was an awful shock for both of us, especially for Borislav." She closed her eyes, trying to hide her emotions. "You know, it could have been a little boy." She held the tears in her throat. "Borislav would have been so happy because he wanted to have son. The first couple of years of our marriage, Borislav spent every evening at our home library reading, while I played with you. Our library was full of literature from all over the world. He used to read to both of us bed time stories from biblical books which belonged to his father."

Radojka touched her mother. "I always think of him as a saint. I could never understand why he was executed."

"Because of his beliefs. He was opposed to communism.

He believed in God and not in communism." Stanislava's tears poured. "I get a terrible pain in my stomach when I think of how the communists took him away from us."

Miloje's chronic cough and footsteps interrupted them. Stanislava dried her face and hid the glasses and wine under the bed.

* * *

Through the American Red Cross and from her Uncle George in Chicago, Radojka got some nice dresses and was able to join her friends at the nicer dance halls. The summer was almost over, but there were a few weeks of hot days left to go swimming and meet friends at the Sava Kayak club, where the Sava and Blue Danube rivers met.

After a couple of Saturdays at home, Radojka asked her mother for permission to go to a school dance with Mima. At the dance she saw Acim playing drums for the band. Radojka wanted to dance, but Acim asked her to sit next to the stage where he could see her. She did not like the idea, but she agreed. Just before Radojka and Mima left to go home, Acim asked her if she would join him at his Sava kayak club to swim and watch him in a kayaking competition.

Acim asked Radojka if she would join him in the kayak. Even though the kayak was a one-seater, Acim told her it was safe. "You are small," he said, "and you can squeeze behind me and hold on while I row."

Acim and Radojka giggled. She held tightly on to him as he rowed down the river away from beach. For a few minutes it was fun. Then the sky became cloudy, and the waves on the Sava river became stronger. Radojka was getting a little scared. "Acim, I have a cramp in my leg. I have to move." As she moved her leg, the kayak suddenly turned over, and both of them were caught under it. Radojka sank deeper and deeper toward the bottom of the river. Acim, who was an excellent swimmer, found her near the bottom and pulled her back to the shore.

Acim was scared, but he knew what to do. He turned Radojka over and pushed the water from her lungs. Finally, he saw signs of life in her and gave her mouth to mouth resuscitation. When Radojka opened her eyes, she asked, "Am I alive?"

Acim gently stroked her forehead and kissed her. "Yes, you are alive." She closed her eyes again. For a brief moment, a reflection came to her mind of the man in the chimney and her father kissing her and leaving through the window.

Acim massaged her hand, trying to keep her conscious. "Look at me. This is Acim, your good friend. Stay awake. Just breath through your nose, let go through your mouth, and relax."

With Acim's help, she sat up and looked around her. "How come it is already dark?"

"Do you know that you almost drowned? You scared me."

"I was very scared. Acim, I have to go home; my mother will worry. She knows I am at the river."

Nearby, people burned wood fires and sang. Acim and Radojka walked toward the nearest fire and warmed themselves. Acim was exhausted, but knew that Radojka should not go back home alone.

It is a Yugoslavian tradition that a girl is allowed to bring her boyfriend home only if they are going to be married. As Acim and Radojka approached the house, Radojka gave him a sisterly kiss on face and said, "Acim, I will be your best friend. Hvala, thanks, Acim."

* * *

When school started, it was harder for Radojka to go out and have a good time. Movies and dancing were more on her mind than school. On the weekends, Miloje and Stanislava chaperoned Radojka at the Topciderska-basta where they listened to live music and watched people dance. No matter how hard it was to buy clothing and food, Yugoslav people always found time for friends, music, and something to celebrate.

* * *

Early one Saturday morning on their way to the Kaleniceva Pijaca, Stanislava and Radojka sat on the right side of the tramway facing the scenic route to Belgrade. Suddenly, the tramway stopped before the Topcider station facing Topcider park. The militia and an ambulance were there. Several people, mostly men, rushed out of the tramway to see what was happening. "Oh, my God, Radojka. There is a girl tied to the tree, and it looks like she...Her clothes are bloody and torn. Oh, my God. That looks like Zorica, a girl from your school."

Radojka jumped toward the windows. "Mama, it *is* her. It *is* Zorica. Who would do such a thing to her? She was such a good girl."

One of the men said he had overheard a militia man state that a young girl had been raped and killed the night before.

When Stanislava and Radojka returned home, Miloje was sitting on the balcony reading *Politika* and looking puzzled. "Draginja, look at this," He pointed at the newspaper and paced nervously. "She was only fifteen years old. What in the world was she doing at two o'clock in the morning?"

"Oh, Miloje, Miloje," Stanislava replied, "Please don't be

so hard on the young people. If you had one of your own, then you wouldn't be so critical of them. Probably the poor girl was going to a dance and got involved with the wrong people." Stanislava hugged Radojka. "This must be a terrible shock for Zorica's parents. This should be a good lesson for all young girls."

Radojka went to bed and cried on her pillow.

Stanislava tossed and turned all night, worried about Radojka being sad. She put wood in the stove, had her coffee and made breakfast for all of them before they got up.

Miloje went for his morning paper while Radojka got ready for school. "Radojka, don't hurry to go to school. You will be spending the day with me shopping."

"But, Mama, what will I tell my professor?"

"I will send a note. Don't worry."

On their shopping spree, Stanislava and Radojka stopped in the alley in the court of a little boutique. Radojka was bending over to see the price of a blouse, when Stanislava pulled her up. "Stand straight, Rado, and view the price with dignity. You are not a chicken or a duckling. Only peasants lean down. Ladies walk straight.

That same day Stanislava had made an appointment with a special brassier couturier for both of them to have new bras made. It was Radojka's first bra fitting and she was very embarrassed. When they arrived at the couturier there was another couple of young girls with their mother; they looked like they were about Radojka's age. One of the girls grimaced and whispered to Radojka. "It's embarrassing. Ahhoooo."

They were just about to sit down, when an attractive lady came from behind the red satin curtain dividing the fitting room from the small boutique. The lady had so much rouge on her face, Radojka felt that they were at a circus. Madame Couturier smiled and politely addressed Stanislava. "Where have you been for so long? Don't you like our brassieres?"

"Yes, I like your brassieres very much, but I did not have mon...I did not have time to come by until now. Rado," Stanislava blinked nervously and turned towards her and gently touched her shoulder. "Since this is your first fitting, I think you should go first."

Madame Couturier agreed. "Yes, yes, young lady you come over here. It will not take long." The lady beckoned to Radojka to follow her into the fitting room behind the red satin curtains, then smiled and said, "Duso draga—dear soul, don't be embarrassed. Every day, I measure many young girls for their first bras. Ajde, come. Do not be shy. Take off your dress."

Radojka kept her dress in front of her chest while the woman showed her different material to design a bra. "This is the best silk-satins today," the lady said.

As the woman left to show the material to Stanislava, Radojka stretched in front of the mirror, happy to get her first bra. She could hear the woman persuading Stanislava. "The thicker satin lasts much longer."

"You know," said Stanislava after a moment of thought, "food is more important than satin."

"Gospodjo, Madam Milinkovic, but you look rich."

"It is not all gold that shines," Stanislava replied.

"Gospodjo, I will have the bras ready in two days."

As they opened door to leave, the woman winked at Radojka and gave her a Mona Lisa smile. "The first bra for a young, beautiful girl like you is free."

* * *

There was not a boring moment in Stanislava's and Radojka's life. One rainy evening, Stanislava was ironing Miloje's shirt and Radojka was reading one of her favorite Agatha Christie stories, when Miloje walked in, soaking wet, with a big smile on his face. "I stopped at the kafana and ran into one of the young athletes who knows Srbislav. Guess what, Draginja, Srbislav is getting married. Hmmm...," he gave Stanislava a long look, "I suppose he will visit us less now."

"That's a very nice surprise," Stanislava said. "Every man needs a good woman. I hope she will be good for him."

"I heard she is very short and very dominating. Draginja, can you imagine, he is going to live with her parents. I hate weddings and funerals, but I will go with you to his wedding. I am curious what kind of girl he picked for a wife. And another thing I forgot to tell you, the man at the kafana said she was a school teacher and they met at Mt. Kopaonik during his ski trips."

Stanislava held both her hands on the top of the iron, and said, "Miloje, don't be so sarcastic. I am sure she will be good for him."

"Mama, look! Smoke is coming from your iron. You're burning something."

"Oh, Miloje," Stanislava said, "If I didn't love you, I would throw this iron at you."

Radojka laughed, buried her head back in her book, and pretended she didn't hear anything.

CHAPTER 26

DECEMBER PARTY

fter Srbislav's wedding Radojka visited him and his new wife, whose name was also Radmila. Each time Radojka visited them, her mind was on the big December party Janko had told her about earlier in the year. Radojka reminded Srbislav how badly she wanted to go to the December party for the Red Star soccer team, so she could see Janko again.

Radojka's fantasies never stopped; Janko was in her heart and mind. Her desire was to have someone who was tall and strong rather than someone like Acim, who was the opposite. Even though Acim was intelligent and came from a well-off family, Radojka had a burning desire to be married to Janko some day. She went to most of his soccer practices, sat all the way in the back, and watched. The times that she could not go to the games she listened to them on the radio. When Radojka heard the announcer mention Janko's name, she closed her eyes and imagined that she saw him. Many times mind she wondered how it would be to have nice clothing, a bedroom for herself instead of sharing one with her parents, and food that the rich eat instead of beans and potato soup.

December arrived, and so did an unpredictable, heavy

snow storm. It was depressing for Radojka to stay in one room with her mother and stepfather. While Miloje would repeat his "Stalag 17" prisoner of war stories, Radojka would run out into the snow to gather wood for the stove to keep warm.

A couple of sunny days melted the unwanted snow away. On December 12, Srbislav came by and brought Radojka the good news that she was welcome to go the Red Star soccer party.

The night of the party Radojka met Srbislav at the entrance of the athletic club where the party was taking place. As soon they passed through the check point at the entrance, Srbislav took Radojka into a quiet corner and said, "Radmila, I have bad news for you. I cannot stay here with you. Rada and I are leaving on a late train tonight for a ski trip to Sarajevo. I am sorry, she arranged it at the last minute without my knowing it. I know how badly you want to go to this party. By the way, Radmila, Janko is aware that you are coming without me and he promised that you will sit with him and his lady friend."

"A lady friend?" Radojka shouted, "Who is she?"

"Well, I am not sure of their relationship. But I have seen her a couple of times with him when she explodes with jealously and anger. She is much older than you," Srbislav added.

"What should I do, Srbo? I want to see him," Radojka pleaded, tears in her eyes.

"Dobro—well Radmila, you have a choice. To go back hungry on a tramway to Rakovica to your stepfather's home or to enjoy food and music, and be seated next to Janko. It is up to you."

Radojka did not like the alternative. There was no better choice than to stay and see Janko.

"Sretan put—safe trip, Srbo," Radojka said and kissed him. "I am staying."

Radojka found Janko's table and sat next to him. For a while they chatted alone, until an older-looking blond woman tapped Janko on the shoulder, interrupting Radjoka's precious moment. To Radojka, she looked funny with her artificial blond coiffured hair. As the woman sat down on the other side of Janko, Radojka peeked at her. Janko introduced them. "Maria, this is my young cousin."

Maria's hand was cold, and her face very unfriendly. Immediately Radojka felt uneasy, not welcome in her company. For some reason Maria was angry at Janko. She got up from the table, got a bottle of mineral water, poured it all over him, then quickly left.

Janko was calm, as if nothing had happened, and said: "It has happened before. Nothing is new. She has a crazy temper. I'm sorry, Radmila, that you had to see this." With a gentle smile, Radojka said, "Not long ago I saw a very nice American cowboy movie where the fancy kafana lady got a bottle of wine and spilled it all over John Wayne."

Janko laughed. "You are funny. I like you." Radojka, shivering all over, tried to keep cool and smile. A lot of beautiful older girls were going back and forth in front of the table, smiling at Janko, but he pretended he didn't notice them.

The band started to play the tune from *Ball on the Water*. Radojka took a deep breath. "I would love to dance to this tune—it's my favorite. I could listen to it all night."

"I...do not know how to dance," Janko replied.

Radojka grabbed his hand. "Come, this is a very slow dance and is easy to follow."

Janko hesitated.

"Please, Janko. I have waited such a long time for this moment."

"Dobro, okay...let me try. But if I step on your feet, don't complain."

It did not matter whether Janko danced badly or well. It seemed to last forever, and still she didn't want it to end.

"Am I boring you?" she asked the yawning Janko. "I know I can't converse with you like the older girls you are used to."

It was after midnight, and Radojka was worried about how she would get home since all the tramways had stopped. Janko suggested they go to his apartment and have some special brandy which he had bought from Italy. Then he would pay a taxi to take Radojka to Rakovica.

Radojka's heart pounded. She thought, "Oh, how I want all my friends to see me, to see Janko dancing and walking next to me." Radojka wanted to touch his hand as they walked, but was scared. What would he think? Am I a bad girl? Better not.

It was a cold night. Radojka shivered. Janko, noticing she was cold, put his arm around her. He walked fast, and she couldn't keep up with him in her mother's high heels. Her feet were sore, and she asked him to slow down. He was kidding and said, "You're young. You can walk faster then I."

"But my new shoes bother me."

"Jump on my back, let my carry you for awhile."

She shied away for a moment, then said, "Dobro." He carried her for a long time, and she giggled and laughed.

They arrived at the center of the town near the city opera theater. He lived in the tallest building, named "Albania," in Belgrade. They took the elevator to his apartment on the fourth floor. As he opened the door, Janko whispered that his roommate was probably sleeping. He turned the light on. Janko's roommate was not there. Radojka waited timidly by the door. He offered to take her coat and suggested she take her shoes off to relax her feet.

She asked if she could wash her hands. As she entered the bathroom, she said aloud, "How beautiful." There was toilet paper, lotions and colognes, brushes, things she had never seen before. She spent a long time brushing her hair and looking at all the luxuries. She tried to figure out how to take some toilet paper home to her parents, but Janko was in the room where her coat was, so she put it in her underwear. Since she was spending a long time in the bathroom, Janko knocked at the door. "Are you all right?"

"I was just brushing my hair and...and...."

"Hurry out and have a cup of hot tea, and I'd like for you to try this brandy." While Janko turned away to serve the brandy, Radojka quickly took the toilet paper from under her dress and put it in her coat pocket.

She sipped the tea.

"Radmila, why don't you try the brandy first? I brought it from Italy," Janko suggested.

"But I've never drank any brandy before. Is that alcohol?"

"Yes."

"I only drink Malina. In the winter I drink hot teas and milk."

"Let me have just a little taste." Radojka took a sip of the brandy. "It is delicious...mmm...it tastes so good. Would you mind if I had a little bit more?"

"No, no, I don't mind. It's good in cold weather."

As she started her second brandy, Janko had his fourth or fifth. He started caressing her, touching her face and hair. Radojka shivered as if she was cold. Even though she had wanted so much to be seen with him by her friends, being alone in his apartment was frightening. Through her mind, a thousand different thoughts swirled like bura – storm on the ocean. "If I give myself to him and he marries me, how wonderful it will be not to live in the same room with my step father and mother. I would be the wife of the famous soccer player and go to be coiffured, have many pairs of shoes and beautiful dresses and lots of books from Agatha Christie."

But suddenly she woke from her day dream and realized she had to make a decision that would suit her as a decent poor girl. His carresses felt wonderful, but she was not sure where they were going to lead.

Radojka started giggling. She felt very sleepy and could hardly keep her head up. She felt Janko lift her from the chair and carry her somewhere.

It was like a dream that she could not wake up from. Someone was chasing her around the room, grabbed and tore her blouse, then it was like a knife stabbing her stomach. She faintly remembered someone in a white long shirt with big wings like an angel lifting her head and pouring warm kamilica tea all over her. Then everything became dark and she fell asleep.

* * *

The next morning, Radojka was awakened by heavy snoring. She felt a body next to hers, but would not dare move. She was confused and could not remember where she was. Next to her, Janko was in a deep sleep, or pretended to be. Slowly Radojka slid to the bottom of the bed and went into the bathroom. She saw in the mirror blue marks on her neck. Her dress was torn and wrinkled. Angry at herself, she spit on the mirror and cried and cried. Radojka felt disgraced; her spirit, her pride, her whole body hurt. On tiptoe, she returned to the bedroom, picked up her coat, and noticed the empty bed. Janko had left without a word.

Embarrassed and sad, Radojka walked out of the apartment and down the stairs avoiding anyone who might pass by.

CHAPTER 27

NINE MONTHS AGONY

t was a very cold, grey morning so common during the winter months in Belgrade. Snow came down so thick that it was hard to see more than a couple of yards ahead. For a long while, Radojka stood at the hallway of a group of little shops and thought about what to do next. In the shoe shop window, Radojka saw the reflection of a school girl-friend, nicknamed Buba, whom she had known from school in Rakovica, who now lived in Belgrade. Radojka didn't dare to move, waiting for Buba to pass.

"Zdravo, hello, Radmila? Is that you? What are you doing here so early in the morning?"

Radojka bowed her head and started to cry. "We can't talk here in the street. I am scared. I need to talk to someone."

"What is wrong? Can you talk to me?"

"Yes. Let's go somewhere."

"What's happened? Why are you crying, Radmila?"

"Something terrible...I don't know how to tell you. I am scared to go home."

"I am so sorry." Buba hugged and kissed her. "Come with me to our apartment."

They took a trolley to Buba's parent's apartment in

Slavia, two kilometers from the center of the city.

"What's new in our old school?" Buba asked.

"Ah, not much. Same thing."

"I heard you met one of the Red Star soccer players."

Radojka took a deep breath, but couldn't hold the tears.

When they arrived at the apartment building entrance hall, Buba said. "Let's sit here on the steps. I want to hear what's happened. Does it have something to do with the soccer player?"

"Yes... He put something in my drink. Some brandy he brought from somewhere.... I never drank before. And... you know... he did it." And she started crying again.

"I am sorry...have you ever done this before?"

"No, never."

"I have," Buba said. "And *I* was the one who got *him* drunk."

"I cannot go home!" Radojka screamed.

"Shh, shh, someone will hear you."

"What will they do to me? I can't face them. They will know what happened. You don't know my stepfather. He will never forgive me. He will make my mother's life miserable. And I'm scared of her too. Very scared."

"Where would you go then," Buba asked. "if you don't go home?"

"I am confused. I don't know. I just know I cannot go home, not now."

"Then why don't you stay with us for a day or two until you start feeling better? Come upstairs."

Buba's family was large; there was no room for an extra person. The only place Radojka could sleep was in the large bath tub. They gave her pillows and a blanket. The first night,

Radojka was very restless. The second night was even worse. Besides being scared herself, she was worried about her mother being upset about not seeing her for two days.

The very next morning, Radojka heard her mother's voice. "Have you seen Radmila? I have been looking everywhere for two days. One of her friends saw Buba and Radmila entering the trolley together."

Buba's mother hesitated for a moment, then said, "Yes, she's here. Don't worry; she's all right. Come in. I am sorry, my daughter was trying to help her. Something happened she wouldn't talk about. She was afraid to go home."

"I want to see my daughter." Stanislava pushed through the doorway into the living room.

Radojka locked herself in the bathroom. Stanislava opened the doors to the other rooms. "Where are you! Radmila?" She came to the bathroom door. "Please, open the door. Open it! I am your mother; I love you. I promise we will just talk."

Radojka slowly opened the door and peeked through the opening. "Mama, please don't be angry. It's not my fault. I, I ... lost the last tramway and was scared to go home."

Stanislava grabbed her hair and shook her.

"What do you think the neighbors are going to say?" Stanislava shouted. "What kind of girl are you to stay all night somewhere? You worried me, terribly. I couldn't sleep."

As she and Radojka were leaving, Stanislava saw Buba. "You keep away from my daughter. She doesn't need fancy girls like you."

All the way home, Radojka did not look her mother in the face. When they passed the Topcider Park, Stanislava said. "You remember what happened to your classmate, Zorica?

Don't break my heart."

* * *

Almost two months had passed. Radojka was so quiet; she refused to go to dances or anywhere except school. Stanislava was puzzled and worried—she knew something had happened.

Stanislava waited for an opportunity to be alone with Radojka so they could talk. The opportunity came the day Miloje went to Belgrade for his invalid pension evaluation. As soon as Miloje had left, Stanislava told Radojka, "I would like for you to stay home today. Now, go outside on the balcony and get some wood to keep our fire going. Later on, I will go with you and explain to the teacher."

"But, Mama, I shouldn't skip school. I have very important classes today." Radojka sensed that Stanislava wanted to question her again about what happened the three nights she was away. The big room was so cold, they had to sit close to the stove to keep warm.

"I'm a woman, I will understand," Stanislava said, "Talk to me. Are you in love with someone?"

For the first time, Radojka looked her mother in the face and bit her bottom lip. "No, I am not in love with anyone." She started crying. "I cannot talk, Mama. Please, leave me alone. I want to go somewhere far away."

Stanislava knew something was very wrong, but was afraid if she pushed her daughter harder to talk, she would run away.

"Since you do not wish to talk about those three nights, perhaps another time. Now...its still early, let's go back to the school."

It was a cold but sunny day. The snow was still hard and crunchy on the ground. As they walked, Stanislava tried to question her again, but Radojka cried and refused to talk.

Another month passed. Radojka was still silent, in emotional pain. Stanislava noticed that Radojka was gaining weight—there was no doubt in her mind about what had happened. She took Radojka aside again, and yelled at her. "Now, I know what happened to you. I want you to tell me who did this to you? Who is he? I want to kill him." Stanislava crossed herself several times. "God forgive me, what is happening to me. I want to put him in jail. Who was the man? Was it Acim, your boyfriend. Did that happen at the river?"

"No, Mama, no. It is Janko. He gave me some brandy. He did something to me while I was sleeping."

"Janko Zvekanovic! Srba's friend? That Red Star soccer player?" she asked in shock. "How do you know him? That man, he's much older than you?"

"Yes, Mama, it was him. I liked him a lot. I hate him now." Radojka shouted and ran to the bed.

Stanislava followed her. "Did he rape you?"

"Leave me alone, please, leave me alone. I do not know how to explain to you."

Stanislava leaned over her and tenderly covered her with her body. "I will protect you."

Radojka's confession stirred Stanislava's blood. Immediately, she grabbed her purse and ran out of the house. "I will show him! Does he think he is God? Just because he is a big star." She slammed the door; the whole room was shaking.

Stanislava went to Janko's apartment in Belgrade. The first two times, she didn't find him. The third time, a blond woman opened the door. "Where is he?" Stanislava asked.

"Who are you asking for? This is Janko Zvekanovic's apartment. I am his fiancee."

Stanislava pushed the door. "I want to talk to him. About what he did to my daughter. That animal." Stanislava pushed the woman aside and found Janko standing behind the door. "What kind of big man you are, hiding behind the door? Hiding behind a woman. And playing games with a teenager."

She hit him with her purse and everything fell out onto the floor. Janko just stood still, saying, "Get out of my apartment! I don't know what you are talking about. Get out now, or I will call the militia."

Stanislava picked her items from the floor and stood up straight. "I'm from Hercegovina, and we are honest and proud people. Don't you forget that." As she walked out the door, she spat on his face. "Barabo! Ruffian! I will take you to court."

* * *

Stanislava didn't know who to turn to for help with Radojka except a couple of older women she knew who could keep a secret. When she asked them for advice, they suggested Radojka should have an abortion before it was too late. Stanislava, having been a nun, would not hear of it. Stanislava decided to carry a pillow under her skirt and tell everyone that she was an expectant mother.

Miloje didn't like the idea of Stanislava telling people she was pregnant because it forced him to lie also. For five or six months, Miloje stayed around the house and did not visit the local kafanas or restaurants. He refused to go out in public with Stanislava, afraid that the pillow would slip out from under the dress even though Stansilava told him it was stitched firmly.

Mima was the only one of Radojka's friend who noticed the changes in her. When Radojka explained what had happened, she also told Mima that she was engaged to be married "someday" to Janko. In the meantime, Mima, who was inclined to gossip, spread the news that Radojka was seeing Janko.

When the time came that Radojka could not hide her pregnancy, Stanislava was in a panic. She wrote a letter to her older brother, Stepan, telling him what had happened to Radojka and that they were both coming to see him.

When they arrived at Stepan's home in Zagreb, they were not welcomed by Stepan. He was angry, but he accepted the situation.

Stansilava stayed for a few days with Radojka. The night before Stanislava was to return to Belgrade, she spent all evening comforting Radojka. They sat together on the floor with their backs to the sofa. Radojka was crying, she did not want to be without her mother.

Stanislava stroked Radojka's hair and face and whispered, "Don't worry. Everything is going to be all right." Looking at Radojka's pale face, she started to cry but tried to hide her tears. "I will cover for you," she said. "I will wear that old pillow under my dress, and no one will know anything until you want them to know." Then Stanislava smiled and said. "Shh. Do not worry about Stepan. He is quick-tempered but good-hearted. Do what they tell you to do and help out in the house."

The next morning, just before Stanislava said goodbye to everyone, she hugged Radojka for a long time.

"I will miss you terribly."

"Mama, it is going to be a long time before I see you again."

"No, time will go quickly. You will see. I promise you."

Radojka stayed with her uncle Stepan until one week before the baby was due.

CHAPTER 28

MOTHER AND INFANT

When Stanislava returned with Radojka from Zagreb, she took her to the hospital to be examined. Just before they entered the hospital, Radojka started trembling. Stanislava quickly comforted her. "You will meet a nice doctor. There is nothing be scared of. She will just look at you and tell you when the baby will come."

Naively, Radojka asked, "How can the doctor just look at me, Mama, and tell when the baby will come?"

"She will not look at your face." Stanislava hesitated. "But she will...look at your... You will see. She will tell you when you lay down on the table."

"But, Mama, it is going to be embarrassing for me."

"It is very embarrassing for me also, but we must go through this. There is no other way. Your life or the baby's life could be in jeopardy if we don't. The doctor's name is Doctor Ljubic. I assure you, you will like her."

Since the doctor was a lady as well as Stanislava's acquaintance from Bosnia-Hercegovina, Radojka did not mind the examination, except for the extra viewers—young interns on their first practice. As the very first doctor's examination of her entire life, it was unforgettable.

"She still has a few days to go," the doctor said to Stanislava. "As soon as the water breaks, call an ambulance or take a taxi immediately."

"Doctor Ljubic, can I speak with you for a moment alone?" Stanislava pleaded, "I don't know where we could go and hide for a few days. We cannot return to our home because my husband would be angry—and our neighbors! Oh, my God. What are we going to do? You see... Doctor Ljubic, no one knows the baby is Radojka's. I have covered for her all this time, and we need to stay somewhere."

The doctor held her hand to her chin and puzzled for a moment, then she said. "Let me see what I can do." She disappeared for a few minutes and returned. "Draginja, you can stay in my room in the hospital, where I usually stay. I will go to my mother's house for a few days." The doctor continued. "No one should know about your stay here, and we have to be very discrete. Radojka is going to stay here under my 'supervision,' and you can visit her every day. After all, we are both from Hercegovina."

* * *

Early in the morning of September 16, the day Radojka had her baby boy, Stanislava walked into the room and said, "I am so happy that you are both alive and healthy. The doctor told me you were the youngest mother and gave birth to the biggest baby. Did you know he weighed 5 kilograms?" She kissed Radojka and the baby. "Rado, I forgive you," she said. "Our baby is so beautiful; we must name him Slobodan. It means 'freedom.'"

"Mama, when they were filling out the birth registration and they asked me who was the father, I told them. The nurse who was there said she knew Janko."

The nurse called Janko to tell him about the baby. The next day, several people who worked in the hospital came into the room, fans of Janko's and had come to look at his baby.

On the third day of Radojka's stay, Janko came. Quietly, he walked into the room, sat at Radojka's side, and watched her nursing the baby.

"Radmila, I am very sorry about what happened." he said.

Radojka turned her head away as Janko uncovered the baby. "He is beautiful," Janko continued as he looked at little Slobodan. "My father would love him. Please let me hold him."

Radojka covered the baby with her hand. "Don't touch him. He is my baby. When my mother came to see you, you denied that you had anything to do with this. And now you come to see *your* baby. How can you say 'your' baby? I was the one who carried him for nine months in agony, and he is *my* baby. Can't you see he's mine?"

"I am sorry, I wasn't aware that you were pregnant by me."

Radojka took her hand out from under the blanket and slapped his face. "I haven't done anything with anyone else but you. And you know it."

Janko held his hand on his face and looked around in embarrassment—everyone had seen him get slapped. In a low voice, he apologized. "I am so sorry I did not know about this earlier."

"How could you not know? Say it louder—I want everyone to hear you." Radojka turned her head away and started to cry.

"I'm sorry I didn't know. Why didn't you come yourself, instead of your mother? You should have told me."

"I did not know I was pregnant...I was embarrassed. I assumed after my mother had told you...that you would come to see me. I fell in love with you like a fool. Part of all this is my fault also." Radojka took a deep breath and looked at Janko. "What do you want now?"

"Please, I just want to hold him. I am very sorry. I will make it up to you."

Radojka's heart softened. "We named him Slobodan."

Just then, Stanislava walked in the room and saw Janko holding the baby. She shouted, "Don't touch the baby, the baby is ours! Get out of this room immediately, you barabo. You don't have any right to be here."

"Mama, he just wanted to hold him. That's all. He wouldn't take him away."

Stanislava grabbed the baby from his hands, still shouting, "You barbarian. You have disgraced my only daughter."

In the room with Radojka were several other new mothers. Embarrassed, Janko backed out of the room. "I'm sorry. Forgive me. I have plenty of money and I will support both of them. I was drunk, I did not know how it happened."

Once more Stanislava shouted, "We will take you to court. You took advantage of a young girl. That is against the law."

* * *

The last day of Radojka's stay in the hospital, Stanislava sat down on the bed by Radojka's feet. "Radojka, I want to tell you something, but I don't know how."

Radojka was so happy about getting out of the hospital and going home that she didn't hear a word her mother said. Happiness showed in her face as she spoke. "Now that I am a woman, I can be open with you. Mama, I feel so proud of my little baby boy. Each time they bring the babies in the big cart, wrapped like little loaves of bread, I can recognize my baby because he is always the longest and hungriest. Always hungry. As soon as they brought him, he wanted to eat."

Stanislava interrupted. "Listen to me, Rado. I have... kind of bad news." She paused again. "I have to talk to you about Miloje. He doesn't think that you should come home with the baby yet. The baby is too young. It might cry all night and keep him awake. He still worries about the neighbors. He's not sure yet, if anyone knows or not. But we have arranged for you and the baby to stay for a while at a home for young girls who have had babies without fathers. It is also for babies whose mothers died at their birth."

Radojka sighed. "Mama, whatever you think is best for me. From now on, I will listen to you."

Stanislava took Radojka to the home for unwed mothers, where she stayed for two months. Radojka matured very quickly. She learned that life was a struggle, and everyone must learn how to survive on their own. At the unwed mother's home, Radojka took turns with the others scrubbing the floors, working in the kitchen, and bathing the other babies. She also attended school in the evenings.

Even though Stanislava visited her every week, life was very difficult for Radojka. A couple of women who were like militia created a lot of misery. They never smiled, and they were always rude to the girls. Many times, they would make the girls clean the kitchen floors over again even though they were clean. Those women had never been married or had any children, and they acted like men.

On one occasion, one of the "soldier" women told

Radojka to share her breast milk with another baby whose mother didn't have any. When Radojka refused, the woman forcefully grabbed and squeezed Radojka's breast to get milk in the bottle.

This happened several times during her stay. In desperation, Radojka would get up early to secretly feed her own little baby before "they" came. Radojka felt they were stealing from her own baby. But hearing the infants crying from hunger, she didn't resent it as she had at first.

* * *

Radojka endured the home for unwed mothers for two months until Stanislava came and took her and the baby back to Rakovica on the day before their family Slava day.

When Stanislava came to pick up Radojka, she was ready with her little Slobodan in her arms, sitting by the door. Stanislava took the baby in her arms and said, "Radojka, from now on I will carry the baby. Since you haven't seen the neighbors for a long time, just say hello and keep calm. I told them you went to stay with my brother for a few months and go to school there."

Fortunately, no one stopped them. Teta, who lived next door, remembered it was the family's Slava day and said, "Sretna Slava, Draginja. Let me see what you have there. Ah, what a beautiful baby," Teta said, then spit lightly, "ptut, ptut." It is an old Serbian tradition that if people say a baby is beautiful they must pretend to spit lightly toward the baby so the baby will not have bad luck in life. Teta turned to Radojka. "You have yourself a very pretty..." she paused for awhile and smiled, "...baby brother."

Miloje overheard them and came out to the balcony.

"Come on in, Draginja, it is too cold to be outside talking." He did not talk to Radojka at all, but looked at the baby and said, "Boo, am I your grandfather?"

"Miloje, shh, don't say it loud. Teta might hear you."

The baby started crying, and Miloje turned away. "I hope he doesn't keep us up all night."

"We are all in it together," Stanislava warned him. "We are parents for both of them now. Let's do the best we can."

Radojka grabbed the baby from Stanislava, kissed him, and rocked him. "Don't cry, don't cry, Slobodan." Stanislava put her arms around Radojka and the baby. "Miloje is a good man," she said. "Tomorrow is Slava. Let's all be happy. We are alive."

No matter what is happening all around or in the world, a Serbian family must celebrate their Slava day. Stanislava deeply believed in Saint Gurigice because Borislav's family also had the same saint, and she strongly felt that everything must continue as in the past. That evening Stanislava baked the Slava Kolach, the big round sweet bread. Radojka molded the dough into the shape of small birds and grape leaves with clusters of grapes to decorate the Kolach.

The morning of Slava day, Stanislava wrapped the Kolach in a hand-embroidered cloth.

"Miloje, you and Radojka must take the Kolach to church for the blessing." she said. "I will watch the baby and finish my baking."

"It is too late now," Miloje answered. "It is almost noon."

"Go, don't talk about it. I know it is late, but I am sure you will find the preacher still talking to some people. He has to bless it. We need blessings. Please, hurry."

Miloje and Radojka hurried to the church. When they came back, Stanislava had everything on the table for them to eat and celebrate. "Miloje, since you are a real Serbian, would you say the prayer, please?" Stanislava lit the large candle at the center of table, and waited for Miloje to say the prayer. Radojka giggled, "Mama, I think you better say the prayer. You know he never said the prayer before. Don't force him."

"Now, we have a young child in our home. He's an angel. We need prayers."

Miloje looked at them and mumbled the prayer quickly. When they started to eat, he complained, "The sarma, the stuffed cabbage, has too much rice in it."

"Miloje, Miloje, be happy with what we have," Stansilava said. "I had a hard time finding even a quarter of a pound of pork." Stanislava took a deep breath, said her own prayer, then she looked at Radojka and Miloje. "Some day soon we will have a big roasted pig for Slava."

CHAPTER 29

STRUGGLING TO SURVIVE

t was the end of December of 1955; Stanislava and Miloje were preparing to go to the Moscow Hotel to celebrate the coming of the new year. Radojka watched as Stanislava used red-colored crepe paper to enhance the color of her face and lips. Then, she lit her cigarette and saved the burned match stick to darken her eyebrows.

Just before they stepped out, Stanislava kissed Radojka and said. "It's my turn to go and have a good time, and you watch the baby. Lock the door and don't let anyone in until we come back."

"And do not burn that pile of wood that I chopped," Miloje said just before they went out the door.

"Mama, you look so beautiful. Go dance for me."

"You know better, Rado. It's more fun to watch people."

Radojka locked the door behind them. It was time to nurse the baby. The big old room was cold, and the fire went out quickly. Contented, Radojka sat by the window, watching the soft snowflakes coming down. As she nursed her little son, she touched his forehead and his little nose. "You know, I would love to go out there somewhere and dance all night, but ... now you are in my life forever." She leaned over, gently kissed him, and whispered, "Oh, my little one, I would not trade you for billions of dinars and dances." A couple of tear drops fell on his mouth, and suddenly he looked at her just as if he were saying, "Mama, your milk is salty."

It was getting colder and colder, but Radojka remembered what Miloje had said. She wrapped another wool blanket around the baby and laid him down in the bed asleep. She went back to the window and back to the last December. Her thoughts were on Janko. Why hasn't he contacted me? Is he really scared of my mother? Or is he traveling to the far lands? Radojka fell asleep on the chair by the window. She was wakened by the sound of the rooster. Little Slobodan was still sleeping. Stanislava and Miloje arrived, very tired. They had missed the last streetcar and had walked the seven kilometers from Belgrade to Rakovica.

* * *

The struggle for the three of them continued. While Radojka went to night school, Stanislava and Miloje watched the baby. They were all crowded in the same room. Miloje could not sleep at night because the baby would wake him up. There were no diapers except some soft kitchen towels. Stanislava boiled them on top of the stove, dried them around the stove, and used them for little Slobodan.

Attending night school, coming home tired and secretly nursing her son Slobodan, was exhausting for Radojka. It was hard for her to study with the noise baby made, clean and cook while Stanislava and Miloje were absent, but she continued to carry her own cross.

To keep their secret from the nosey neighbors, Stanislava, when she saw someone coming for a visit, would go in the corner of the room and pretend to nurse the baby.

* * *

Stanislava or Radojka waited in long lines in the freezing rain to get a few grams of meat and bread. On several occasions, just when their turn came, the store manager would announce, "Come back tomorrow. We are out of everything."

Even in freezing weather, Radojka would walk to the school. It no longer embarrassed her to walk in her mother's or her stepfather's shoes. She went to school, came home, fed her infant, then went to work at odd jobs so she wouldn't be a burden to her stepfather. Watching her hardworking mother made Radojka determined to do the best she could to help all of them.

Between school hours Radojka never refused little jobs, whether they were hard or easy. For some of the jobs she did not get money, but vegetables or a smoked meat. Food was very hard to find even for people who had money, but Radojka never came home empty handed.

One evening, when Radojka brought home money from her first paycheck, she found her little Slobodan crying while Stanislava and Miloje argued.

"Everybody else is going out to kafana and listening to music, but we are always at home," Stanislava was crying.

"We simply do not have the money," Miloje said. "We can not."

Radojka waved an envelope. "Perhaps this will help," she said as she pulled the money from the envelope and gave it to her mother. Stanislava and Miloje were both so struck by the radiance in her face that they momentarily forgot their argument.

All three of them spoke at the same time: "Let's go to

kafana and have some cevapcici (pork, beef, and lamb rolled into small link sausages)!"

"And hear a good singer," Miloje added.

With Radojka and Stanislava taking turns carrying little Slobodan, they walked a kilometer or two to the kafana Livac where they could smell the meat on the grill. They were greeted by the head waiter and sat at a table near the singer and the accordion player who accompanied her.

Stanislava counted the money. People usually ordered a minimum of ten cevapcicis from the grill and had either wine or beer to drink. They decided to split two orders among the three of them so they could have something to drink. Miloje had a few extra beers, not hearing what Stanislava had said about the money. The music was loud, and little Slobodan was grabbing at Miloje's beer, wanting to drink some.

When the time came to leave, Stanislava gave Miloje the money they had and left him behind saying angrily, "You drank it, you handle it."

* * *

Between Belgrade and Rakovica was President Tito's indoor vegetable garden where tomatoes, lettuce, peppers, and other vegetables were grown for the budjas in the government. Radojka fortunately got a job there on the weekends. It was an undesirable job, working from 3 to 6 in the morning, but rewarding in other ways.

On the mornings that Radojka worked in the garden, Stanislava got up much earlier than usual. She put wood into the old stove, lit the fire to warm up the room, boiled the milk, and put lard on thick slices of homemade bread. "Radojka," she always said, "You most put something in your stomach. Please stay healthy for us."

At the garden, Radojka took every opportunity to bring home a small tomato or a cucumber and some lettuce. Normally, gardening and harvesting time were in the early summer; no one in Belgrade had ever heard of such a thing as having fresh vegetables in the middle of winter.

Getting up before dawn every morning, picking the vegetables, carrying the heavy baskets on top of her head, and loading the trucks was finally too much for her. After a couple weeks Radojka was so exhausted she had to quit.

* * *

Miloje continued to receive his invalid pension, but it was not enough. He was not allowed to work full time, but he found part-time work in a large optical company as a legal advisor. A time came when the company invited the whole family to a picnic, and Miloje took Stanislava. At the company grounds, while they were waiting for the truck to take them to the picnic area, there were more women than men.

When the picnic was over, they transported the people back to the company grounds in the truck. All of the men, including Miloje, were gallantly helping the women jump down. One of the heaviest women, whom Miloje was helping to jump, lost her balance and her weight crushed poor Miloje and caused the ring finger on his right hand to be broken.

Since Miloje was afraid of doctors, he let the finger heal by itself, and the finger was twisted to the position inward permanently. In the Balkan countries, when men are being forward with a woman they hold the middle finger inward when shaking hands—this was, in effect, asking them to go to bed. This was very embarrassing for Miloje whenever he had to shake hands.

* * *

Not too far from Rakovica in another suburb of Belgrade, Radojka had a summer job working in the Topcider mint, where she cut sheets of freshly printed money and stamps. Radojka was soon promoted to a position where she counted large currencies, initialed them, and stored them in the safe. There were many times when Radojka was tempted to take money home.

One day, just when she was tempted to take some money, her supervisor called her into his office. He told her, "Since you are one of my most honest and best workers, take this for your family." It was a big smoked ham. The times were still very hard; food was very expensive and hard to get. To get a smoked ham was like getting a month's salary for a man.

When Radojka came home with the ham, Stanislava was very proud of her and very happy. She hugged her and hugged her, but Miloje didn't say anything; as usual, he was aloof as if nothing had happened.

* * *

Several months passed. Little Slobodan was getting bigger and almost too big for his age. Stanislava was worried that the preacher would not be able to hold him during his christening ceremony.

One evening Stanislava talked aloud that it was getting late and that little Slobodan should be christened in church. "We must decide who will be his kum—godfather," she said.

"Rado, shall we christen him as a Catholic or a Serbian?" Stanislava asked. "What do you think?"

"Of course, Serbian," Miloje shouted from the corner of

the room.

"Mama," Radojka said. "You once told me that when you changed religion to Serbian, you adapted and said God is one for all of us. That is all that counts."

"It will be Serbian, then."

As they continued talking, Miloje reminded Stanislava. "Do you remember when we stopped at Topciderska basta for dinner? We met a big, heavy-set man who was very pleasant and treated us with wine? He was a Serbian."

"Rado, duso moja," Stanislava said. "I have solved the problem. I will go and find that man. Even though we did not get his address, he told us where he works. He will make the very best Godfather for our Slobodan. He is an engineer, intelligent... plus, he is rich."

* * *

After the christening, Miloje suggested that Janko should support the child. Stanislava and Miloje submitted papers to the courts. The courts had to send a subpoena to Janko three times. He did not come the first two times, saying he was out of the country. The court demanded that he take a blood test as soon as he returned, have the results sent to the court, and appear in front of the court himself.

The day of the court hearing, Radojka was uneasy. Stanislava purposely dressed her as a school girl in a black dress with a white lace collar. Miloje didn't want to go into the courtroom, but stayed in the hallway.

In the court room, Janko was sitting in the back with a couple of his friends and his parents. The judge called the names, Radojka's and Janko's, and asked Radojka to stand up. After the judge listened to Radojka's testimony, he told Janko to stand up.

"Do you know you are charged with rape?"

"No, we didn't have anything to do with each other."

The judge pointed towards Radojka. "Do you know this young girl with the child?"

"Da. I met her a couple of times. But we didn't sleep together."

"Then why did you go to the hospital to see her when the baby was born?"

Janko lifted his hands up and covered his ears. "Uredu. Yes. We were drunk. We were both at fault."

Stanislava stood up and shouted again. "No, he is at fault. He gave her a strange drink. He made her drink. And he ran out on her like a rat without facing her the next day. He should be put in prison. He is a rat, not a mouse."

The judge looked sternly at Janko. "You know that your blood test matches the baby's. You are responsible, she was a minor. You have a choice. A month in prison or pay double alimony."

"Uredu, I admit it was my fault. But since the mother is still very young and lives with a stepfather in the same home, the baby would be better off with my parents."

Stanislava screamed. "The baby has to stay with us! We will never let him go. He is ours. Look at our baby. The baby looks healthy, big, and strong."

Stanislava was shouting so much, she had to be ordered out of the court and the judge declared a recess. During the recess, Janko's father, who was a communist, talked to the judge for a while.

After the recess, the judge asked Radojka if she would voluntarily agree to have Janko's parents raise the baby.

Radojka squeezed little Slobodan. "No, no. He is mine." she cried out as she ran out of the courtroom.

The judge addressed Janko and said. "The baby stays with the mother. And you will pay her monthly alimony."

When the judge named the amount, Stanislava shouted from the back. "It isn't enough. She needs much more."

"Chuti .." the judge said, "before I throw you out again."

* * *

The court case was settled. A few months passed, but Radojka had not received alimony, and the struggle to survive continued.

After Radojka finished high school, Stanislava insisted that it would be good for her to continue some kind of schooling. Stanislava kept little Slobodan in the evenings while Radojka took courses again. One was stenography, short hand and typing and the other was a basic secretarial class. She was not happy with the courses, but she continued.

One day Radojka was not feeling well. She was excused from class, and went straight home. When she opened the door she did not hear anyone and started to call, "Mama? Slobodan? Where is everyone?" As she come closer to the bed she heard her mother snoring in a deep sleep. Suddenly she heard little Slobodan say something like "I make soup from chicken" while he was holding a butter knife over Stanislava's neck.

Quickly, Radojka approached him saying "Ne, ne, ne, Slobodan." But he repeated again, "I am killing the chicken like mama do."

Fortunately, the butter knife was dull and Radojka caught Slobodan in time. Stanislava quickly woke up after hearing their voices and jumped from the bed. "I am so sorry,

Radojka, I must have fallen asleep. Oh, I'm totally exhausted. Our little boy is full of energy. Rado, you came home early today. Are you happy with your secretarial training?"

Radojka turn her head way and very hesitantly replied, "Da, Mama, da ..."

"Duso moja, tell me the truth."

Radojka looked at her mother. "I want to quit. I do not think I would happy being a secretary, sitting on my dupe—fanny—all day, and becoming an old maid."

"Than what do you want to do?" Stanislava was upset. "You have this little child, and he needs food and your love. I want for you to have some kind of secure job."

"Mamo, don't be upset with me, please. Tomorrow I will look for something better."

Radojka stayed at home for a few days and, instead of reading the comics as she usually did, read all the business opportunity pages in the newspaper. A large ad said: "Yugoslav-Italian film to be made on location at Kosutnjak. Extras needed. Victorio De Sica, Italian film director, will be directing, and Gina Lolobrigida, Silvana Mangano, Curt Jurgens and many other famous film personalities will be there."

Radojka very exited. The next morning she got up early and dressed in her best dress which she had received from the American Red Cross. She walked up the hill at least five kilometers to the Avala Film production facilities. She carried her shoes in her hands until she arrived close to the place where the auditions were being held.

Only a few people were waiting in the line, which gave Radojka a chance to get acquainted with the important film production personnel. From them she found out all about the new film to be shot in Kosutnjak. When she was auditioned she was asked to fluff up her hair, and they give her a colorful gipsy skirt to put on.

An old gramophone was playing gypsy music. She was told to take her shoes off and dance to the music. Radojka shyly looked around her, closed her eyes, and danced. She danced joyfully and could not stop. In her mind, she was back in her childhood, when she was taught to dance with the gypsies by the fire.

There was loud applause. With a touch of the hand, someone woke her up from her day dream. A pretty actress— tall, slim, brunette—stood next to her. With a smile, the actress said, "Here is your schedule to report to work. You were great."

When Radojka heard that, she was so happy she kissed her.

"We want you to come back. Here is some advance tramway money. We will see you tomorrow."

The scene for the movie was set in a barbed-wire camp. Radojka played a gypsy girl with a big woven basket full of clothing, running and falling in a crowd of gypsies. Horse solders were chasing them with a whip and the gypsies were falling on the ground in front of them. The scene was repeated over and over.

Even though Radojka's knees hurt for a long time, her experience as an extra had been so exciting that she was allured by the idea of participating in films.

CHAPTER 30

ESCAPE ACROSS THE AUSTRIAN BORDER

he people at Avala productions advised her to sign with BFA, the Belgrade Film Academy. Radojka took their advice and applied. At BFA, she studied all the phases of film making, art, and foreign languages.

Through the academy, she met several interesting people. In the afternoon after their classes, the students would go to a korzo, or promenade, where friends met and talked in front of the 3 Sheshira (3 Hats) restaurant in the artist district. The korzo was from Slavia, the major intersection for all the trolleys and streetcars in Belgrade, to the old fort of Kalemegdan.

One afternoon after her class, Radojka ran into Acim, whom she had not seen for a long time. Acim invited her to join him and meet some of his friends. When Radojka met them, they were all talking about escaping to Austria.

After seeing many foreign films, especially American films, most of the younger generation in Yugoslavia would have given anything to run away or even visit another country. Life outside Yugoslavia looked like it was full of everything, especially food and clothing, which the Yugoslavs were hurting for.

Radojka also wanted to escape the oppression in Yugoslavia, to spend at least one Christmas in Vienna. She was determined to save some money and make the attempt, but she was reluctant to go alone to the meetings. She renewed her relationship with Mima and asked her to come with her to the next meeting.

At the meeting, Radojka told Acim and his friends that a couple years ago her brother Srbislav had introduced her to the Austrian hockey player Robert Wagner. "We exchanged addresses," she explained. "I've written to him several times and he has written back. He wrote about how much he loved the Yugoslavian people and said if I ever came to Vienna, alone or with friends, all Yugoslavs would be welcome."

After several meetings with Acim and his friends, a definite time was set to leave Belgrade.

Early in December, just before Radojka and her friends were to leave, Radojka received a letter from Robert which read:

"Dear Radmila,

You are a very precious girl and dear to me. Forgive me for not writing sooner. I remember well how you expressed your desire to come to Vienna. Since Christmas is coming soon, my wife Inga and I would like for you to be our guest. We are looking forward to seeing you.

Yours truly R.W.

Robert's letter gave Radojka confidence that she had a place to stay in Vienna. Her plans to escape were set, and she was determined to pursue them. Radojka was afraid to tell Stanislava and Miloje the truth about her "travel" plans. She just told them that she was going on a trip with her friends and would be back in a few days and to please keep her little Slobodan.

* * *

Six of them—Isad, Acim, Petar, Misa, Mima, and
Radojka—met at the kafana at the Belgrade Train station. Isad
was in his second year at the film academy. Misa was a high
school senior, and Petar had one more year to go at the film
academy.

It was a cold December night. They purposely met in the
kafana because it was so loud. Since everyone was preoccupied
with their own conversation, the six of them felt they could final-
ize their secret plans.

Everyone had barely saved enough money for the train
from Belgrade to Zagreb. From Zagreb they would have to hide
in the train latrines and different passenger compartments all
the way to Maribor, the closest city to the border. Since the night
train conductors were older and usually tired, they often didn't
check everyone's tickets, so they would have a better chance of
getting through without tickets.

"In case one of us gets caught," Petar said, "Give whatever
money you have to the conductor, so you don't get delayed for
our meeting at the border."

The six of them traveled without any suitcases, only
money and jewelry to bribe the border guards. The plans were
memorized; they were all ready and excited. Acim had a small
revolver and Isad had a small knife, weapons that would only be
used in an emergency.

After two days on the train, they arrived in Maribor,
where they spent the night. The next day they found a jeep in
front of a hotel with the keys left in it. Petar carefully looked
around, then they all piled in and drove to a small town called
Shentilj where they were supposed to meet a man, nicknamed

Brka because of his long moustache, who was their contact to take them over the border.

They danced and celebrated in advance their long awaited freedom. Everything was going as planned. They stuffed themselves with the region's famous "Kranjske kobasice (smoked sausage)." They had a couple of hours left and needed to rest, so all six of them crashed in a room which was rented for two.

They had only three hours before dawn. Three unforgettable hours. Even though they were tired and needed to rest for their dream to come true, it was almost impossible to sleep. Excitement and fear was showing on all their faces. The men were much more at ease. Radojka and Mima, fragile in many ways, were more frightened. They all slept restlessly with one eye open; half of their bodies and minds alert and prepared, perhaps, for an impossible task. Since every moment was so valuable, they slept with their clothes on.

Radojka and Mima snuggled tightly around Misa's body and squeezed their hands across him to keep warm. In spite of their thoughts of escape, they found a few moments to laugh over Misa's snoring. As the girls giggled, Petar whispered, "Pssh, chuti, sleep now. This is a very serious matter. Life or death. You must take this seriously. Now, go to sleep."

"Would you like for us to cry instead of laugh?" Radojka replied.

"I'm serious. Mima, Radojka, sleep now."

Restless, Radojka slowly got up from the bed without disturbing Misa and Mima, and peeked behind the dirty curtains to see if anything was moving outside. For a few moments she watched as snow flakes fell in many different directions, carried by the indecisive winter winds.

One by one, they tiptoed out of the room and through the hotel lobby, where the desk clerk snored with his head on the front desk and an almost empty bottle of slivovica next to him.

Finally, they were all outside. It was very cold and still dark, but there was enough visibility to see if someone were coming. They walked silently, each knowing their position and what to say in case they were stopped by the town police. If they were stopped, they would say they were on a school break sight-seeing around town, and were too excited to sleep.

The snow fell thicker and thicker, but they decided to proceed with their plans. As they walked, Acim slipped in a deep hole and sprained his ankle. For a few minutes he was in bad pain, but he kept in good spirits. Isad took his shawl from his neck and wrapped Acim's foot tightly.

"Acim," he said, "hold tight, in less than a couple of hours we'll all be in Vienna and get you a doctor."

Petar was stronger and bigger than either Isad or Misa, and he volunteered to carry Acim.

Dawn was creeping slowly over the mountains, and they were concerned about being late. Suddenly, they heard footsteps crunching in the snow; Misa turned his head and whispered, "Don't worry, it's Brka. I recognize his limp."

As Brka caught up with them, he said with a guilty laugh, "Everything is going to be *uredu*, don't worry." He also apologized for being late. "Now, everyone, I need my payment in advance before I take you over the border. If I die, I want to die with gold in my pocket."

All of them emptied their pockets—taking out money, gold rings, and watches—and give it all to Brka. "Now, follow me," Brka whispered.

Even though it was still pretty dark, Radojka could see shadows in the surrounding valleys and mountains, and the tiny lights in the watchtowers along the border. Soon Brka left them on their own. Radojka and her friends hurried on, scared and worried about being late. Before he left, Brka had instructed them, "As soon as you approach a certain point and see the guard patrolling back and forth, crawl on your knees until you reach the second point of the guard exchange."

It seemed that it was the coldest night of the year. The snow had stopped, but they had to go on. They crawled in single file, the men in front. Petar helped Acim with his sprained ankle; at times it seemed to Radojka that he was almost dragging Acim. They all watched the hand signals of Isad and Petar as their lead. Their noses dripped, and icicles formed on their eyebrows.

"Psssst," Petar whispered. Everybody stopped immediately. They were very close. They could see the guards, with bayonets attached to their rifles and their German shepherds, exchanging places, going back and forth. Time was passing too fast; they had to move. Radojka prayed for snow: "Please God, make it snow. So we can blend in with it." Just that moment, it started to snow. "Thank you, God," she whispered.

Petar and Isad were next to the barbed wire. The guards were apart again. It was the moment for them to go through. Petar went through silently; Isad went also.

One of the German shepherds was sniffing, sensing something in the air as he closely walked beside the guard. Acim panicked and started running. With a scream he started shooting straight towards the guard and accidently shot the dog, then ran through to the other side of the border.

In a few minutes about ten dogs and twenty militia and

guards surrounded the three who were left. One of the dogs pinned Radojka on the ground. She was petrified, seeing this huge mouth full of teeth like the large spikes of a rake next to her face, nose to nose. His paws were on her chest and she did not dare breath. After a few seconds, the guard called the dog off and they were all arrested.

* * *

Radojka, Misa, and Mima were caught. They were slapped around, kicked, pushed, and rolled all the way down to the base of the hill where a militia truck was waiting for them. They were ice-cold and bloody. Misa was so severely beaten that Mima and Radojka had to help him to get into the truck.

They were taken back to a small border village and thrown into the basement of a large, old house. The basement was full of coal; rats and mice ran back and forth. The only light Radojka could see was coming through the opening of the little window used to shovel the coal into the basement.

Misa was very scared about what could happen next, so he decided to escape through the window high above them. Since Mima was much taller and stronger than Radojka, she was the first support on the bottom; then Radojka climbed on top of her back, so Misa could have a human ladder. All this was done very quickly and Misa escaped, but not for long. He was caught before he even got out of the courtyard.

The next day the militia took the three of them out of the dungeon-like basement to a small "office" where the officer in charge of the border guards interrogated them. Later that same day, a militia bus took them to a prison in the city of Maribor, Slovenija.

In a few days, Radojka and Mima were brought to court

and sentenced to six months in prison. That was the day Radojka swore to herself that she would never do anything again that would put her in prison and away from her precious baby.

The day when Radojka got on the stand, the judge shouted questions at her: "Why are you against communism? What is so much better on the other side of the border? What do you have against your country?"

Radojka, with tears in her throat, tried to talk and express herself, but no matter what she said, the judge shouted her down, screaming, "Fascist daughter, you should be shot like your father."

CHAPTER 31

MARIBOR PRISON

Radojka and Mima were put together in a large room with twenty other women. The women guards insulted them almost every day. Mima did not talk to Radojka, blaming her for the escape. Mima was a year older than Radojka, but she assumed that Radojka was supposed to be smarter because she had a baby.

The room was extremely large. Double bunk beds were all around the room against the walls. The toilets where holes in the ground. To use the toilet they had to bend their knees down just like female dogs do. In the prison, the women joked that when they pulled the string chain to flush the toilet, they had their shoes polished and feet washed at the same time.

In the middle of the room were two large tables and two long wooden benches. Food was served "elegantly" in old beat up metal plates, most likely saved from the World War I. In the morning they received black coffee and a piece of hard dark bread.

Lots of women received packages of food from their families. The new prisoners, like Radojka and Mima, could only watch, salivate, and look in other directions. Although Radojka was starving and had lost several kilograms, she was too proud to ask for any of the food. She was also afraid to write home, knowing that her mother and Miloje would be furious about her trying to run away over the border in that most critical time.

One day Mima received a package from her mother, with a nasty note for Radojka. That was all Mima shared with her.

A week later Radojka was delightfully surprised when she received a package of her own. Stanislava sent her little cookies called kiflice which were her favorite. Radojka hid the kolache from everyone like they were made of gold. Another surprise was a chunk of a smoked pork called slanina and a couple heads of fresh garlic. The package also contained some items of her personal undergarments, a long letter, and a couple of photographs of little Slobodan.

The note said:

Draga Rado,

I do not know where to begin. As I am writing, little Slobodan is trying to tell me that he is cold and he is crying. Now, duso moja, this big room is so cold. No matter how much wood we put in the stove, it seems never enough. We need a new stove and much more wood to be able to survive this hard winter. Oh, please do not worry about your little one. I have knitted several wool long pants and tops for him to keep him warm. Miloje is trying to stretch the wood a little longer, and he makes small fires. Most of the day he spends in the kafana reading all of the newspapers and keeping warm there.

I took little Slobodan to one of our neighbors to see her English white pig and their twelve little piggies. Now he wants to go to look at them every day and to hold one in his arms. Oh, moja Rado, I miss you so much, much too much. Even what you did, I cannot keep angry. Miloje is angry at you, but what he can do?

Yes, yes, moja Rado, I almost forgot to tell you that our little Slobodan is talking and learning fast lots of words, even bad ones, credit to Miloje for cuss words.

One more thing: the smoked bacon came from our milk delivery woman whose daughter Laka was in school with you. Somehow she heard of you being imprisoned. She came one evening to tell us that your friend Laka sends her love to you.

Your loving mother

Radojka sat in the corner of the room and read the letter three times and looked at the photograph. It was the most precious gift of all.

Radojka was sad because she did not have any visitors. Because of the harsh winter, the great distance, and the expense, it was impossible for Stanislava to travel with a small infant and visit Radojka.

* * *

Even though the room was already overcrowded, new people kept arriving. Soon the women had to double up in the beds and bunks. Since Mima was not talking to her, Radojka didn't have a choice for a bunk mate. For a couple of nights, Radojka slept in a corner room with her designated blanket and got a bad cold. She spent two days in a hospital, where she wished that she could stay longer. How she loved the feel of clean white sheets again, a soft pillow and hot soups and tea. It almost reminded her of home.

When they took Radojka back, she got a new bunk mate, a very pretty ladylike woman, who had a son much older than Radojka's. The woman's fiance had escaped to Italy, but she was caught.

Everything went fine until one night when the woman was fondling herself. Radojka tried to sleep but could not. She pretended to be sleeping, afraid that the woman was crazy. The following night the woman put her hand on Radojka's breast and grabbed her. Radojka had never been exposed to such a thing before. She slapped the woman's hand and said, "Only men do that." She pushed the woman away and told her she would scream if she touched her again.

The next morning when breakfast coffee came, Radojka was prepared to do anything to get way from the "bad pretty woman." A woman guard who watched the prisoners opened the door to bring in the coffee and bread. Radojka leaned on the door and "accidentally" fell, pushing the door all the way open and spilling hot coffee all over the woman guard. She grabbed Radojka, slammed the door shut, and threw her ten feet away. After that Radojka was left in solitude for 3 days.

* * *

When Radojka returned to the big room, Mima softened toward her and their friendship was renewed. They started talking to each other and sharing food.

Radojka received another package and a note from Stanislava saying that she would come on the day of her release to travel back to Belgrade with her. "I have so much to tell you," the note concluded, "All good news. You will be very happy. I cannot wait until I see you."

The day of Radojka's release, she was taken to the courtroom to receive the final release papers. There were also many other people waiting. While Radojka was waiting, she heard someone say, "Psst." Then she heard a child's voice say, "Rado,

Rado." She turned her head and looked toward the back of the courtroom. There was Stanislava standing by the door with her little Slobodan in her arms. Seeing the both of them together suddenly made Radojka feel she was the happiest person in the whole world.

Since Radojka was the first one to receive her release, she ran to greet her mother and little Slobodan. When she hugged them she realized they were both soaking wet, but it was a very happy moment for the three of them to be together again. Radojka cried and hugged her mother and her child. "I promise, Mama," she said. "I will never do anything foolish like this again."

It was a warm, rainy early summer day. Down the street from the prison, they found a small restaurant where they had a little lunch and caught up with the past.

"Radojka," Stanislava said, "we don't live in Rakovica any more. We have moved back to the city to a very elegant apartment on Bulevar Revolucije, a couple of blocks from the Skupstina, parliament building. It has two bedrooms, a bath, and a large balcony."

"But, Mama, how can you afford that? Where did you get the money?"

"Miloje had his invalid pension raised, and he sold some of his land in Kragujevac. Now, let me finish my story. Do you remember the opera singer Andrasevic? He let us have his old piano for a while. It doesn't work very well, but it makes the apartment look nice. And we are subleasing half of the apartment to an English diplomat."

"Mama," Radojka replied, "I'm so proud of you; I promise I will go back to school and work to help you out. How is Miloje doing?"

"He's the same. Always sick and complaining about different problems. But I bet he will outlive me."

On the way to the train station, they stopped and bought some bread and cheese to eat on the train because it would be a long trip. Little Slobodan was unmanageable on the train. Radojka tried to hug him, but he didn't want to be hugged by her and sat closed to his "Nana." Stanislava took him in her arms and rocked him to sleep, singing, "Ljulja ljulja (rocking, rocking), Nana sina Slobodana." Just before he fell asleep, he looked back at Radojka with suspicion.

They were all tired and slept for a while. When Radojka stepped out from the compartment for a short time, she came back and found little Slobodan crying. "He was asking for you," Stanislava said, "he was afraid that you would not come back. You see, he knows you."

Radojka grabbed little Slobodan and kissed and hugged him, cleaning his face with her handkerchief, lovingly saying, "I will never leave you again."

Radojka played with little Slobodan, but at the same time she was looking at her mother and noticed how tired she looked. Through Radojka's mind, she realized that her mother was carrying a heavy cross, taking care of her baby and a sick step-father. It was time for her to seriously keep the promises she had made. Also remembering how her grandfather, when he got angry when something was not done properly, would raise his voice saying, "God has given you brains, use them."

CHAPTER 32

THE CORPS DIPLOMATIC PARTY

Upon returning from Mirabor prison, Radojka again blended perfectly into her new city life and continued her studies at the Film Academy. Radojka, an extravert and survivor, quickly met a lot of new people. At the foreign language classes where Radojka was learning English, she met Ann Marie, a young English lady, who was learning Serbo-Croatian. The two of them became good acquaintances, almost friends. They practiced and helped each other with the languages. Ann Marie was married to Lord Norwich, the assistant to the English attache. They had a three-year-old girl.

Ann Marie was a very tall, slim blond, introverted and intelligent. Her favorite form of transportation was her small jeep; her dresses were always simple and plain, but for embassy occasions she dressed with exceptional elegance. Only one thing worked against her in Radojka's mind: Ann Marie always had runs in her stockings.

On several occasions Ann took Radojka to the English Embassy to shop in the small commissary and afterward to a little pub at the Embassy to have lunch. For Radojka it was a luxury, an exceptional treat, to see lots of chocolates, boxes of perfumes, lipstick and face powders, fine-textured white toilet paper—things she couldn't buy in the Belgrade market.

The Film Academy students were advised to take art classes, held at the main gallery close to the hotel Majestic, for their own benefit. Students from other universities also attended and, during the lunch breaks, everyone mingled with each other.

On one lunch break, Radojka met another tall, beautiful blond who became her friend, a girl named Lili. She was impressed by Lili's beautiful clothing and her blond hair, which few Serbs had. Lili was a music academy student who worked part time at the American Embassy and occasionally baby set for the embassy families. Radojka learned that she came from a very poor and large family. Since there were several Lili's at the art classes, she nicknamed her "American Lili."

A couple of weeks later, Lili invited Radojka to visit the Music Academy next to the exclusive Excelsior Hotel. Radojka came early, before Lili's class was over, and waited in front of the hotel. Curious, she walked through the lobby and looked around, noticing people eating in the hotel restaurant. Then she quickly exited, walked around the hotel window, and looked. Her hunger pains filled her with envious thoughts and made her mouth drool.

When Lili came out, Radojka said. "I have a few dinars. Do you think we could go to the hotel to eat something?"

"No," Lili whispered, "this place is expensive. It is only for big budjas and diplomats from the different embassies."

Radojka looked back at Lili, "You know, Lili, someday I will go to America. My uncle lives in Chicago, and he promised to send me a guarantee letter for a visit. Sometimes he sends us packages. One day I will go to America and come back rich. I will stay at this hotel and also eat here."

The friendship between them grew. One day Radojka took Lili to her home to meet her mother, but during all their conversations she did not mention anything about her little son. When Stanislava opened the door, little Slobodan peeked from behind her skirt.

"Lili, this is my mother," Radojka hesitated, then she said, "this is...my little brother, Slobodan."

Usually, Stanislava would shake hands when she was introduced, but this time she didn't. Radojka immediately saw from the expression on her mother's face that Lili was not welcome.

Lili's visit was short; for some reason she was in a hurry. Stanislava could not wait to express her feelings. "That girl is not good, Rado! I can feel it. She looks too rich and is too old for your friendship. Plus, dying her hair! Where did she get the money in these days to buy those expensive clothes? What do you know about her?"

"I do not know anything about her mama, except what she has told me. Her mother is crippled; she has lots of brothers and sisters at home. And she has a part time job at the American Embassy."

"Hmm, she works with those rich Americans. How 'nice.'"

"Oh, Mama, do you want me to have friends in rags and ugly? She is smart, and she looks rich. And I would like to look rich also."

"It is not rich or poor, my Rado. But something about her tells me she is not a good girl for you."

* * *

Through Lili's friends at the American embassy Radojka

was invited to attend a gala party. Radojka's first invitation to a Corps Diplomatic party was like having a major role in a film.

Just before the gala party, Radojka had lunch with Ann Marie. After their chat Ann Marie asked Radojka if she could baby sit for her little girl. It was the same night as the party Lili had invited her to. Through Radojka's mind ran many thoughts. She needed money to feed her baby and help her family, but it was also her heart's desire to meet people. Rather naively, Radojka decided she could handle both in the same day.

The night of the party, she took a streetcar to Ann Marie's villa, which was located on Diplomats Avenue in Dedinje where all the foreign embassies resided. As soon as Radojka arrived, Ann Marie gave her instructions that the little girl must be in bed at 7 p.m. and they would be back close to midnight.

When Ann Marie and Lord Norwich had left for the evening, Radojka quickly telephoned Lili and explained to her what was happening. "Do not worry," Lili said. "I know what to do." A few minutes later, Lili arrived with her fourteen-year-old sister who would watch Ann Marie's little girl once she was asleep.

Lili took a look at Radojka's dress and said, "Well, I don't think the dress you have on would be good for the party. I know what we can do, let's look in Ann Marie's wardrobe."

"But I tried them once," Radojka replied. "She's too tall, and they were too long for me."

"Do you know if she has any safety pins somewhere? You have to look nice."

After trying several dresses, they found a beautiful, floor-length, multi-colored sequined dress. It was bit long, but a few pins worked a miracle. The high heels were also too big, but they stuffed them with newspaper and cotton. When they were finished and Radojka looked in the mirror, her excitement was worth a million dinars. She felt she was like Elizabeth Taylor in one of her happiest films.

Lili, who spoke excellent English with a distinctive British accent, called the embassy's limousine to be driven to the party. She warned Radojka not to say a word in front of the chauffeur until she told her. "I don't want him to know that we are Yugoslavs."

Arriving at the embassy entrance, Radojka stepped on her dress and tripped. She was embarrassed, but quickly recovered. In the elegant hallway of the entrance, a handsome man in his twenties approached her and asked, "Miss, if you please, may I assist you?"

Radojka's English, which she had learned from school and from American films, was poor. The young man's handsome smile as he extended his hand got her attention, but she was not quite sure what he was talking about. Her common sense told her that it had something to do with her falling, so she smiled and hand waved that she was okay.

Lili guided Radojka by the arm. "Put your head up," she said, "and give me a Mona Lisa smile." As they entered the entrance of the ballroom, music started playing. Lili was stopped by a male friend; while she was talking to him, Radojka watched the people interacting with each other. Some were dancing, some drinking.

When a waiter came carrying a tray with several glasses of champagne, Radojka asked Lili if she should have some. Lili took two glasses and gave her one. Radojka held the glass in two hands and observed how the other ladies were holding their's. She noticed that some of them had their little fingers out and were holding the glass at the stem. The man behind her came closer to her, and whispered, "Ladies hold the glass this way." Taking her glass from her hand, he showed her how it was supposed to be held. He stuck his little finger far out.

Just when the party was starting to be lots of fun, Radojka thought she saw a ghost, actually a pair of ghosts—Ann Marie and Lord Norwich were coming through the door! Just as they walked into the ballroom, the young man who had tried to help Radojka when she tripped over her dress, approached her again and took her to the dance floor.

Radojka's eyes were on constant alert. As she danced she tried to hide her face behind his face, forgetting that the rest of her body and her dress could be easily seen. For a few moments Radojka tried to forget the trouble she was in and pay attention to her dance. Suddenly a hand touched her shoulder. "Pssssssshhhhh." Radojka jumped.

"Oh sorry, I didn't mean to scare you," Lili said, "but do you know who just arrived?"

"Yes, yes," Radojka mumbled. "Please take me back as soon as possible. Stand in front of me. Don't move. I see them talking to people over there. I know she's going to see her dress."

Hiding behind Lili's back, Radojka glided into the lobby and waited while Lili telephoned the chauffeur to take them back. In the meantime, Ann Marie had seen her. She was so angry, her pretty face looked like a baked sour apple. In a low voice, clenching her teeth tight together, she said to Radojka, "How in the world could you leave my child alone? You... wearing my dress! I will never put it on again. You can keep it, you little b... I don't want to see you ever again!"

Radojka started to apologize and Lili interrupted, trying to explain that the little girl had a baby sitter and everything was okay. But Ann Marie wouldn't listen. "If I weren't a lady, I would slap you and throw you on the floor."

The embassy car drove up and the chauffeur took them back to Ann Marie's villa. Radojka quickly changed into her own dress, put away everything that belonged to Ann Marie, and asked Lili to wait with her until they returned. "I am afraid to face them again," she said.

So Radojka, Lili and her sister sat in the corner quietly waiting. "Well, here we are," Lili said ironically. "Waiting for the BRITISH TO COME."

Soon, the door opened and Lord Norwich entered with a pleasant smile. "Ladies, my wife is quite upset and does not wish to socialized with you at all." Then he rushed to the other room to check on his little daughter. "Wait," Radojka whispered to Lili, "I want to see if he is going to give me some money for baby sitting."

Lord Norwich returned, again smiled, and said, "Thank God, my little girl is alright and sleeping. Now I would like to ppp.... show you my gratitude." He stammered as he jingled the change in his pocket and counted the shillings. Radojka took a deep breath. He looked at her, then at all three of them, pulled out his wallet, and said, "So sorry. I do not have any Yugoslav money at the moment." He took several English pounds and give it to the three of them.

That evening at the embassy party was the last time Radojka and Ann Marie saw each other.

CHAPTER 33

MAN FROM THE EMBASSY

That same night, when she returned from Ann Marie's villa, Radojka could not sleep. She was frustrated with the thought of breaking up her relationship with Ann Marie, a friend whom millions of Yugoslav teens would love to have. Now Ann Marie could not be a doorway to the West.

"UrrrUrrrUrr." The sound of a make-believe truck, which little Slobodan produced with his mouth, woke Radojka up early from a short sleep. Little Slobodan was rolling a toy truck over her toes. She tried to move slowly, but a little voice said "Rado cekaj, wait, I must go over those hills." Radojka was not angry but lovingly patient with him.

As usual, Miloje had gone early in the morning to kafana to read *Politika*, still hopelessly believing that the communists would lose and the king's dynasty would return. It was still very early in the morning when Stanislava returned from the indoor peasant market carrying a small knitted bag and a live chicken for their Sunday lunch.

For a long time, Radojka didn't attend any embassy parties or other exciting events. She just went to school and worked. At the Film Academy the students occasionally received free passes for the theater or the opera, but the seats were far back in the balcony or downstairs. However, it was a must for Radojka to see her favorite composer Giagcomo Puccini's La Boheme.

Saturday evening at the opera, during the first intermission, Radojka and her friend Lili silently moved closer to the stage to an open seat. The lights came on, and everyone started to move around. Radojka saw several young men sitting alone. One of them smiled and waved to her. She knew him, but could not remember where they had met. "Lili, I know that second man who is looking at us this way. But I cannot recall where I met him."

"Radmila," Lili said, "they look like foreigners."

"Oops, I remember, the American Embassy dance party. He danced with me. I think his name is Don." As Radojka said his name to Lela, Don touched her shoulder in greeting. Radojka's inadequate English had just barely improved. But Lili was interpreting. During the intermission, they chatted for awhile and set a date to meet again.

Over the next few weeks Don and Radojka became friends. Don encouraged her to take extra classes to learn English.

Several months passed. Radojka's parent's apartment was vacant and ready for a new tenant. One day Don offered to help find someone to rent from them. It was a warm spring evening just before Easter. Stanislava was making a dress for Radojka and trying to save electricity. The balcony was her only source of light. Radojka and Stanislava with little Slobodan sat on the balcony watching people passing by. They watched in amazement when a Corps Diplomatic car pulled right to the curb below the balcony.

Radojka recognized Don, coming up with another man to the entrance. Radojka, excited, jumped up. "Oh, Mama, my new friend is coming up. Let's check the house and make sure that everything is in order." They ran over each room, huffing and straightening things.

The doorbell rang twice. Stanislava went to their room and kept Slobodan quiet. Radojka went to the door and opened it. Don smiled and in broken Serbo-Croatian said, "Dobar dan, good day, Radmila." Then he introduced the man with him. "This is Edward Sherman, an assistant to the Air Attache at the embassy. He needs a small apartment."

Edward had blue-green eyes, black hair, and a handsome face. He was about twenty-eight years old, American, single—perfect. Radojka looked at him without blinking and asked, "Is your Mrs here? Perhaps she would like to see it, too."

With a serious face, he answered, "I am alone. There is not a 'Mrs.'"

Radojka showed him around the living room, dining room, kitchen, bathroom and one bedroom, rather large. She called her mother and Slobodan and introduced them. "This is my mother and little brother."

Radojka told Edward that they would use the living room, dining room, and bathroom, but only when he was not there. She also said they would maintain the apartment, even his bedroom if he wished.

Edward liked the apartment, left a deposit, and asked if he could move in immediately. The next day he moved in; everything was quiet.

* * *

After Edward left for the Embassy each morning, Stanislava would clean the bathroom and apartment. Just before Edward's return at 5:00 o'clock, Stanislava would light a fire in the water heater in the bathroom, so that he could have hot water for a bath.

Radojka would come home late every evening. Several times Edward asked Stanislava, "Where is the girl, your daughter?" Stanislava couldn't understand what he was saying, but she realized he was asking about "Radmila."

"No, no Radmila," she answered, "School."

One evening when Radojka returned early from her English class, Edward was sitting in the living room reading. She quietly greeted him and tried to go to her family's room.

"Good evening, Radmila," he said and looked at his watch. "It is still early in the evening. Would you like to join me for dinner?"

"Yes, I would love to. I would like to ask my mother first if she has cooked anything." Radojka went to her room and excitedly kissed her mother. "Guess what?" she whispered, "Edward asked me to go to the embassy for dinner."

"I hope you didn't refuse," Stanislava answered, "Go, go now. Fix yourself; look pretty. You have to bend the metal when it's hot. He looks like a nice young man. And his eyes are so blue-green, just like Harry James."

"Yes, Mama, that's the first I noticed about him."

"Go, fix yourself, hurry."

After they left the apartment, Stanislava rushed to the balcony to catch a glimpse of them leaving. She lit a cigarette and stared out at the distance. The sky was darkening over the city. "Oh my, Jesus help me," she thought, "What would happen if Radojka married him and he takes her to a far away land? Oh, no, no. And my precious child, my loving Slobodan!"

Radojka and Edward had dinner at the embassy club. After dinner, they saw a film. Since he was quiet through the whole evening, Radojka decided she had to be a little more aggressive. At the theater, she touched his hand. He looked around, then he touched her's. That was all.

Radojka felt confused and did not know if he was cold-natured or just trying to be a gentleman. Through her mind ran thoughts of the hot-blooded Yugoslav boys who would jump high from their seats, kiss the girl, and grab her breast if she touched first. Well, she thought, I bet he is a gentleman

The embassy car took them back to the apartment. Just before they entered, Edward smiled for the first time and said, "I would like to take you shopping at the best clothing boutique and buy a couple of pretty dresses for you."

Radojka stuttered and asked him to repeat what he had said, only slowly so she could understand. "Oh, yes, yes I love nice dresses, but here in my country if a girl accepts gifts from a boy, she must be his fiancee or wife."

Edward did not reply to her comments. He yawned and said, "Sorry, but I am very tired tonight. Good night, and I hope we see each other again."

After that night, Radojka went everywhere with Edward. He took her to the theater, the opera, classical concerts, and to the embassy for dinner. One evening Radojka was very sad and bitter because she had begun to like Edward a lot and wanted to tell him her secret about her little Slobodan. But she postponed telling Edward anything until the right time.

Radojka was so disturbed by her thoughts about how to tell Edward, that she got sick at school and came home early. Stanislava was sitting on the balcony, smoking and patching a pair of Edward's socks. "Mama, I am sick in my stomach. I need to tell Edward about Slobodan, but I do not know how. He is a very nice man. I think he is serious about me, and I should be honest with him."

"Rado," she lit her cigarette again, puffed in to the air. "I want to tell you something that you probably already suspect. Do remember when you were fourteen years old and I went to Mostar to the house of a man named Jovan? He was ill and asked for me to come. Do you remember?"

"Yes."

"He was actually asking to see you. Because he was very ill and dying. He was your real father." There was a silence for a few seconds. "Oh, Mama," Radojka said. "how did it happen? Why did you keep it secret for so long?"

"I was going to tell you when we went to see him, but I didn't want you to think bad about me. You know I was a holy sister. He raped me."

"Oh, my poor Mama, you went through the worst." She hugged her mother and they both cried. "For all these years, I never knew until now what you have gone through. Oh, Mama, I will never feel bad about you. After all you have done for me." Radojka took a deep breath. "I love you, Mama. Since we both have secrets, I feel better now. Moja Mama." They embraced and kissed again. "You have given me the strength to tell Edward."

Radojka wondered if her secret was a legacy, a curse or a blessing. More likely a blessing.

* * *

When the Barnum Brothers' famous circus came to Belgrade, Edward got tickets through the embassy for Radojka and her family. Radojka had tried several times to include little Slobodan in their activities where children were permitted, but she did not insist, waiting until Edward suggested it.

That evening, after the circus premier, all of them went to a very nice restaurant for a late dinner. Miloje suggested sitting outside in the basta close to the singer and not too far from the grill. Everyone was having a great time, even little Slobodan who stared at the pretty Hungarian gypsy singer. Edward, however, was very quiet the whole evening. The next day Edward told Radojka to tell her parents that he was shy by nature and that he apologized about last night.

That evening at the American Embassy after dinner, Edward and Radojka stayed for the movie at the embassy theater. Edward acted kind of nervous and whispered, "Let's get married."

"Please, repeat," Radojka asked, not certain about what he had said. So he did, but she still had a hard time understanding him.

"You be my wife," he said twice.

Radojka did not answer.

"Say yes you will marry me."

"No, I cannot, not yet."

"That means yes," Edward said aloud. Someone behind them said, "Shhhhhhh, do not talk. Sshhhhhhh." Edward grabbed Radojka's hand. "Let's go outside," he continued. "When, when will you tell me then?" Radojka bowed her head down. "I..... have ... something to tell you. It is a very big secret."

On the way home, through tears, Radojka said, "I do not know where to begin. I was a good girl," she mumbled, "but he made me do it."

Edward took his white handkerchief from his blazer pocket, which had been tucked there the whole evening for style, and wiped her eyes.

Radojka looked him straight in the eyes, "Slobodan is not

my brother but....my son."

* * *

For a few days, Edward did not see Radojka. Then one evening he brought Radojka a large bouquet of flowers and asked if she would bring her mother, her father, and her little boy so they all could sit together and talk.

Edward was shy and did not know where to begin. As he talked to Radojka, she struggled to translate for her parents. He said he would like to adopt her little Slobodan and marry her. When Miloje and Stanislava heard the news, they were kicking each other under the table, thrilled and happy. Miloje suggested that they should celebrate by going out to dinner somewhere in the Basta where music was playing. They went out and celebrated and when the bill came, Miloje was slow to pull out his wallet. "Let the American pay," he whispered to Stanislava.

* * *

One day Radojka took Slobodan to play with the other children in the park near their apartment. A man in a black leather coat approached her and addressed her in a vulgar way, "Is an American man a better lover than a Yugoslav or Russian?" He called her bad names again and said, "This is not the end."

Radojka came home crying, very scared and upset, and told Stanislava what had happened. Stanislava said, "I bet it was one of those UDBA men, like the KGB. I have not told you, but we had gotten a summons from them in the mail a couple of times. They want to see you. I did not want to scare you."

Again in the park, the same man appeared. This time he handed her a piece of paper which said to meet him at a certain time downtown so they could talk or her family would be threatened.

When the time came, Radojka went to see the UDBA man. He asked her a lot of questions about Edward: who was he, who came to see him, who else lived in their apartment? Because she did not have an answer for him, she took a chance and ignored the UDBA man's demand. One evening when she was coming back from school, the UDBA man waited in the entrance hall of the apartment building, grabbed her hand, twisted very hard, and threatened her that he would break every bone in her body unless she informed him about Edward.

Radojka was hiding a long time, avoiding the parks. Stanislava found a note at the doorstep. It said that her daughter and baby would be kidnapped by 2 o'clock on Tuesday if she did not have the answers to the questions she was asked. Stanislava, in panic because she remembered what had happened to her after Borislav's death, showed the note to Radojka.

Monday night when Edward was taking a bath, Radojka sneaked in his room, looked in his wallet, saw a card that said Private Pilot; then purposely, she did not look for anything else. She wrote on a piece of paper: "Edward Sherman is an embassy pilot." This was not true. The pilot's license was really for a private pilot. When she handed the note to the UBDA man that was the last time she saw him.

* * *

Edward's mother was Catholic and his father was Jewish. Since Radojka was also Catholic on her mother's side and Serbian on her father's side, they both agreed to get married in the Catholic Church.

On December 31st, the wedding took place in a Catholic Church, followed by a large reception at the American Embassy. After the wedding, adoption procedures took place in the city hall of Belgrade. Just before the adoption, Janko heard that Slobodan was being adopted. He protested, but didn't succeed in stopping it. Slobodan was christened again, this time in the Catholic church as Robert Sherman, Edward nicknamed him "Bobby."

* * *

Three months later, in March, Edward received notice that he was being transferred. He was to report to his new duty in London and had to leave in a month's time.

Stanislava was very sad to see Radojka and Slobodan leave her, but she was also happy for them because they going to freedom in another country. They could have rented to another foreigner and stayed in the apartment, but Stanislava was very sad at Radojka's leaving. There was no need to make more money. The two of them could live on Miloje's pension and her dealings in the black market.

When the day came, it was very hard for Radojka to say goodbye to her mother. Stanislava and Miloje, who were moving to the outskirts of Belgrade that same day, had rented a small truck and loaded everything in it. As the truck was being driven away, Radojka waved from the balcony of the empty apartment. She could see her mother sitting on a piece of furniture in back of the truck with one hand holding her handkerchief to her mouth and waving with her other hand. Radojka followed the truck with her eyes all the way until it turned. That was the last time Radojka saw her mother.

CHAPTER 34

LAST LETTERS FROM STANISLAVA

Radojka was like most young people who do not take their parents and their problems seriously. Arriving in America was very exciting and quite different from her native country. She was solely responsible for her child. They were both going to school and learning a new language, and at the same time she was responsible for the house and staff. When Radojka wrote to her mother and relatives, her letters were brief and the content was often:

"My schedule is enormously busy. Everything is so big here and we have anything our souls desires, except time and patience for each other. Yes, this is America."

After Radojka had lived in American for a couple of months, her mother became seriously ill.

The last letters from Stanislava, some of which had been written by Laka, an acquaintance of Radojka's from her high school days, were very sad. They were followed by two letters from Mila Aleksijevic a friend of Stanislava's.

THE LETTERS

March 5 1959 Beograd
Rado, my precious child;

After you and Slobodan went to America with Edward, I become very depressed, stayed in bed, and cried for a several days. I could not eat or sleep. On top of my depression I had a bad cold and urinated on myself in bed. A couple of days later Miloje called the ambulance and took me to the hospital. One of the doctors who I saw before you left me, Rado, told me that the tumor in my bladder was enlarged and that an operation was necessary.

Oh, my Rado, I had bad thoughts, but here I am—a brand new woman, healthy again. Before the operation, I prayed to God and St. Gurgic to help me to survive. I took a picture of St. Gurgic out of its frame and put it inside my gown next to my heart. The picture was with me at all times during the operation, and I know it saved my life.

Dearest Rado, sometimes in the past when you and I went shopping, you told me that you smelled urine on me. You were right. Just before your trip to America, the doctors told me that I should have a hysterectomy, but I postponed it until you had left Yugoslavia. I kept it secret and suffered. Today is the second day after my operation and, really, I feel great.

Oh, I almost forgot to tell you that I have ordered two custom-made, large brown leather suitcases. Slowly, I will start to get ready to visit you in New York.

Oh, my sweet Rado, here in the hospital next to me are a couple of much younger women who have been operated on for the same tumors that I have. I beg of you, don't work hard to have more material things, keep your health, please Rada. God forbid, if something would happen to you, who will Slobodan turn to? He only has you in that big foreign land of America.

Your Mama Draginja

*** * ***

April 25, 1958 Beograd
My dear sweet Rado and nana's little Slobodane,
In my last letter from the hospital I forgot to tell you that Miloje and I have moved to the outskirts of Belgrade close where we used to live. A small town called Knezevac, also very close to the train station. This time we are sharing the large old house with two older widows. We have one room with two big windows facing the train station like we used to have before our elegant Belgrade apartment. We are now alone, and that is more than enough; Miloje needs fresh air all the time, not just by walking to nearest park. It is about seven kilometers to the center of Belgrade. Even though, occasionally, we are awaken by the sounds of pigs and roosters, we do not miss the city. I am worried that when you come to visit us it would not be in elegant rooms with parquet floors like we used to have.

Oh, my Rado, how much I miss you and Slobodan. I cannot help thinking of you two constantly. I am smoking now, two packs of cigarettes a day. I am trying to keep busy and not to worry about you, since you are in the rich America.

My doctor, Dr. Gikic, who operated on me suggested that I should try the new experimental treatment called radiation to heal my operation faster, so I am visiting the hospital twice a week. There were several other "guinea pigs" and they were younger people. I feel great now after the operation, except I am getting fatter in my stomach, faster than other parts of my body. I went back to Dr. Gikic for an exam and he took some kind sample inside of where the uterus was. The result came back negative, whatever that means. A few days later Dr. Gikic called and said that I needed more exams immediately. I am scared, my Rada, if something was wrong from those radiation experiments. Well, my sweet Rada, I am packing a few things and early in the morning I will catch the local train to Belgrade. Pray for me........

Love, love, love, you Slobodan and Edwarda. Please Rado, always remind Slobodan of his Nana and Deda.

Your mama Draginja

* * *

Excerpt from Laka's Letter:

Dear Rada,

I am writing to you for your mother. She is very ill. She stayed in the hospital for a while, then had surgery. During her hospital stay she has had many visitors including her older sister Dragica with whom she hadn't had contact for many years.

Your mother says that they come constantly asking her whom is she going to leave the gold and dollars that her rich daughter in America has sent her. She told them, she doesn't have any of that. And she told them, "Please leave me alone, can't you see that I am sick." Suddenly she gets stomach pains and started to cry and calling for a doctor or nurse to help her, to give her morphine to ease her pain.

Some of her visitors went and visited her home without permission and took clothing, jewelry, and anything valuable. After they discovered that she did not really have gold and many dollars, those "visitors" suddenly faded away.

When your poor, lovely mother discovered the truth of her cancer and did not know who to turn to for help (if anyone was left), but to write to you, Rado, and beg you to come to see her and to stay close with her.

* * *

Stanislava's Letter 15 May 1959 Beograd

Dearest my children, Rado, my sweet child and Slobodan,

Please do not get upset with me for not informing you of my situation. Again, I am so sorry that I was unable to keep my promises. Since the doctors have recommended these radiation treatments, I have been in and out of the hospital several times. Now, the worst is here.

Rado, my child, here I am totally helpless laying in this depressing room alone. The room looks like people have been walking upside down. The walls are dirty, so are the squeaky, old wood floors. In a way, I like the squeaky floors; they alert me if someone is entering in my room, even though visitors rarely come anymore. Here, light comes from the ceiling. Would you believe one single light in the large room with a high ceiling and not a single window? For a few days I was not told why I was isolated from others, and when the nurses come they run in and out like they were chased by ghosts.

Finally Dr. Gikic came. He was dressed in some kind of plastic suit and mask (oh, he also had heavy plastic gloves), but he sat next to me. The moment Dr. Gikic sat at my bed side I felt that everything was alright, except when I saw his forehead and his face under the mask starting to grimace like he wanted to say something important. He grimaced sadly, tilted his head, and with his hand touched my forehead. Suddenly my whole body turned into bumps and chills. Then I asked him, "Please, Dr. Gikic, what can be worse than the news you already have given to me?"

He mumbled under the mask: "I have written to your daughter and informed her that she needs to come as soon as possible to see you once more."

I got very upset hearing the unpleasant and ugly news

again plus to hear that you, my Rado, know now. I jumped from the bed and screamed aloud at him. "Please, please," I begged him. "I do not want my Rada to see me dying," I cried aloud.

He grabbed my hands and, with a tears in his eyes, said, "I am very sorry, my daughter also lost her mother last year." Then he briskly walked away.

P.S. My sweet child Rado, please do not be angry at Dr Gikic. He is a gentle and good man, he is trying to save my life. Also, my wishes are long, but one of them I want to tell you, my Rado: Do not work hard, even if you only eat food every third day. Health is something we must manage ourselves. We must draw our own road maps and choose better roads for our lives.

I have almost forgotten. Please Rado, help Slavka to get out of this rotten life, she is an orphan. Her parents were killed in the war, Slavka's aunt is my good friend. Oh, poor Miloje, he does not know anything if someone is sick. If I die, what is going to happen to him? Please, my Rado, help him as much as you can. Now, my sweet children, goodby. I have always suffered in my life time, and sweet God has granted you life, a good one in America. Keep my little Slobodan and tell him about his dear Nana. Also, say goodby to Edward. Now and forever I am kissing this letter. With my lips I will seal it forever. Goodby my sweet children...

Your loving mother.

* * *

Letter from Mila Aleksijevic
15 June 1959 Beograd

Dear Rado,

As an old friend of your mother, I wanted to contact you and tell you that there is no hope at all. Do not come, just remember her the way she looked when you left to the far land.

Your mother was released from the hospital with incurable cancer. She is restless and her body is very ill, but her spirit and her heart, are amazingly, keeping her moving. *Poor Draginja, several days earlier she took her Singer sewing machine and other valuables on her own, sneaked out the house on the streetcar, and went back to the hospital to beg the doctors to help her live just a little longer. She dropped her sewing machine into doctor's office, threw all the jewelry and dollars, and begged on her knees to save her life. Doctor Gikic, who saw how bad she looked, took her to one of the hospital rooms and quickly put her to bed.*

Draginja refused to go to her home and die. She requested to telegram for her parents to come immediately. Since her mother was ill and could not come, her father Djurin came with his two youngest sons. One unforgettable moment was, when we all entered the room, seeing Draginja surrounded by several women in black weeping loud, then, a silence began. Draginja lifted her head and whispered, "Oh, my chacha, my father, you came after all." Then she motioned with her hand to everyone to get out except her father. "I want to be alone with my father," she whispered again. We all stepped outside the room. It was silent, no one said a word nor did we hear anything.

My dearest Rado, that was the most sensitive and touching moment for all of us, the reunion of a father and his dying daughter.

The next day was my turn to stay with Draginja. Miloje came and brought her oranges and some little cookies. When I saw Miloje, he looked awfully tired and unshaved. Draginja was upset when she saw him, and refused to see him. She had heard from some of the neighboring woman that when her father and her brothers come to the house to spend the night, Miloje called the militia in the middle of night to have them out of his house. Draginja claimed that one of her oldest sisters brought the candle, put it under her pillow, and whispering said to Draginja that she hoped she would die fast. My Rada, your poor mother had suffered lot. The day before she died, some women visited her and took her gold ring with a diamond.

Your weak stepfather Miloje arranged for her burial in the most beautiful cemetery Topcider, even though Draginja's wish was to be buried at some small cemetery closer to where they lived.

Draginja suffered bad constipation, and I came to give her an enema with camomile. A couple hours later she was relieved and showed signs of energy.

I was extremely tired and needed to rest for a while, went to my house which was just few minutes by streetcar from the hospital. I had just arrived in the front of my doorway trying to unlock the door, when I heard the telephone ringing. My key was not opening the door as usual, so I pushed the door forcefully and grabbed the still ringing phone. I found myself stone still and suddenly ice cold in the middle of a warm June day. The voice on the telephone said that our dearest, loving friend Draginja had just passed way with a smile on her beautiful face.

Even I expected Draginja's departure, but I thought she would live at least a week or longer. I wanted to collapse and cry my heart out, but knew that I should be back at the hospital and see how I could help.

* * *

Letter from Mila Alexsijevic
24 June 1959 Beograd

Dearest Rada,

I'm so sorry, my child, today we have buried our long time loving and never-to-be-forgotten Draginja. After all the complications to get permission to be buried at the Topcidersko groblje everything went as poor Miloje and a few of our close friends had planned.

Rado, do you remember a steep hill from the Mint bank where you had worked a summer job? Well, four strong men had to carry the casket almost a mile up to the cemetery. Step by step, around fifty of us had to follow the casket up the hill. Some of the women wore high heels. Just before we came up the hill close to the cemetery chapel, it started to rain. Following Serbian tradition, the casket of the deceased was brought to the chapel first and opened for viewing. The prayers and blessing of two Serbian preachers were performed. Rajko, Marija, my Slavka, Srbislav and his wife Rada with her mother and small little daughter Mira were there. I saw only your aunt Catica with her younger son Ivica.

The rain stopped slightly, and the burial procedure continued. People were pretty quiet and with sad expressions. After the ceremony at the chapel, all of us followed outside to Draginja's new home. After about 13 rows of graves there were a couple of evergreen shade trees near the grave where our loving Draginja was going to rest. Two men were still digging out wet soil. Miloje started to cry aloud saying, "Moja Draginja, please don't leave me alone." Then, my Slavka screamed, "Oh, my mother, oh aunty, why must you go so young?" Then Slavka's foot slipped on the muddy grave site and she almost fell into the grave.

Other women were crying aloud also. The saddest moment was when those two cemetery workers were shoveling muddy soil over the casket. Miloje kneeled down, spread his hands towards the grave and helplessly yelled once more, "Can't you hear me, my loving one."

Rado, our tradition is when someone has passed away, after the burial, zito, cooked wheat with walnut is served first, than food and slivovica, wine and beer also, for the soul of the passed one.

* * *

EPILOGUE

The moments of agony and unbearable pain that my dearest mother went through were described, word by word, in the sad letters which I have kept together with photographs from her funeral for thirty years now.

Since death had struck my mother so early in her life, I wanted to expand the record of her life beyond those last few letters. There was so much about her that needed to be remembered: her kindness, her love for people, and her love for life. She wanted to live. A poet once said that after death a person's existence continued in the memories of the living. This is my way to continue her life in our memories.

Many of the other people who touched my mother's life in this novel are also gone. Jovan died shortly after my mother and I visited him in 1950. Djurin and Andjelka sold their mountain home in Raketno and moved to the city living with their son Grgo and his family, in Slavonska Pozega. One Sunday morning on her way to church on her ninety-third birthday, slowly crossing a road, Andjelka was struck by a speeding truck. Djurin spent the last three years of his life sadly, missing his love Andjelka, and left the earth at the age of one hundred and two.

Shortly after Djurin's death, Grgo lost his life in front of his house in 1977, also struck by a truck, and left a wife and five children behind. Ivo, who ran away from home at age 15, before passing away in 1986 in Canada, became financially quite succesfull thru various businesses of his own in Germany and Canada. He also sponsored three of Grgo's sons to emigrate to Canada and start their own businesses. He was Stanaslava's favorite brother. Ilka died of old age in Mostar before the current civil war started.

Miloje, who never remarried after Stanislava's death, enjoyed the best years that Yugoslavia could provide a retiree on a small pension. His last few years were spent at a retirement center in Belgrade for pensioners; he left the earth a month before his eighty-second birthday and the collapse of Yugoslavia. Janko who became a leading athletic coach in Yugoslavia had a heart attack and died in 1989 while coaching soccer.

The war and the communist regime after World War II left many unpleasant memories, invisible and visible scars on my mother's body and soul, but my memories of her beauty cannot be erased. My mother now exists in my memories of her, and this novel is my attempt to preserve those memories and her struggle for life that has made me stronger. These memories of my mother are like irreplaceable treasure.

Terms

Avlja	Courtyard surrounding mosque
Allah	God. (Muslim word)
Bog	God (Serbian word)
Boga mi	God help me
Basta	Garden, park
Babushka	Head scarf
Bura	Storm
Chorba	Stew with vegetables and meat
Cevapcici	Mix of ground pork and beef rolled into a small sausage and then grilled.
Chuturica	A carved and decorated wood bottle
Chiko	Friendly nickname used by children for a strange man.
Chacho	Daddy, expression used in Hercegovina
Chuti	Quiet Shut-up
Dido	Grandfather (in Hercegovina)
Dobro jutro	Good morning
Dobar dan	Good day
Draya dusa	Dear soul
Dovidjenja	Until we see again
Dimije or Shalvare	Genie or Turkish pants
Dodji	Come here
Dunja	Quinci (Quinci)
Fijaker	Horse drawn carriage
Gibanjca	Cheese or meat pastry
Gospodin	Sir, Mr.

Gospodja	Madam, Mrs.
Hodja	Muslim preacher
Izvinite	Excuse me
Kum	God father, Best man.
Kocijas	Horse carriage driver
Kajmak	Sweet butter
Kolachi	Cookies
Majko	Mother
Mlada	Young lady
Moja	Mine
Palenta	Cornmeal
Putnike	Passengers
Popa	Serbian preacher
Slava	Family holiday to celebrate their Saint (Orthodox)
Slatka	Sweet
Spomenik	Monument, large stone or bronze statue
Slivovica	Aged plum brandy
Sunie Moje	My sunshine
Sretan put	Safe journey
Tata	Daddy
Teta	Aunt
Tiho	Quiet
Uredu, Gospodine	Alright, Sir
Vrelo	Underground mountain spring

dj-g as in George; lj-i as in lure; j-y as in Yugoslavia z-s as in measure